DANGEROUS ADDICTION

PIPER STONE

Published by Stormy Night Publications and Design, LLC.
www.StormyNightPublications.com

Stone, Piper
Dangerous Addiction

Cover Design by Korey Mae Johnson
Images by Shutterstock/FXQuadro and Shutterstock/marchello

CHAPTER 1

"*When Anger and Revenge get married, their daughter is called Cruelty.*"

—*Russian Proverb*

Walker

Darkness.

Flashing lights.

I leaned my head against the cold glass surface, staring out the window of the train car as lights flashed all around me. The brakes screeched, the car jerking as it slowed dramatically. From somewhere in the back of the train, I heard a distinct moan. Some drunk guy who'd been passed out the entire time was finally coming to.

Exhaling, I dragged the coat around me, loathing the chill in the air, the brisk wind that cascaded across Lake Michigan bringing bone-chilling temperatures. Lately, I'd been forced to remind myself this was the city I'd always planned on moving to, the dream job the only one acceptable to me. However, getting home at two in the morning, enduring the assholes lurking in the shadows as well as the wretched cold temperatures made me long for summer days.

As the train pulled into the station, I moved to a standing position, grasping the metal pole as the car vibrated under my feet. Maybe I should feel lucky my poor little car hadn't been moved in almost three weeks. Between the subway system and being able to walk to my favorite destinations, I'd certainly saved money on gas. Thank God for that.

And for my glorious condo, the high-rise building capturing a perfect view of the gorgeous lake. Even though there was little furniture inside, it was mine. How it'd happened, I still wasn't certain.

After stepping off, I slipped my hands into my pockets, keeping my head down as I walked up the stairs and onto the street, scanning the area before heading toward the secure building. Even in the upscale section of town, working late nights kept my anxiety high. There were far too many violent crimes in Chicago, enough I'd stopped paying attention to the news. I dealt with enough of blood and gore on an everyday basis.

I walked quickly, crossing the street and noticing just how deserted the road seemed tonight. Maybe because it was a

Monday. At least I had the next day off, although I doubted that I'd have any energy to leave the condo. Maybe I'd just stay in my PJs, watching movies.

Clang. Clang.

The noise echoed, but loud enough it gave me pause. I stopped short, taking a few seconds to look in all directions. Maybe a cat had turned over a trashcan. After taking another two steps, I heard a scraping sound, as if something metal was being dragged across brick. A trickle of fear skittered through me, and I walked faster.

Then I heard footsteps.

Oh, hell, no. I tried to keep from running, but as the pounding sound of heavy feet matched my own, I flew down the sidewalk, looking over my shoulder only once. While I couldn't see who was following me, that meant shit.

Go. Go. Go.

I pumped my legs harder, grateful I had on running shoes. As I neared the building, I heard a distinct, deep and evil laugh.

And I could swear the bastard whispered, "Next time."

I wasted no time smashing my hand against the security panel, suddenly grateful for the extra security. When I was safely inside, the massive glass doors shutting behind me, I stood just inches away, glaring out into the night.

No one was going to scare me away. I'd worked too damn hard to get where I was.

Now I was no longer frightened, just pissed off. While I had a can of mace, I'd been thinking about getting a concealed weapon's license. I knew how to use a gun and wouldn't hesitate if it meant saving my life or that of someone else. Bad guys did exist in every walk of life. There were very few people who cared about their fellow man, and even fewer heroes.

Maybe I'd become too jaded since moving here.

I rubbed my temple and hurried toward the elevator. I could use a glass of wine after the horrible day. Everything was so quiet inside what I called the mausoleum, the building barely forty percent occupied. While gorgeous, the massive foyer exquisite with hundreds of thousands of dollars of marble, a beautiful fountain off to one side, it was cold.

Zero personality.

Still, I couldn't look a gift horse in the mouth. I was one lucky girl.

The elevator seemed to take forever but when I stepped onto my floor, I finally breathed a sigh of relief. I had plenty of food, wine, ice cream, and popcorn. What else could a girl need?

After opening the door, I struggled as usual to find the light switch, but even before my hand managed to touch the plate, a sickeningly sweet and pungent smell wafted into my nostrils. I'd know the odor anywhere.

Blood.

Against my better judgment, I flipped on the light, not paying any attention as I pushed the door closed and walked further inside. My feet heavy, a knot formed in my stomach as I took several steps more.

I'd been a trauma nurse for almost three years, working the emergency rooms in two hospitals, including the one I'd recently been hired. The horrors I'd seen had created nightmares, but I'd found a way to push them aside, joyful when victims of catastrophic car wrecks or violent crimes were saved, allowed to enjoy the rest of their lives.

But this was something I would never, ever be able to forget.

Oh, my God. He's dead. Dead. Someone killed him.

Blood. So much blood.

It was everywhere.

All over the walls.

I was woozy, unfocused.

Terror clawed through me as I tried to steady myself, barely able to keep standing.

What if the perpetrator was still inside? What if they were hiding?

The man was dead. Decapitated.

I moved closer, crouching down before I reminded myself there was no need to check for vitals. He was dead. Dead!

My God. I knew him. I… bile rushed into my throat, my stomach lurching. I'd just seen him, the good-natured guy wishing me a fabulous day just like he had from the evening I'd moved in. Who would want to kill a maintenance man?

After jerking to my feet, I pressed my hand over my mouth, staring down at the huge crimson stain on the floor. There was so much of it.

As I stood over his headless body, his lifeless eyes staring into my own, blood already coagulating on the new tile floor, I did something completely out of character.

I threw my head back and screamed.

* * *

Maksim

Sekrety.

The word meant secrets in Russian. There was no reason I had that single word imbedded in the forefront of my mind, but I did. My mother used to say it when talking about the old days—the years she'd grown up in Kazan before moving to Moscow.

Then she'd fled her native country without turning back. She'd enrolled in college, finding the man of her dreams and getting married, the perfect American dream. She'd kept her accent, something I'd acquired even after spending my entire life in Chicago. I'd felt closer to her than anyone else, my father always working, never taking the time to spend with his small but loving family.

Until his cold, calculating methods of handling business had been the only thing that I'd gained from our relationship. Now I hated him, his pretenses nothing but a joke given he was a soulless man, at least with regards to his only child.

Instead of following in my father's footsteps, I'd made an alternative decision to enter the world of the Bratva, working alongside an uncle whose name had almost never been mentioned in our house. As the *Pakhan* of a ruthless crime syndicate, Ivan Novikov had held Chicago in the palm of his hand for almost twenty years. His power and influence only continued to increase, yet it hadn't been without sacrifices or bloodshed.

Violence.

It was the way of the Bratva and one I enjoyed. Some would call choosing the life of a ruthless mafia leader a foolish choice. I could have become a lawyer or an accountant, even a doctor, but I'd chosen the life of crime instead, infuriating my father to the point he'd basically disowned me. I'd fought my way into being involved with the sacred organization even though my mother had

7

begged me to stay away. Her last words of warning I would never forget.

"Ivan will turn you into a monster. Everything he touches is destroyed. Everything he desires, he takes. You're going to become just like him."

Just like him.

That had been eight years ago, the ninety-six months spent learning my craft, proving myself to a brutal leader who had no problem gunning a man down in cold blood. I'd been cut from the same mold, our family ties only a small part of the reason I'd sacrificed a traditional way of living. Maybe what few stories my mother had told me about the old country, Mother Russia, had inspired me more than they should have. Whatever the case, I'd shed most of my American upbringing for the half of me that had never been allowed to fully explore my Russian heritage.

My methods of punishment were considered cruel and unusual, which often kept our enemies from seeking revenge. My cold-hearted abilities had also provided me the respect within the organization that I deserved.

However, it didn't matter that I was Ivan's nephew. Our close relationship just meant he held me to a higher standard. Especially given who'd sired me.

But I'd learned to enjoy the same merciless tactics, inflicting pain when necessary. Even the majority of other soldiers in his employ were terrified of me.

As if I gave a shit.

At least I'd earned Ivan's respect.

This wasn't about competition or forming friends. I couldn't care less about anyone else working for the most powerful man in the Midwest. I had my own agenda to follow, a kingdom to run.

Darkness had become my way of life. Every action I'd taken over the last eight years, every thought entering my mind.

Dark.

Black.

Obsidian.

Very little calmed the savage beast lurking inside of me, which continued to horrify my mother. Nothing seemed to still the rage festering inside of me or the need to exact revenge on those who made my life complicated.

As I stepped out of my beloved Mercedes, I took a deep breath of the night air. Cold. Crisp.

Perfect.

My Capo pulled close beside, cutting the engine on the Escalade and immediately climbing out. "They've made progress."

"Yes, but not nearly enough. Winter is setting in, which means additional delays."

He snorted behind me. "I don't mind lighting a fire under their asses if necessary."

"We'll see, Brick."

I took a few steps away from my car, marveling at the sight of the project, construction almost halfway complete. Novikov money had funded the thirty-acre parcel, the incredible design coming from one of the most brilliant architects in the industry. When finished, the multi-use parcel would become one of the finest business, residential, and entertainment facilities in the city of Chicago.

Sadly, for the brainchild behind the project, he'd attempted to muscle out his deep pocket investors. Shame on him.

"Get him out of the vehicle," I instructed my most trusted soldier, Brick, not only my Capo but a man I considered a friend.

"Gladly," he said, a dark chuckle rumbling from his throat.

I didn't wait for the asshole to be pulled out of Brick's SUV. The draw of the construction site had already captured my attention. As I moved toward the newest addition, staring down at the black pit of the foundation, a smile crossed my face. As I reached into my jacket, pulling out both my weapon and the silencer, I wasn't certain why I was bothering to eliminate the sound of the kill in the first place. Production had been shut down for the long holiday weekend, eliminating the possibility of anyone bothering me while doing business.

Still, it paid to be cautious, especially since we didn't control the construction workers hired for the project.

Something that had troubled me from the start. While expanding our business was prudent, doing so without absolute control stuck in my craw. Recent events had been a prime example.

I heard the man's screams through the gag as he was dragged in my direction and sighed. Some men faced their destiny with courage while others reverted to childish methods of begging for mercy. The latter irritated the hell out of me.

Even the stench of the man pissed me off. He reeked of cheap perfume, a product of his sexual proclivities, something else that eroded the concept of providing salvation for his crimes.

As I turned to face him, I gave Brick a single nod, my Capo ripping away the thick duct tape.

The man gasped, still struggling with the thick rope binding his hands. The bright moon lit up the sky, also highlighting the terror riding his face.

"Mr. Chamberlain. You've been a naughty boy," I said with zero inflection. I had no emotion regarding my upcoming action whatsoever, but the irritation at disrupting my evening remained in the forefront of my mind. Gregor Chamberlain had been a major player in the world of real estate development for years. He was well educated, highly intelligent, and had a good nose for success. Sadly, he'd forgotten that loyalty was the most important attribute to have when doing business with the Novikov family.

"Mr. Calderon. Please. I've done nothing wrong," he pleaded.

"Nothing wrong?" I shook my head, taking a few seconds to enjoy the stunning view. "Look around you. This is an incredible development, but there'd be nothing here but dirt if we hadn't taken up your cause."

"I... I know that, but..." He didn't bother finishing his sentence because he knew there was nothing to say.

Brick continued grinning as he held the man by the back of the neck, enjoying every minute of the asshole's weak attempts at making excuses.

"Not only did you attempt to push our organization out of the existing contract, but you ran and hid like a fucking rat, unable to own up to what you did. That's unacceptable. I'm afraid that there's nothing I'm willing to do to provide you with a reprieve."

"This is my baby. Mine. You attempted to take control. I couldn't allow that! You don't own the place." He dared to look away from me, ignoring my admonishment.

I took my time before answering. "Hmmm... Even worse, Gregor. That wasn't your only mistake."

He seemed confused, sputtering several times, even trying to take a step away.

Brick grabbed his hair at the scalp, a quick snap of his wrist yanking Gregor's head to an awkward angle.

I'd grown weary of the game. I walked closer until I was only a few inches away, taking another deep breath of the fresh night air. "You were working with Samuel Rossi, the two of you planning on shoving us out of the project completely. Isn't that the truth?" While I was taking a calculated stab in the dark, I could tell almost instantly that my intuition had been correct. Kudos to me.

Samuel Rossi had managed to extort a large sum of money right under Ivan's nose. That had been seen as a significant weakness given Samuel had been the Bratva's accountant for years, a man trusted with the family's fortune. The man's death for his betrayal had been vicious, sending a very distinct message to anyone thinking about betraying the Novikov family.

"I… No… I mean…" Gregor whined like a baby.

"Which is it, Gregor? Yes or no?"

He swallowed hard. "You don't understand."

"You're right. I don't but at this point, I no longer give a shit what you have to say. However, this project was your baby from inception, and I know just how important it is to you. Therefore, I'm going to make certain you remain a solid part of the foundation of the enterprise knowing the Novikov family will be moving forward without you."

My Capo knew when to move away from the man, allowing Gregor to stumble toward me.

Then I fired a single shot, the bullet catching him in the throat. As he tottered to the side, his eyes open wide from horror, Brick gave his arm a single push, dumping him into the pit ready for concrete to be poured.

Maybe it was time to push the project along. I shifted my gaze toward the awaiting concrete truck, laughing softly.

"Let's give our construction workers a little surprise when they return to work tomorrow morning."

Laughing, Brick moved toward the massive vehicle. "You got it, boss."

At least a certain amount of information had been confirmed. However, I had a feeling I should have interrogated the man even longer. Our former accountant had been working behind our backs for several months from what we'd been able to tell. Given what I knew about Samuel, that surprised me.

Unless he was working with another organization altogether. My thoughts returned to Gregor. That pissed me off even more.

As I headed for my waiting Mercedes, I turned and studied the construction site one last time. Maybe I'd changed my mind. It was definitely good to expand our business.

CHAPTER 2

alker

Coffee.

I stared into the dark brew, marveling at being able to catch a portion of my reflection in the track lighting bouncing against the side of the refrigerator. While I brought the heavy mug to my lips for a third time, the stench alone was enough to make my stomach lurch. Hissing, I pushed it across the counter, moving slowly toward a cabinet on the other wall, grabbing one of my four wineglasses.

Even the oversized galley kitchen was suffocating, the window with an incredible view of downtown Chicago doing no good. My pulse continued to race, the adrenaline rush I'd felt before ebbing.

Dead. A man is dead inside your condo.

I'd managed to block out most of the muffled voices coming from the other room, but the noise continued to give me jitters. There were at least eight people in my condo. Police. Forensics. Even a detective had already been assigned to the case. I was surprised the murder had taken a high priority, although no one was telling me anything.

As I poured a glass of wine, I realized just how badly my hand was shaking, strings of red wine trickling down onto the granite counter. I knew there might be a stain if I wasn't quick to react, but my mind was like sludge, unable to process anything. I stared down at the kitchen floor, studying my bloody footprints. All I could think about was how difficult it was going be to remove the stains.

"Are you certain you want to do that?"

I almost dropped the bottle, the deep baritone of the detective's voice shattering my last nerve.

"It's either this or a few shots of tequila," I answered, managing to grab one of my kitchen towels. "If you'd like to join me, Detective, there's plenty, although at this point, I'm not certain I actually have enough to satisfy both of us." I heard my nervous laugh and frowned. Nothing about this was funny. Finding a dead man—not just dead but slaughtered like some animal—was straight out of a horror movie.

"Unfortunately, I'm on duty and I still need to ask you some questions. Are you up for it?"

I turned to face him, studying his craggy face. He didn't need to provide a resume to tell me that he'd seen more than his share of violence in his career. "Detective Declan. Do you really think there's a right time to talk about the fact I found a dead man murdered in my condo after coming home from a long shift at the hospital? Would you like to start with the fact his head was severed from his body or that he'd been beaten to within an inch of his life prior to that happening?"

While I heard the anger in my voice, I didn't care about being the nice girl at this point.

The detective chuckled and leaned against the counter. I was surprised he wasn't taking copious notes. Maybe he was recording me for his listening pleasure later.

"Did you know the victim very well?"

I closed my eyes, doing everything I could to block out the repulsive vision. "I moved here a little over a month ago. While I've seen Mr. Springer on several occasions, I've only talked to him a couple of times. I wouldn't say that's knowing him very well."

"Did he have any enemies?"

Sighing, I tried to thoughtfully answer his question. "Jack kept to himself. He was pleasant and from what I could tell, well liked. I have no idea how this happened given the building is secure."

"Interesting."

I rolled my eyes, trying to keep my temper in check. Adrenaline continued rushing through my system, although I had no doubt that I'd crash into a heap soon enough.

"What did he do in the building?" the detective continued.

"He was the maintenance man, but as far as his job description, I wouldn't know."

"Why was he in your condo?"

"I don't know," I snapped, shaking my head and taking a sip of wine. "I'm sorry, Detective. It's not every day I come home to find a dead man inside."

"Yes, I can imagine."

I can imagine? If I didn't know better, I'd say he was hinting at something. "I don't know how else to help you, Detective. I worked long hours and barely had time for myself."

"At Chicago Hospital. Is that correct?"

I tugged on my identification badge, glaring him in the eyes. "Do you need to make a copy?"

He lifted a single eyebrow, a slight smile curling on his face. He was amused. I was angry. Damn him.

"I've already confirmed you're an employee," he said, almost in passing. "Unfortunately, Ms. Sutherland, I do need to ask you where you were between the hours of ten p.m. and midnight."

"Are you kidding me?"

"I'm not in the habit of kidding with regards to a brutal murder. Can you please answer the question?"

My anger continued to increase, my patience level shot. While I knew he was just trying to do his job, I was incensed I was considered a suspect. I took another sip of my drink, cringing when all I could think about was the color of the wine. "If you really want to know, I was helping a well-respected surgeon in his attempt to save the life of a man who had three bullets lodged in his spine. While we were able to save his life, it's still questionable whether he's going to be able to walk again. If you'd like the name of the entire team who worked with me until I walked out the door at one thirty-seven a.m., then I'm happy to provide that to you."

He didn't seem flustered in the least about my outburst, but he finally retrieved a small notebook from his pocket, scribbling on the pad furiously. I looked away, images of Jack's broken body remaining in the forefront of my mind. I walked away from him and into the doorway, my nerves shot. Daylight was already streaming in through my windows, the forensics team finally zipping the black bag around Jack's body.

"Do you know of any reason why Mr. Springer had a gun on him?"

I opened my mouth, trying to remember if I'd noticed before. "Not really. The building is very secure." Or so I'd thought. I envisioned the moment I'd found him and come to think of it, I had seen a weapon in the corner next to the floor-to-ceiling windows. Why hadn't the murderer taken it? "Did he manage to get off a shot?"

He lifted a single eyebrow, the question obviously strange as hell. "As a matter of fact, he did." The detective didn't say anything else, but he continued staring at me.

"Oh," I managed. Oh? My God. I was acting suspicious. Swallowing, I looked away, trying not to chastise myself too badly. Even coming from New York, I'd never been the victim of a crime or seen anyone shot.

"As you might imagine, this investigation is just beginning. I will need to confirm your whereabouts and I'm certain I'll have additional questions for you after the evidence has been processed."

Processed. He said the word as if this was just another day on the force instead of a man bloodily losing his life. For all I knew, Jack had a family, kids and grandkids. He'd been taken from them and for what? Who murdered a maintenance man?

"I'm sure you will and other than my day off tomorrow, you can find me at the hospital almost every day," I managed, my voice little more than a whisper. "Am I a suspect, Detective? Do I need to hire an attorney?" I turned my head to study him. He continued to jot down a few notes, taking a full minute to turn his head in my direction.

"At this point, Ms. Sutherland, everyone is a suspect until I rule them out. As far as an attorney, that's entirely up to you; however, I will need you to remain in town."

My God. The man was staring at me like I was some femme fatale.

"But I can go about my life? You know, helping people?" I asked, although I had no clue how I could ever return to the condo. From where I was standing, the sight of the bloodstains wrapped around my mind like sharp claws.

He chuckled as he walked closer. "Of course." He produced a business card and I couldn't tolerate looking at it. "If you think of anything else, give me a call."

While I accepted his card, I had a feeling he'd been the one hounding me. If only I had something more concrete to tell him. Jack had been overtly nice to me, maybe because I seemed out of my element, a girl who had no business owning a three-million-dollar condo. He'd checked on me several times, although my hesitation in telling the detective that bit of information surprised me. The older man had been sweet, almost like he'd been looking out for me.

Why had he been inside? I hadn't reported any issues and there wasn't any scheduled regular maintenance that I remembered.

"Of course." I slumped against the doorjamb, shivering.

After he walked out of the room, he stopped, taking a few seconds before shifting so he could look me in the eyes. "I'm going to suggest that you stay with a family member for a few days. That's going to be the only way you rid yourself of the nightmare."

Another anxious laugh slipped from my mouth. "I doubt I'll ever be able to get rid of the horrible sight, and I don't have any family in town." I chewed on my lower lip, realizing the only person I could call was a friend from the hospital, although we'd only recently gotten close outside of our work.

"Well, just a suggestion, but you will need to email me where you're staying. My address is on the card."

"Very well, Detective. I'll let you know. When will I be able to return?"

"You should be able to gather your things tomorrow. I'll give you a call."

"I would appreciate that."

"You may want to consider contacting a crime scene cleaner after we're finished."

I knew what he was talking about. I'd been forced to talk with several members of law enforcement during my career. I'd picked up on how a crime scene was handled. I'd just never expected to be in the middle of one.

"Thank you, Detective. I'll consider that."

He took another few steps then stopped again. "Ms. Sutherland, you seem like a very nice girl. I'm going to give you a piece of advice. Be careful. This is a dangerous city. There are people who enjoy the act of violence, murdering anyone who gets in their way. I wouldn't like to see that happen to you."

His statement was startling. What the hell was he getting at? "That almost sounds like a threat, Detective Declan."

Huffing, he shook his head. "Not at all, Walker. Just a piece of advice after spending years picking up the pieces."

When he walked away, all I could concentrate on was the sound of his loafers moving across the tile floor toward the front door.

After he left, I shifted back into the kitchen, sliding down the wall, the cold chill remaining.

And for some reason, I thought I could hear Jack's screams.

Maksim

Blood.

I'd been responsible for my share of brutal deaths, the elimination of Novikov enemies necessary in order to

23

carry on our way of life. And I rarely if ever questioned the reason why. I'd learned early on that a single moment of hesitation meant weakness, a trait I couldn't afford. Given my penchant for violence, I'd garnered the respect of almost everyone in the Bratva.

Almost.

However, a nagging feeling remained in the back of my mind and had since the incident with Chamberlain.

I took a deep breath before knocking on the door.

When it was opened a few seconds later, I tried to keep all emotion from my face.

"Cousin. Come in," Vadim said, the usual hateful grin on his face. The fucker liked to lord over me the fact he was Ivan's only son, prepared to take the Novikov throne when the *Pakhan* was either assassinated or arrested. That could be at any time, Ivan's murderous rampage increasing any time an enemy dared attack us. Even now, there were rumors a turf war was set to begin, although the identity of the other player coming to the party had yet to be confirmed.

I cocked my head, narrowing my eyes but remaining quiet. I noticed he was favoring one of his arms, which I found curious. The man usually required his soldiers to handle his dirty work.

He laughed softly then opened the door wider, allowing me entrance, but not before murmuring his usual nasty condemnation in Russian.

"Grebanyy glupyy amerikanets."

As if using the term 'fucking stupid American' bothered me in the least. From what I'd learned about the Bratva, my American upbringing had been an added benefit in securing our position within various powerful corporations, just like the development Chamberlain had owned. I could talk the talk, hiding the Russian accent gleaned from my mother at will.

But my heritage remained strong, an attribute that I never allowed Vadim to forget.

"Bespolexnyy russkiy pridurok." 'Useless Russian idiot' was my reply. The fact I was fluent in several languages, including Russian, had intrigued Ivan as much as my Harvard education.

He seemed amused by our exchange, merely tolerating his son's hatred of me up to this point.

Ivan usually sequestered himself behind his desk, puffing on a thick cigar. On this early morning, he stood by the window, which meant something, or someone had pissed him off even more than normal.

"Maksim. Thank you for coming on such short notice," he stated. A man like Ivan never requested anything. He demanded it just like I did, refusing to accept anything less.

While I'd been given my own territory almost a year before, brought into the fold as if I were one of his sons, that meant nothing when he required orders to be followed.

"Of course. What do you need?" I asked, darting another glance in Vadim's direction. He was studying me carefully. Was this nothing more than an additional test of my will and my loyalty?

Ivan took several additional puffs of his cigar, flicking the ashes onto the refurbished teak wooden floor. He didn't care. He wasn't the one who would clean up his mess, which is what I expected I'd been called into his office to do. Someone had failed him, and my merciless nature earning me a reputation as being born without a soul. He needed my handiwork.

"You managed to hunt down Mr. Chamberlain," he said without any emotion.

I chuckled half under my breath. "New travels fast."

"Even my Capos and other trusted men had been unable to do so. I applaud your efforts." Ivan turned slightly, giving Vadim a dark look, one that told his only son that he'd failed the powerful man. I didn't have to glance in my cousin's direction to realize he was boiling from the acrid venom flowing through his veins. At some point, he'd send all that bitter hatred in my direction.

And I couldn't wait for that moment to occur.

"Eliminating a problem was necessary," I answered without bothering to give Vadim the time of day. Fuck him and his self-righteous bullshit.

"Yes. Now the project can move forward, but I want the damn construction site controlled and watched. That's your baby, Maksim," Ivan stated, taking another puff of his cigar.

I nodded, my instinct telling me Ivan was more concerned about something else. When news of Samuel's termination had leaked in the streets, tensions had risen.

"I am curious. Did Mr. Chamberlain provide you with any useful information before his unfortunate demise?" Ivan asked offhandedly.

"He confirmed that Samuel Rossi was working with him," I answered, watching Ivan's expression turn from amusement to fury.

"The little cocksucker," Ivan hissed as he finally turned to face us. "I should issue an elimination of everyone in Chamberlain's company."

"Mr. Chamberlain has powerful friends, Pops. You should be mindful of that," Vadim told him. "I don't think going on a killing spree is in our best interest right now."

The sharp look Ivan gave him was one I'd seen many times. The man didn't like to be questioned.

"First of all, I don't think Chamberlain was working with anyone else within his company. Second, I doubt his *friends* will attempt to point fingers," I said quietly. "Or attempt to issue trouble of any kind. Two warnings were sent. They will be heeded, at least for a period of time."

27

"While that would usually be the case, I'm concerned we might have other issues to contend with," Ivan huffed.

"That Samuel was also working with someone else." My statement brought cold stares from both men.

Ivan took a few seconds to gaze down the length of me, still puffing on his cigar. "Yes, which is why the rumors keep sweeping through the streets of Chicago, something we can't allow to continue."

"Unfortunately, I think that's impossible," I said, Vadim laughing instantly before spewing out his thoughts.

"Samuel was a two-bit accountant at best. He didn't have the nerve to do anything else underhanded against us."

"That two-bit accountant managed to steal a significant amount of money. Might I remind you of that?" Ivan's face turned beet red, the embarrassment of going over his losses again not something he was used to.

Vadim cursed, walking around his father toward the bar. "Then we eliminate everyone who might have been working with Samuel. Period. After that, we'll have no more issues."

Smirking, I had a feeling I knew what Ivan was about to say. Vadim was short sighted at best, unable to think about the future within our industry. Times were changing, the need to keep a low profile while handling business vital if we wanted to stay alive. Plus, there were other methods of eliminating issues when necessary.

"We're not handling this like a bulldozer, Vadim. We need to tread carefully until we know what we're dealing with. To that end, Maksim, I need you to carry out something else, but you'll need to be careful."

"I will do my best," I answered, noticing the *Pakhan*'s voice was strained.

He chuckled as he came closer. "I have no doubt you will. You've proven to be very worthy of my trust, which is why I'm expanding your territory. It's become clear to me that you do well with all our corporate venues while walking a fine line in ensuring our employees follow our rules. We'll talk more about your heightened responsibilities after you finish this task for me."

I could tell Vadim was furious, which pleased me more than it should. The man was a pompous pig with zero moral character and no understanding of the need for detail. "I appreciate the nod."

Ivan walked even closer, taking another puff. "Rossi caused us too many problems, but it's not over yet. I find it interesting that we never recovered the money. Not a penny. After everything Vadim put that man through, he continued insisting that he had nothing to do with the theft. I have to give him credit in the end. He had balls. That's something I admire. Still, locating the cash is important to me. Given the fact he was successful in stealing from us has leaked onto the streets, the unrest continues to grow."

"I understand. That doesn't bode well for keeping control. Do you have any ideas what Rossi could have done with the money?"

"He had less than ten thousand dollars in his bank accounts when he died. There is no sign of offshore accounts or other investments. No boats. No expensive sports cars. Even though my Capo was given decent tips from a trusted informant, he ran into a dead end everywhere he looked. As you might imagine, that angers me tremendously. However," he said as he held up his index finger, "all is not lost. I managed to find out he purchased a condominium in South Loop three months ago."

"South Loop?" I questioned. The area of Chicago was known for exclusive and very expensive pieces of real estate. While Samuel had been paid well for his duties, the multimillion-dollar condos alone would have been a stretch for him.

"Fascinating given Samuel never wanted to leave the old house he once shared with his wife. It took me pulling in a favor to find that juicy piece of information since Rossi did everything in his power to hide the purchase and the transfer. So, I think it's time for you to handle a brand new hunt, your expertise in these particular matters quite useful."

Ivan grinned, his gray eyes twinkling.

"Who are we hunting this go around?"

"It would seem that there is another person involved, some cocksucker who just moved to the city. I just found out he's staying in Samuel's condo. And it would seem the place was deeded over to this individual after Samuel's death. Even if the man paid cash, there is still at least three million unaccounted for." Ivan cursed in Russian.

"Brazen asshole needs to be taken out. I can handle that for you, Pops," Vadim suggested.

Ivan threw up his hand. "This isn't just about eliminating the man, although that might become necessary. He'll need to be manipulated until he provides the information we need."

Manipulated. He meant interrogated, taken to a facility I'd designed for that specific use in mind.

"That can be arranged," I answered, lifting a single eyebrow as Vadim continued to fume. He and I would need to come to terms with his increased level of anger against me sooner versus later. Questions started forming in my mind. Had Samuel paid cash for the unit? Why leave it to someone?

"Good," Ivan huffed. "The asshole thinks he's going to play me for a fool, using my own money against me. I need you to hunt this interloper down and find my freaking cash. Then I want you to seek revenge in any way you desire. *Bespolezntt kusok ploti.* Do you think you can handle that for me, Maksim?"

A grin crossed my face as I flexed then fisted my hands. *Useless piece of flesh.* That's all the son of a bitch would have left when I was finished with him. No one stole from the Bratva. "No problem."

"Just so you know. I had certain baggage handled beforehand, which should put the fear of God into the fucker, but I have a feeling the man doesn't scare easily. However, do whatever is necessary. And I do mean whatever." Ivan's eyes narrowed, his chest heaving.

Chuckling, I shot Vadim one last look before a slight smile crossed my face. Perhaps Vadim had been the one assigned to 'handling' this piece of business and had gotten hurt. "I already have a few ideas in mind." What continued to bother me was that if another player had moved into town, the fact Ivan had allowed such a huge sum of money to disappear could mean additional trouble including bloodshed. Loyalty was something that could be bought, allowing some of our employees to be hired by whatever organization that had dared to set foot in our territory. There was far too much information to be circulated that could prove deadly to the family. The shit would need to be handled quickly, issuing the kind of warning that no one would soon forget.

He patted my arm, giving me a nod of respect. "You will be paid handsomely for your endeavor. I'll have my Capo provide you with the information and whatever else you need. *Khoroshey okhoty.*"

Happy hunting. It would be a pleasure.

CHAPTER 3

 *alker*

He's dead. Jack's dead.

My inner voice nagged at me, my head throbbing from intense pressure. My chest ached from trying to catch my breath, another wave of adrenaline the only thing keeping me going at this point.

"You're really not going to call in a crime scene cleaner like the detective suggested?" Jessie asked.

Blood. Blood. Blood.

The single word had woven throughout my mental faculties. Why it'd bothered me more than the dozens of times I'd been in a bloody operating room was something I hadn't been able to fully answer.

Other than a headless man caused the pool of blood.

There was that.

I chewed on my inner lip, finally shaking my head. "I can do it myself."

"You're a nurse, for Christ's sake. You know as well as I do that his blood could be contaminated. You could get an infection."

"That's why I purchased a few things. Remember?" I'd ceremoniously purchased every type of cleaning supply I could get my hands on.

"Damn it. You're hardheaded," she snapped.

"That's why you love me. Stop worrying. Okay?"

"Are you certain?"

The question seemed rhetorical. I managed to smile even though Jessie's face was a stark reminder of what had happened the night before. She'd dropped everything, rushing to pick me up. Then we'd spent the night huddled under blankets in front of her television. I hadn't gotten a wink of sleep, the ugly visions continuing to ravage my mind. I glanced at the top floor of the building, swallowing hard.

Evening had already fallen, dusk creating creatures in my mind waiting to jump out of every bush. A lump would remain in my throat for a long time.

"I have to do this, Jess. I can't allow the tragedy to rule my life. I feel horrible for the man and his family, but I didn't know him."

"But it happened in your place."

"Yeah, I know. I'll clean it and everything will be fine."

Her mouth twisted, her eyes flashing her disapproval. The thought of cleaning the bloodstains was revolting, but it had to be done.

"You could sell the place. You don't even know the man who gave it to you."

I snorted as I reached for the handle of her car door. She was right. I had no idea who Samuel Rossi was at all. "He was friends with my dad. Okay?"

"You mean a father you never met?"

Hissing, I shook my head. I didn't need to be reminded that my father had skipped out on my mother long before I was born. "Besides, do you honestly think someone is going to buy the place once the information about the murder leaks?"

"Maybe. It might take some time," Jessie insisted.

"I don't have time. I can barely afford the condo fees, let alone the electricity. Where am I supposed to live in the meantime?"

She wrinkled her nose, her eyes finally lighting up. "You can live with me!"

35

Laughing, I shook my head. "You have a teensy tiny bedroom but it's much larger than your kitchen. And you only have enough hot water for a ten minute or less shower. I don't think that's going to work."

Reaching out, she grabbed my hand. "I'll stay with you if you'd like."

"First of all, you have a shift in about twenty minutes. And second, no. I need to do this on my own or I'll never be able to get over it. Besides, Nurse Breckinridge was kind enough to allow me to have tomorrow off as well." I rolled my eyes before making a face. We both worked for the same woman. While she was a talented nurse, she was a terrible people person.

She sagged against her seat, groaning. "Okay but call me later."

"I will if I don't fall asleep from exhaustion. Okay? Stop worrying about me. My mama raised one tough girl."

"You're tough, but I've seen the marshmallow inside of you."

"Get out of town." I teased, even though the tone sounded flat.

"Okay. I'll just a phone call away."

I climbed out, grabbing the cleaning supplies and closing the door behind me. I'd left the condo without taking anything but my purse. As I stood on the curb in the brisk wind, staring up at the building, a small part of me felt adrift, as if I'd lost someone important to me. I felt terrible that I hadn't taken any time to ask Jack any decent questions other than about the building. He'd always been so kind, even helping me with groceries a couple of times. I realized I hadn't mentioned that to the detective either the night before or when he'd called to let me know forensics had finished.

Now was the moment I regretted not setting up the last security measure, a scan of my handprint. At least my key worked without incident. When I walked into the building, I was pleased seeing the interior for a change. Nothing had changed, the same beautiful ficus trees adorned with white lights sparkling when I walked toward the elevator. My freshly washed tennis shoes skidded across the slick marble surface as usual. The elevator button pressed the same way as it had the night before.

No, one thing had changed. The elevator ride didn't take nearly long enough.

I stood in front of my door for almost two minutes before finding the courage to unlock it. At least when I went inside, the place no longer had the odor of blood. I turned on as many lights as possible, avoiding the area like the plague. For some reason, I expected there to be crime scene tape everywhere, what little furniture I had in disarray. The forensics team had done an excellent job of keeping everything intact.

However, the crime scene itself remained. I dropped my things in the foyer, heading toward the living room, trying to remain clinical about what I was going to do. As I peered down, I realized the stain wasn't as large as I'd remembered, the splatters on the wall contained to a small area. Still, my stomach lurched from the thought of what needed to be done. After a full five seconds I turned away.

You can do this.

We would see.

I set to work cleaning and disinfecting the area, trying not to think about what I'd walked into the night before. Why would anyone want to hurt the man? How had they gotten inside the building in the first place? Why had Jack kept a gun with him given the tight security?

The questions continued to churn in my mind, enough so that by the time I was finished, I couldn't think clearly, and my clothes were drenched in perspiration. I tossed the garbage bag toward the front door near my purse, unable to stand another minute without taking a shower.

After tossing the scrubs I'd been wearing the night before into the laundry basket, I changed my mind, nearly ripping the material in my forced effort to dump every-thing into the small trashcan. Then I started the water as hot as I could tolerate it, enjoying the burning sensations against my skin.

As the water tumbled down over my head, I stared at the drain.

Then I began to shake uncontrollably even though I refused to cry. I hadn't shed a tear for as long as I could remember, always remaining tough on the outside. I would continue that effort now. Damn it.

At least the shower soothed my aching muscles. I made a promise to myself that I'd had my last meltdown. I'd cleaned up the mess. Now I had to rely on the police to do their jobs, finding the murderer.

If that was possible.

After drying off, I grabbed my robe, trying to pretend like nothing bad had happened in the middle of my condo.

But it had.

Images continued to flash in my mind, ugly and violent. I had to get rid of the bag. I couldn't sleep with it inside, even stashed in the foyer.

After tying the sash, I glanced at myself in the mirror. I could swear I'd aged since yesterday. As I walked out of the bathroom, shutting off the light, my gut told me that whatever the reason Jack had been murdered would come back to haunt me.

And I had no idea why.

I grabbed the bag, heading for the door. At least I could dump the entire contents down the trash shoot, even though I was no longer certain who would be required to deal with the bloody mess.

Poor Jack.

Poor. Dead. Jack.

*　*　*

Maksim

Baggage.

I'd learned that Jack Springer, a maintenance man for the condominium association where Samuel had purchased his condo, had been killed to send a warning to the new resident. While there didn't seem to be a connection between Jack and Samuel, I didn't believe in coincidences. Jack had been snooping around the only unit on the top floor when Vadim had come to have a chat with Walker Sutherland, the man taking up residence in the high-rise. The transfer still intrigued me, which is something I would chat about with the man once inside.

From what Brick had told me, the murder of the maintenance worker had been messy, even more so than usual, the cops called. That had put Ivan in a bind, especially if any evidence had been left behind or if Walker had seen anything. Whatever the case, I had a job to do. It was probable that Mr. Sutherland knew exactly the location of the stolen funds.

There wasn't a building I couldn't get into no matter how secure. While my studies at Harvard hadn't included breaking into facilities or hacking into computers, that had been a fascinating hobby belonging to my roommate.

I'd learned an entirely different trade, even though testing his knowledge had almost landed both of us behind bars more than once.

As I headed for the back door of the expensive high-rise, I was surprised that the heavily trafficked street wasn't busier. Then again, it was almost midnight. Maybe all the Fortune 500 superstars were safely tucked away in their beds. Snickering, I held my phone to the hand scanner. I'd researched one of the owners, obtaining his handprint for this very event. While I'd tried to find Walker's for a bit of irony, I could find nothing on the man. I'd heard he was new to town, but as of yet, he hadn't made an address change and my quick search of the internet didn't answer any questions about who he was or what organization he was connected with.

That was the other item necessary to find. Who were Walker's associates? When the question was answered, there would be additional eliminations.

The skill I'd perfected worked beautifully, the door clicking, allowing me entrance. The fucker lived on the thirtieth floor. While not a penthouse, he certainly had an excellent view of the city. I could only imagine the kind of cocksucker he was. Some rich dude who thought coming into our territory would be easy.

Maybe Jack Springer's untimely death had sent him a warning, something Ivan never did. I found that... fascinating.

I moved toward the bank of elevators, taking my time. The asshole wasn't going anywhere. When the elevator pinged, I checked my weapon, once again shoving it into my suit jacket. I was a crack shot, my reflexes better than anyone else in the organization. If necessary, I'd put a bullet in his leg to keep Walker from attempting escape.

Then I'd drag his sorry ass to the facility I called the playhouse, a location designed for questioning anyone who crossed us. My methods were highly effective, my success rate hovering at ninety-two percent. In my opinion, that's why I'd skipped the ranks, moving from soldier to leader without enduring working with Vadim directly.

As I moved down the hall, I scanned the area, checking for possible escape routes. There was always a chance Walker was expecting a visit. I had to be prepared for anything. I rounded the final corner, moving to the end of the hall. My keen hearing allowed me to catch a few sounds coming from behind the secure door. However, I preferred the element of surprise.

When the door was thrown open, for the first time in as long as I could remember, I was caught by surprise. The person standing in front of me wasn't who I was expecting. A woman. She was leaning over, wrapping her hand tightly around a white trash bag, the slight transparency allowing me to see various colors of red.

Jesus Christ.

She'd been tasked to clean up the mess Vadim had left. Was that the reason for the sexy purple silk robe and bare feet, her long dark tresses still damp from a recent shower?

When she finally lifted her head, there was shock as well as a flash of terror in her deep violet eyes, the hue matching the color of the robe perfectly. For a minute, I allowed myself to become mesmerized by her beauty. Shimmering porcelain skin. A voluptuous hourglass figure with full breasts and rounded hips, the kind of woman meant for a man's hands to explore.

My hands.

Her robe had come slightly undone, revealing the swell of her breasts, her bend at the waist coming dangerously close to allowing her nipples to show. I envisioned exactly what they'd look like; perfect areolas the color of sun-kissed rose petals in the summer. My mouth watered at the thought of having her tight little nipple in my mouth, sucking and licking.

The thought was just as surprising as the sight of her. I hadn't desired a woman in a hell of a long time. I narrowed my eyes, drinking in her scent as she stared at me unmoving.

Then she dropped the bag, instantly pulling the two edges of her robe together with one hand.

I said nothing for a few seconds, attempting to determine what should be done with her, but I continued raking my eyes down the length of her body. I could tell by her mixture of expressions that she'd gone through myriad emotions from surprise to terror and finally fury. I'd invaded her space.

After quickly scanning the opulent rooms I could see over her shoulder, I had the distinct feeling she was all alone, but I still couldn't be too careful. Maybe this was Walker's main squeeze. The bastard. I could imagine he'd force her to clean up the shit he'd been a part of creating. I could only imagine a brutal murder like what Ivan had described didn't happen in this part of the city very often.

I cocked my head, my nostrils flaring. Whoever she was, sadly, she was going to become a casualty of war. Then again, she would be fun to play with, enjoying the spoils of battle. With one hard shove, I pitched the door against the foyer wall, moving past the threshold, shocking her even more.

I was amused when she attempted to shove the door in my face, using all her weight and managing to push me back by a few inches. Good for her. It was obvious she'd been given some amateurish training on self-defense. Sadly, that wouldn't matter. Not when millions of dollars were at stake.

"Get out of here, whoever you are," she spit out, her lower lip trembling as her eyes flashed anger as well as defiance.

She had no idea how sultry and delicious she looked to a brutal man like me. I could devour her without a second thought, taking what I wanted. Maybe that's exactly what I would do. However, I certainly didn't need an audience.

Without addressing her question, I slammed the door, moving further inside. She backed away, her entire body shaking. I could tell she was contemplating securing some kind of weapon in her hand. I was almost eager to see the sexy little bird try. I had a few minutes to kill.

As I walked further into the condo, I continued sweeping the location with my eyes, prepared to pull out my weapon if necessary. However, there was no sound other than her heavy breathing. I returned my gaze toward her, marveling in the fact she'd yet to freak out. Most women in this position would've started screaming by now. She was still attempting to figure out what the hell was going on.

She raked her hand through her hair, giving me another defiant look. But I'd seen the quick glance toward her purse, which remained by the front door. If I had to guess, I'd say she had a weapon hidden inside, was calculating how to get to it before I managed to stop her.

"I told you to get out of here. I have a gun and I know how to use it." Her demand screamed of rebellion while her voice was quavering. I resisted smiling, taking another long stride in her direction.

She glanced toward her purse again, her chest rising and falling as fear continued to increase.

A growl erupted from my throat, and I leaned over, yanking the leather strap into my hand. Let's see what the lovely little creature was attempting to hide from me. As I slipped my hand inside, I shifted my heated gaze in her direction, daring her to challenge me.

"Those are my things. Who are you? What do you want?" Her commanding voice held a haughty tone, as if she thought she could get control. I continued to admire the woman, even more curious what relationship she had with Walker.

I narrowed my eyes as I yanked out her phone, tossing it against the wall. She yelped when the expensive communications tool broke into a hundred pieces. I certainly couldn't have her attempting to contact anyone. Then I continued searching through her things, chuckling from finding the usual items found in a woman's purse. Keys. A makeup bag. Tissue. A small notebook. When I managed to locate her wallet, I jerked it from her purse, flipping it open to take a peek at her identification. What the hell? I studied her driver's license for longer than I should have.

Wait a fucking minute.

She was Walker Sutherland? That was impossible. I almost laughed from the chilling realization. Women weren't usually behind betraying a powerful mob. That made her even more dangerous, her innocence and fear likely faked.

That roused the beast deep within me.

She chose that awkward moment to bolt away from me. Was she kidding? I dropped the bag, including the wallet, shaking my head. Where in the hell did she think she was going? She made it into the kitchen, yanking out the drawer as I took long strides toward her. When she decided to grab a large kitchen knife, a wave of anger rolled through me. She needed to be taught a lesson in obedience. I wrapped my hand around the back of her neck, yanking her against me, smashing her hand against the edge of the counter with enough force the knife flew out of her fingers.

"Let go of me," she managed, although her voice was strangled from the pressure I was using.

I jerked her again, forcing her against my chest, surprised at my body's reaction to her. I should think of her as nothing but someone who needed to be dealt with. Instead, my pulse kicked up a few notches, a bolt of electricity shooting through every muscle and tendon. I breathed in her scent, intoxicated immediately from the freshness of her shower gel. Just the feel of her body against mine allowed a moment of pure euphoria. I debated what the hell I was going to do with her, the adrenaline flow rushing through my body enough to tighten my throat.

"Who are you?" she asked, undulating against me until my cock was rock hard. God, I wanted this woman, which was completely out of character for me. This entire situation made no sense.

"Are you Walker Sutherland?" I growled into her ear, resisting sliding my hand under the thin layering of material keeping me from touching her luscious body. My Russian accent was more pronounced than usual, which was another surprise. She brought out the savage in me, tossing aside everything about humanity my parents had taught me.

I could do vile and filthy things to her without looking back.

"You already know the answer. What does it matter? Now, get the hell out of here or I will call the police." Her defiance, while adorable, was starting to get on my nerves. Interrogating her was going to be difficult, if not impossible.

I snickered. She would soon find that continuing to fight me wasn't in her best interest. I tightened my hold around her neck, allowing my hot breath to cascade across her face.

Walker refused to stop fighting me. Using both hands, she grabbed my arm, yanking hard in some ridiculous attempt to break my hold. I squeezed even tighter, nuzzling against her neck. "Be a good girl and maybe I won't hurt you." I pulled a deep breath into my lungs, my cock aching to the point I wasn't certain I'd be able to get her out of there without finding some relief. I shoved my groin against her, grinding back and forth, barely able to control my needs.

Then I pulled her away from the cabinet, sliding my arm around her neck, pulling her even closer.

"Son of a bitch. Let me go," she barked.

"I'm afraid, Walker, that I'm not going to be able to let you go." I wasn't inclined to take her to the playhouse, but there were few other choices. Still, my gut told me that her interrogation needed to be handled carefully. For all I knew, she could be an operative, extensively trained to withstand all levels of torture. That meant I needed to get creative.

"Why? I've done nothing to you. Nothing."

"Mmm… It's not what you've done. It's what you haven't done. And for that, you're going to be punished." A hard spanking would be a good start. As far as whether or not she was involved, of that I had no doubt. Her attempts at playing me like a fool hadn't worked. It was time to shift the little game we were playing onto another level.

Her heavy breathing was a sweet acknowledgement that she realized she'd met her match. As my carnal needs increased, I made my decision about how to handle her discipline.

As well as securing information.

I would entice the darkness I knew existed inside of her. Then I would break her, becoming her only source for fulfilling her needs.

After that, she'd surrender to me without question, providing me with everything I required.

She continued to struggle even as I slid my hand down her arm to her thigh, crawling several inches of silky material into my hand.

While my decision of how to handle her initially was risky, I no longer gave a shit.

I would taste her.

Then I would force her to submit.

After that, I'd fuck her long and hard.

And that was just the beginning.

CHAPTER 4

alker

No. no. No!

Please let me get out of this alive. Please.

I continued struggling, but there was no way to get out of his grip. The Russian was far too strong. His heavy breathing continued, whatever he was saying in his native language full of rage. What money? What the hell was the man talking about?

"The money. I know you have it."

Money? Was he kidding me? This was just a robbery? Wait. Wait. None of this made any sense. "Buddy, I don't have any money. If you'd like me to pull up my bank account on the computer, you'll see I used almost every last cent I had moving here from New York, barely able to provide what little furnishings you see here." Why was I explaining anything to him?

Several additional words flew out of his mouth that I couldn't understand, likely cursing that I wasn't more accommodating. Well, fuck him.

"You're lying."

"Why would I lie about something like that? What you see is what you get. Whoever gave you information like that, they were wrong. And stupid. I'm a nurse. I work eighteen-hour days. I don't have time for friends or anything else, including whatever you think I did to take money from you."

I could tell by the stern look on his face that he didn't believe a damn word I said. Money. I racked my mind, trying to figure out what he could mean. Did Jack owe the man money? Is that why he was murdered in my apartment? Several thoughts raced through my mind, none of them making any sense.

Maybe Jack had gambled and lost money to some mob group. He'd never struck me as the gambling type, but who knew about a person any longer. Besides, why slaughter the man in my condo?

Jack. What the hell were you involved in? Wait. What if this had nothing to do with Jack. What if…

I knew nothing about Samuel Rossi. In fact, my mother had refused to talk about him other than her single statement that he'd been an old friend of my father's. I'd grilled her for a half an hour. When she'd flown off the handle, demanding I not accept whatever item had been left for me in the man's will, I'd been shocked at her fervor. She never raised her voice. Even her body had been shaking.

Of course that had yanked my curiosity to the surface.

I'd only found out Samuel's name when I'd received a letter from an attorney in the mail telling me I was a part of the man's will. The knots in my stomach confirmed what my gut had been telling me since the day I'd received the damn note.

Samuel Rossi hadn't been a good man, which meant my father hadn't been either. Was that why my mother had refused to talk about him all these years? There was no other explanation why my mother had reacted that way. Now I was going to pay the ugly price for something done by a dead man.

"Who is Samuel Rossi to you?" he demanded, the tone even harsher than before.

"I… I don't know him."

He narrowed his eyes then burst into laughter. Seconds later, the brooding Russian dragged me closer to the living room, staring down at the spot. *The* spot. I shuddered, doing everything I could to pull away.

"You're still lying, which mean I'm going to be forced to resort to other tactics, little bird. None of which I think you'll enjoy."

"What? I don't... understand. I'm not who you think I am."

"You will understand in time, my precious little bird. But first things first, *moya vkusnaya ptichka*," he whispered in my ear.

I didn't need to know what he was saying to understand what he hungered for, but he made certain I knew exactly what was going to happen. He was going to take me.

Use me.

Dear God. The man was going to... fuck me. I slapped at his arm, squirming so hard that within seconds I was exhausted.

"I'm going to learn every inch of your gorgeous body, little bird. Because as of this moment, you belong to me."

"Like hell you are." I tried to remember all the self-defense training I'd learned a couple years before, a birthday gift from my mother. I'd laughed at her choice then. Now I was grateful. I stomped on his foot first, elbowing him in the gut seconds after.

Grunting, his grip on my neck loosened. That was all I needed. I bit down on his arm, shaking my head back and forth, enjoying his howl. Then I slammed my foot into his knee. That did the trick.

I flew out of his hold, racing into the bedroom, slamming and locking the door. I knew a piece of wood and a brass lock wasn't going to keep him out but for so long. However, I had a nice weapon of sorts courtesy of my old boss, the statue thick and heavy with a couple of sharp edges. That should do the trick.

As he bellowed from the other side, I rushed to stand behind the door. Just as expected, he kicked it in, the wood splintering easily. He was barely inside the room when I smashed the statue against his head.

His body immediately jerked, his muscles tensing as he roared another bellow of anguish. I hit him one more time, waiting until he toppled over before jumping over his legs and heading straight for the front door.

This wasn't going to be like one of those horror movies where the dumb chick fumbled to get out of harm's way. I concentrated, refusing to allow fear to stop me from getting the hell away from him. Within seconds, I was in the hallway, moving toward the elevator. As soon as I hit the button, I realized I was a stupid fool. It could take thirty seconds or more for the elevator to make its way to my floor.

The stairs.

There was no other choice. Even in my bare feet, I figured I could race down the thirty flights within a couple of minutes. Right? The man was far too bulky as well as injured to keep up with me. I flew around the corner, cursing the fact the stairwell was all the way at the other end of the floor.

As my blood pumped through my veins, the sound of my heart thumping irregularly echoing in my ears, I ran as fast as possible. With only a few yards to go, I'll be damned if I didn't hear heavy feet behind me.

Running fast.

Faster than I was.

Oh, dear God.

Only when I flung open the door did I allow myself to look over my shoulder. I might be one of those girls with issues judging distance, but it was clear he was gaining on me. The only hope I had was keeping my momentum going as I rushed down the stairs. The door closed behind me, which was almost comforting.

As my feet hit the hard concrete, I gripped the metal railing, pummeling myself forward. By the time I made it down one floor, he was right behind me. How the hell could a two-hundred-and-twenty-pound man with muscles like a damn body builder move that fast? I was small and wiry, which should help.

It wasn't.

Panting, I refused to give up, even as I heard his dark laugh pulsing in my ears.

"You really think you can get away from me?" he asked, the low rumble echoing in the dense space.

The bastard wasn't getting an answer.

Run. Run. Run.

I made it four floors below when the asshole shocked me by jumping down a full flight of stairs, landing just behind me.

I shrieked, praying someone, anyone would hear me. My knees buckling, I was stymied by a few disgusting images floating in my warped brain, every one of them sexual in nature. I had to get myself out of this ridiculous desire that had ripped away my sanity. He wasn't some bad boy fulfilling a fantasy. He was a brutal criminal who wanted to kill me.

I skidded across the cold floor, jumping down several stairs, panting uncontrollably,

He was gaining.

Faster. Faster.

With a single hand, he snagged my hair, jerking me hard enough agony burst into my neck and shoulders.

"No!" My scream also bounced off the thick walls.

He snapped his other hand around my mouth, making a tsking sound. "You shouldn't have run from me, little bird. That pissed me off."

Pissed him off?

As the brute pulled me against him once again, I realized my robe had come untied. Why hadn't I bothered to put on underwear? He took several deep breaths before brushing his fingers down the side of my neck. I couldn't believe the number of tingles floating through me, tickling every one of my nerve endings. I was hot, both from the race as well as from his touch.

He didn't seem bothered in the least that at any time someone from another floor could open the stairwell door, although from what I'd been able to tell, very few of the owners would ever consider using the stairs. Whatever exercise they got was probably from a high-priced gym where they had a fabulous trainer.

As the random, ridiculous thoughts continued to rush through my mind, he tossed me over the railing, keeping his hand wrapped around my hair at the scalp. He tugged once, causing another shot of anguish, leaning over so his hot breath cascaded across my cheek.

"Now, I'm going to punish you. If you make a sound or try and get out of my hold, the punishment will become much worse. Do you understand me?"

"Yes," I managed through gritted teeth, although I wasn't planning on following his commands. "But you have no right to touch me."

"I have every right since I own you."

"That will never happen."

"It already has. You see, you ventured into my world, disrupting my life. In turn, I'm going to take yours." He jerked the robe away from my body, exposing my naked backside. "And you are going to obey everything I tell you or you aren't going to enjoy a moment of what will happen to you. Do you understand what I'm telling you?"

I understood alright.

The words weren't just haunting as hell. They were revolting, keeping my anger at the surface. Tears finally formed and while I did everything I could to shove them aside, a single salty bead floated past my eyelashes, trickling down my face in yet another ugly reminder that I was his captive. It had taken a brute to make me cry. I would never, ever give him that satisfaction again.

Moaning, I glared down the floors below, nauseous as hell, my hands already sweaty from trying to hold onto the railing. When he brought his hand down against my bottom, stars shot in front of my eyes. He smacked me several additional times, the pain increasing, my mind nothing but a huge blur. How? Why? Why?

The asshole kept me pinned to the railing, his hold only getting stronger as he peppered my bottom with brutal swats, one coming after the other. I was thrown into a combination of unwanted, toxic desire and the longing to drive a knife into his heart. My mind remained a blur, the echo of his palm smashing against my backside matching my rapid pulse.

There wasn't an inch of me that wasn't tingling, which added to the disgusting moment. Even the sound of his large palm slapping against my skin became a powerful aphrodisiac. The robe had come undone, but still covered my hard-as-pebbles nipples. His rough actions forced them to slide back and forth, only adding to the ache that seemed to envelope my entire body. I opened my mouth to scream, ignoring his horrible demand, but nothing came out.

After several additional brutal smacks, I found myself melting against the railing.

"Stop. Just… stop," I begged, but only once. I wasn't giving the bastard any additional acknowledgment that his actions bothered me in the least.

"You want me to stop, little bird?"

God, I hated the nickname he'd given me. I wanted to loathe his deep, resonating voice, but that was growing increasingly impossible. The huskiness wrapped around me, adding to the anxiety threatening to shut me down hard and cold.

His hulking mass of a body leaned over again, pressing me so tightly against the thick metal pole that my breath was knocked out of me.

"Yes," I struggled to say.

"And what will you give me in return? Huh?" He raked his nails down my spine, dragging aside the robe until it was hanging off one shoulder. My naked breasts were crushed against the cold metal, and I was no longer able to feel my legs.

"Fuck you."

He laughed, the sound deep and throaty as he resumed the hard spanking, moving from one side to the other. I was shocked at my body's reaction, the longing that spilled into every part of me. This wasn't normal, and all I could think about was my brain's wiring had malfunctioned, leaving me incapable of understanding what was really happening.

"That will come, little bird. Let's see just how wet you are." His breathing remained labored as he kicked my legs apart, never releasing his hold on my long strands of hair as he rolled his fingers down the crack of my ass, tickling my inner thigh. I held my breath, my legs trembling as he dared to slide them closer toward my pussy.

"You won't get away with this."

His dark laugh rumbled in the dense space. "That's where you're wrong. We own every inch of this city."

We? Who the hell was 'we'?

As he slipped a single finger between the folds of my pussy, I let off a strangled cry, throwing out my arm and extending my fingers. When he shoved the long digit inside, I clamped my eyes shut, unable to understand what the hell was happening to me.

"I can tell how much you hunger for me, little bird."

"Never, you pig."

"Deny if you want to but your body provides the truth. You long for a dominant man."

A strangled laugh bubbled to the surface. "Over my dead body."

"Hmmm… That can be arranged. Be careful what you wish for."

When he lowered his head, his heavy breathing electrifying every inch of my skin, I couldn't manage to stop shaking. As he thrust his finger deep inside my tight channel, I gritted my teeth, the dazzling yet unwanted sensations nothing I'd been prepared for.

"Yes, you are one hungry little girl. Aren't you? Soon I'll take care of that, but in my time." He smacked me several more times, then jerked me into a standing position. "Now, we're going to go upstairs to your apartment where you will put on some clothes."

"Then what? You're going to kill me?"

"That remains to be seen. After that, you're coming with me."

"Where in the hell do you think you're taking me? I have a life. A job. Friends." I demanded, although I doubted that I was going to get an honest answer.

He pulled me close to the stairs, forcing me to take several steps. "We're going straight to hell. We'll see if you deserve salvation after you pay your penance."

CHAPTER 5

$\mathcal{M}$aksim

A woman.

I'd been sent to collect a freaking woman, which continued to piss me off. Ivan hadn't been honest with me, which was the first time that had happened I could remember. There had to be a reason. I certainly knew Vadim would have beaten her by now, uncaring about the fact she might not deserve his wrath. Then again, she could be one damn good actress. I had to keep that in the back of my mind. While I had no issue ending the life of scumbags like Samuel or Gregor, I still considered myself a decent man for a single reason.

I'd never injured or exacted revenge on a female, no matter their crime. Perhaps that was a weakness that would get me killed one day, but I refused to change my convictions.

Maybe my mother had managed to influence me to some degree.

However, the fact remained that she was the only person who knew where the large sum of cash was being kept. Perhaps she'd thought that feigning her innocence would convince me to free her.

The woman was wrong.

She'd tangled with the wrong person, even if I found it difficult to keep my eyes off her. I wanted to taste every inch of her, fuck her. My reaction was irrational, but she was that special. Special. I hadn't thought of a woman that way in as long as I could remember.

After taking a deep breath, I allowed my gaze to fall, studying every inch of her as she yanked the thin robe around her luscious body. Even the cotton candy pink color on her toes was enticing, pulling me further into the darkness of lust. I shouldn't feel this way, allowing even a slight consideration of acting on my carnal needs.

Granted, she was absolutely gorgeous, awakening something deep inside of me I'd long since thought dead and buried. However, in my mind fucking her should be forbidden. But as a growl swept up from the depth of my being, I knew there was no way to avoid taking what I wanted. I'd forsaken the pleasures of the flesh for a number of years, preferring to soothe my beast with the use of violence. My decision had worked up until now, until the moment she'd opened her huge violet doe eyes, peering at me as if studying a monster.

I'd expected to find a pompous, entitled asshole given the exclusive address. There wasn't a studio apartment in the sleek high-rise that didn't cost somewhere in the neighborhood of two million. That meant the unit transferred into her name easily cost four, maybe more.

Purchased with our money.

I seriously doubted she had no idea what I was talking about. There were no coincidences in my world, only those who believed they could steal from the Nikolovs. Still, her presence presented an entirely different set of challenges.

Instead of finding the job easy to do, dumping the arrogant bastard who'd stolen our money into the trunk of my car after beating him senseless, I'd found her.

Her.

A beguiling flower.

A breath of fresh air.

A woman whose voluptuous body called to me, her scent permanently staining my skin. Just touching her soft skin had electrified dead tissue, my cock aching to violate her in filthy, unimaginable ways.

And I would.

But all in good time.

The fact remained she was continuing to fuck with us, her lies pitiful. I couldn't allow her stunning raven hair or full breasts meant for a man to fondle to overrule what I'd been sent here to do. Yet as I pulled her around to face me, I found myself unable to resist allowing my gaze to fall, drinking in every inch of her. Tasting her would be dangerous on several levels, but even the way she pursed her lips in frustration as well as anger was tempting.

She had the kind of figure that no red-blooded man could ignore, rounded in all the right places. The woman was a tiny thing in comparison to me, barely reaching my shoulders, but I could still imagine her long legs wrapped around my waist as I fucked her like some crazed animal.

I found it difficult to breathe around her, my needs increasing just as the heat had built in my hand. Spanking her had been a pleasure, but mild in comparison to what I'd had in store for her.

No, not her. A man.

This changed everything.

She'd added a fire in my belly, a need that couldn't be denied.

While I relished the fact that I was unforgiving, refusing to accept any kind of crap as an excuse, I would find it difficult if not impossible to end her life after retrieving the information I sought. Hissing, I cocked my head, using a single finger to lift her chin. As she'd done before, she glared at me with venom in those huge intense eyes of hers.

The woman had moxie. I would give her that.

My balls tightened over the thought of taming the wild filly, forcing her into complete submission. She wouldn't go down without a fight, but it would be worth every scratch she issued or attempt at running away.

Walker had battled with me like a masterful fighter, the gouge on the back of my head providing a dull ache that would remain for at least a full day. I was both impressed and irritated as fuck with her attempts to get away. She would soon learn that ignoring my rules wasn't in her best interest.

As far as the money? Women were excellent liars, using their feminine wiles to get exactly what they wanted. But I wasn't convinced she had any knowledge of what Samuel had gotten himself in the middle of, and I wasn't certain myself. However, the gift of the condo could have been payment for a job well done. I just had to learn for what, and I couldn't allow her any leeway until I knew for certain what the hell was going on.

Even then, her fate had been sealed.

She'd found herself smack in the middle of a nightmare.

"Go," I hissed, pushing her toward the stairs.

Her expression remained harsh, her body still trembling. I could tell she was furious on two levels, not just because of what I was demanding of her, but also from the fact I'd brought out her hidden desires.

Walker kept her glare hard and cold as I lowered my head, drinking in the fresh scent of some fruity shower gel. My thoughts returned to the bag of trash she'd been holding in her hand, the bloody rags a reminder of the kind of life I lived, one that had never bothered me until now.

She'd been forced to clean up the mess, showering off the gore. No woman should ever be forced to scrub away remnants of business, no matter their crime. Maybe she was used to it, her hard, cold nature allowing her to process murder scenes as I did.

Why was my gut gnawing at me?

"I said, go. Don't make me punish you further." Although my hand itched to spank her again.

She turned sharply, muttering words of hatred under her breath as she stomped up several steps. I lingered behind, watching the muscles in her calves, still envisioning her legs wrapped around my naked body.

While the building was soundproof, the condominium she now owned the only occupied space on her floor, that didn't mean the pesky detective who'd been assigned to the case wouldn't drop by to have additional questions answered. Removing her from the premises as soon as possible was the only option.

As expected, the moment she got within a few feet of the door leading to her floor, she bolted. I was forced to admit, I was losing patience with her. She had no phone, no weapon, and no way of getting out of the situation, yet she refused to back down. Stupidity was often disguised as bravery.

I didn't bother racing after her this time. There was nowhere logical for her to go other than attempting to lock herself into her condo. I shook my head when I heard the door slam, finally taking long strides down the hallway. While the game was enjoyable as fuck, it was time she began to understand that she was no longer in control of her destiny.

Unless she gave me exactly what I wanted.

Even then, it would be impossible to let her go. The local authorities were itching to find anything they could use to convict a prominent member of the Novikov family. And she was a screamer. There was no doubt she'd go the police if released.

After taking a deep breath, I kicked in the door. At least it would take the owners of the building a while to hire another maintenance man, but I would try to prevent the police from realizing she'd been taken. Growling, I closed the door behind me, narrowing my eyes when she came into view. Damn, the woman was pushing every button.

Her chutzpa was confirmed by the way she held a knife in her hand, shifting back and forth from one foot to the other.

"Don't you dare come any closer," she stated, even swiping the blade through the air the second I took a step closer.

Everything about her intrigued me, dragging my desire for her closer to the surface. No other woman had ever attracted me as much, forcing my possessive nature to the surface. As I headed in her direction, she snarled viciously. My balls tightened even more, my throbbing cock pinched from the way it was pushed against my zipper.

"I am coming closer, Walker. You can either hand over that weapon or I'll take it from you. I don't think you want to push me any further."

"Or what? You're going to shoot me just like you did an innocent man."

Innocent. I'd always considered myself an excellent observer of people, knowing instinctively when they lied. Her eyes alone gave me an indication she wasn't acting.

"Why did you kill a maintenance man?" she pushed.

"You'll get answers only if you supply them."

I exhaled as I walked even closer, studying the way her eyes shifted down to my crotch in a slow and easy fashion. She was as aroused as I'd become, fighting her natural urges since good little girls weren't supposed to be interested in ruthless killers. There was no need to answer her given she remained where she was, her body frozen perhaps from finally surrendering to a moment of panic. There was nowhere for her to go, no possibility of escaping me. She'd begun to accept that fact just like she would soon learn to submit.

However, she would need to be urged, coerced into allowing her intense desires to breach the surface.

"Please," she finally said in a soft voice, the tone reminding me of a kitty cat purring from the touch of her human.

"Please what, Walker? Please fuck you? Please fulfill all those dark desires you've buried deep within your mind? Hmmm?" I closed the distance, easily able to remove the knife from her fingers. When I tossed it across the room, only her lower lip quivered from another trickle of fear.

She should be terrified. I was one nasty son of a bitch.

"Answer me."

"No. Never. That's insane."

"You're lying to me again, and I don't like liars."

A nervous tic appeared in the corner of her mouth as she looked down, although she wasn't focusing on anything. As I'd done before, I lifted her chin with a single finger then cupped her jaw, caressing her face. The softness of her skin brushing against the rough pads of my fingers created a series of vibrations. That even surprised me.

"I'm not… lying. I would never want scum like you."

Scum. I hadn't been called that in one hell of a long time. It was interesting it made my cock twitch again. I clenched my hand around her chin, shaking my head. "If you want to play hardball with me, you should know the rules. I play dirty and I play for keeps."

"And I don't play at all. There's nothing you can do to me that will ever make me want you."

"Want is implied when two people have as much chemistry as we have. Need is something else entirely. Need is when you can't breathe if that person flaming your desire isn't in your presence, your pulse racing the moment they are, your heart skipping beats from a single touch alone. Need is when everything in your life takes a back seat to sharing passion with the only person who can satisfy your yearning, exciting every cell deep within your body." I lowered my head, daring to lower my face to within inches of hers. "Then the burning need becomes an obsession, something you'll die without. Do you understand the difference?"

She continued shivering, but by the way her lips twisted, I could almost read her mind, her thoughts nearly as dark and sadistic as my own.

As I took a deep breath, holding the sweet scent of her in my lungs, I realized even her intoxicating fragrance could become a dangerous addiction. That didn't bode well for a man in my position. She would be seen as a weakness,

Novikov enemies doing everything in their power to use her against me.

But for tonight and many nights to come, I would partake in what already belonged to me.

"I think you do and just for tonight, I'm going to give you exactly what you want and what you need," I whispered hoarsely. "That means I'm going to taste you. Then I'm going to fuck you."

Her eyes opened wide, her jaw clenching from her fury. "You're an asshole."

"Yes, I am. You're going to learn just how much so in the next few weeks."

I could tell her mind was trying to wrap around what I was telling her, her wheels turning to the point she was just about to promise me anything in order to get her life back. She'd yet to comprehend that there was no turning back. She would be kept in a gilded cage until she talked.

And she would be punished on a regular basis.

Maybe I would take her to the playhouse after all.

I took my time, removing my jacket and placing it across one of her chairs, even taking the time to unbutton my sleeves, rolling them up to my elbows. She watched me intently, her lovely lips twisting.

"Why are you doing this? I already told you I don't have any money. If I did, I wouldn't be here."

Here. Did she mean in this condo or in the city? At some point, she would tell me all her secrets. In the meantime, I'd allow her body to do the talking. "You see, Walker, men like me don't ask for permission to taste and enjoy what we hunger for. We take what we want. That's our right."

Her long eyelashes flitted against her shimmering cheeks, her shoulders tensing as she took a single shaky step backwards.

I took the same step closer.

She pushed out her hand, palming my chest. Every cell in my body burst from the boost of energy she'd just given me, my desire off the charts. "No."

"Yes," I repeated as I looked down at her long, thin fingers, my hunger continuing to swell. I took her hand into mine, slowly moving it down the length of my chest to my groin.

Her shudder was the sweetest music, the way her fingers stroked me the beginning of her acceptance.

And her acquiescence.

"Please," she repeated, her eyes now glassy.

"You can tell me anything. How can I please you, little bird?"

"Don't call me that. I'm not your anything." She jerked her hand away, the same beautiful shade of crimson creeping up along her jaw. "And I definitely don't *need* you, no matter what you think in that warped mind of yours." Her body continued to betray her, her breath coming in short gasps, the delicious scent of her pussy becoming more intense. My mouth watered, the filthy thoughts only increasing. I wanted nothing more than to drive my tongue deep between her luscious folds, licking up every drop of her cream.

I wrapped my hand around the back of her neck, pulling her onto her toes. "Then I guess I'm going to be forced to choose what kind of pleasure I provide."

She pushed both hands against me this time, although her action was feeble at best, another telling statement.

I tightened my grip around her neck, holding her in place as I slowly brushed my finger down her arm, crossing over to her waist then down to her rounded hip. When I wrapped that same finger around the looped end of her robe, she gasped, swatting at my hand.

"Stop fighting me," I growled and yanked the thin tie keeping her gorgeous body from me.

A single whimper escaped her mouth until she bit it back, shaking more from rage than fear. In her eyes, I saw such a will to fight me, not just to get away, her defiance just adding another layer of juicy complexity to the woman who'd already captured my interest.

When I brushed my lips across hers, she forcefully turned her head, allowing a disgusted sound to slip past those rosy lips of hers. In turn, I cupped her breast, squeezing for several seconds before flicking my finger back and forth across her nipple lightly as I watched her expression change from utter hatred to a moment of pure bliss. That pleased me to no end.

"Let yourself go, Walker. There's no one here to chastise you for wanting a man as unseemly as myself." I rolled my finger around her lips then down the side of her neck, the end of my finger seared from the light touch alone. I couldn't help but marvel at the vibrations shooting through my spine.

She swallowed hard, her pulse thumping against the side of her neck. My nostrils flared as I glanced down at her nipples. They were swollen and the rosiest color of pink I'd seen. Utterly beautiful. I dragged my tongue across my lips, several guttural sounds rushing up from deep inside. I was amazed how pent up I'd been, the release even by the simplest touch one of the greatest pleasures I'd had in a hell of a long time.

Then I crawled my hand gently down her stomach to her inner thigh. The heat between her legs cascaded across my fingers, adding to the rush of sensations. When I darted my fingers against her pussy, she closed her legs, shifting her hips in an attempt to block my access. That didn't prevent me from swirling my finger around her clit. I took my time, teasing her as her body swayed back and forth.

"You do hunger, Walker, more than you've allowed your-self to believe."

"No, I..." Her sentence faded away, a strangled sound pushing past those luscious lips of hers.

A single moan was my first reward. My second was watching her tension ease, enough so she unclenched her legs but wrapped her delicate fingers around my shirt, fisting her hand as her breathing became more ragged.

"Your lower lip quivers when you lie, little bird. That's something you should remember." I slipped my fingers just inside her pussy, flexing them open before pumping deep and hard.

"That's... I just..."

I continued finger fucking her for a full minute before pulling them away. Then I rubbed them back and forth across her lips.

"Open your mouth, Walker."

She pursed her lips closed.

"Do as I say. Now."

After a few seconds, she obeyed me, opening them a few centimeters. I thrust my fingers into her mouth, my actions more brutal than before. My patience was all but gone.

"Do you taste your desire?"

I knew she wouldn't answer me, but those glorious eyes of hers spoke volumes. Her longing had turned into need.

Now I would take her.

From this moment on, Walker Sutherland belonged to me.

My prisoner.

My possession.

My addiction.

CHAPTER 6

 *alker*

Possession.

I could see it in his eyes, that obsessive look that I'd only witnessed in movies. He was a man possessed by the kind of dark need that would terrify most women, including me. The bastard was brutal and more like a savage than anything else.

Yet his deep baritone and the dirty talk had kept me completely and irrationally aroused. I was hot and wet, which was a terrible combination. My head also ached from the rush of blood as the pressure rose. His words about need continued to shift in my mind. While they held a ring of truth, admitting it made me sick to my stomach.

When he pulled away entirely, a cold chill shifted down my spine. But as he dragged the robe off my shoulders, pushing the material to the floor, I was once again unable to move a muscle.

His eyes flashed, his nostrils flaring as he gazed down to my breasts then moved beseechingly slowly to my legs. I threw my arms over my chest in some pointless attempt to cover myself.

"Don't do that, Walker. You don't have permission to hide from me," he said, his voice laced with the grit of lust.

Unable to swallow, I eased my arms by my sides, continually darting a look toward the door, praying that someone would come knock on it.

He sneered before he dragged his shirt over his head, tossing it aside. "No one is coming to save you, *malen'kaya ptitsa*. Only I can be your savior, but that only comes from being a very good girl."

I fisted my hands, unable to control my eyes as they raked over his sculpted chest. He was a creature of beauty, every muscle toned to perfection. He had to be a former body builder. Or maybe he tossed bodies he'd killed as his way of exercise. There was a single ragged scar running down the front of his chest, a portion covered in brilliant ink. Every part of him was dangerously gorgeous.

I almost laughed nervously until he wasted no time finishing undressing. The sight of him completely naked did little to calm my nerves. He was huge in every department, his cock long and thick, the tip so purple I realized my mouth was watering. How in the hell could I want a man who had already told me I belonged to him?

I backed away, taking long strides until I walked straight across the area, the horrible section of floor that I'd cleaned a man's blood off of only hours before. When I hit the window, I gasped, realizing I couldn't go any further.

The Russian took decided steps toward me, the leer on his face more pronounced than it had been before.

"You aren't going anywhere," he said mostly under his breath.

He was close, far too close, the heat of his body shifting through me like a wave of fire consuming every inch. When he was within a few inches, I slammed my fists against him, realizing that my attempts were futile, but it made me feel better to try. I glanced from right to left, staring out the window down to the street below. Thirty stories above the rest of the world seemed so far away.

He planted his palms on the glass, piercing my eyes with his. I was thrown by how enigmatic they were, drawing me in. He exuded power in the way he carried himself, his quiet yet demanding demeanor, although he seemed to have the weight of the world on his shoulders.

Or maybe he was just trying to prove himself.

It didn't really matter at this point. He'd identified me as enemy number one and I would be forced to pay for my sins.

"How did you get inside the building?" I asked as he lowered his head, taking several shallow breaths.

"Is that what you really want to know, Walker?"

"As a start."

He laughed in that deep, sexual throaty way, sending another rush of shivers all the way to my toes. "I can get into any building. There's no security system that can't be cracked, not a single person alive who can't be bought."

I wasn't certain what he was trying to tell me, but it was likely I'd never learn.

"No more talking. Now, I fuck you." With that he crushed his mouth over mine, his body still a few inches from mine but the heat even more explosive.

I pushed against him then dug my fingernails into his skin. He didn't budge and if I had to guess, I'd say he was impervious to pain. As his tongue pushed past my pursed lips, sweeping inside then dominating my tongue, I raked my nails down the front of his chest. Without realizing it, I wrapped one hand around his cock, squeezing before pumping up and down twice. Then I jerked my hand away, horrified at my actions.

He merely wrapped his fingers around mine, pushing them back in that same position. I closed my eyes, doing his bidding even though I became even more disgusted by the thought. But as the kiss continued, the taste of him tingling my senses, I found myself stroking him without hesitation.

My entire body ached as another blast of desire roared through me. None of this made any sense, my mind refusing to provide any decent answers. As I tightened my hold, he emitted a series of growls, the sound floating all around us.

Stars floated from right to left, keeping my vision as cloudy as my mind.

I didn't want to feel the passion roaring between us but there was no point in denying the way he made me feel. It was strange and amazing, terrifying and surreal. I'd never felt this way before and that bothered me even more.

When he finally broke the kiss, he pulled my hand away, easing back and lifting first one arm then the other over my head. As he wrapped one hand around both wrists, I studied him even more carefully. He had such soulful eyes, the kind any woman could get lost in. However, I had a feeling there was nothing but empty space in his soul, as if he'd sold it to the devil himself.

He cupped my chin as he'd done before, keeping my head held high as he rubbed his thumb back and forth across my lips.

"So beautiful," he muttered then slid his hand down to my breast, flicking a finger across the surface of my nipple before pinching it in between his thumb and forefinger. The pain was like a rush of adrenaline. Instantly, my legs began to tremble, the knot in my stomach growing in size.

He took his sweet time exploring my body, shifting his hand to my other nipple, twisting and pulling until both ached from the rough touch. I panted, blinking in order to keep tears from forming. The thought of giving him any additional satisfaction repulsed me almost as much as what he was doing.

When he opened his large hand, running his fingers down my breasts to my stomach, I rose onto my toes, unable to stop a gasp from erupting from my throat.

"We're going to be very close, you and I," he said out of the blue.

Was he kidding me? "We will never be friends, no matter what you think."

"You don't want me as an enemy, Walker. That's why you're going to learn to be a very good girl."

"I thought I already was your enemy."

He smirked, the slight dimple in his chin too damn attractive. "If you were a true enemy, you'd already be dead." The bastard continued his exploration, following the trail of his fingers with his heated gaze, his nostrils flaring.

"Just like the man who was murdered right here beneath our feet?" My question seemed to surprise him.

"A necessary evil in my line of work."

"Evil is right. You're a monster."

"I didn't kill him."

"Then who did?"

He cocked his head before sliding his entire hand between my legs. When he added pressure, rubbing my pussy gently, there was no way to keep from moaning. I tried to control my breathing, but everything seemed impossible around him. Every bodily function I'd taken for granted before was coming to light. My breathing was out of control. My mind was lost in some irrational moment of insanity. My body was betraying me, the scent of my leaking pussy assaulting my nose.

I was sick inside. Sick. A terribly sick woman, something I'd never realized.

"Someone equally as powerful as I am."

I took a calculated guess, realizing I could face additional punishment for being so bold. "Mafia."

"You are as intelligent as you are stunning. Now, I suggest you stop asking questions that I know you really don't want answers to."

"What if I do?"

He glanced into my eyes, that damn smirk remaining. "Then that would make you more like me that you would choose to believe."

"I could never be like you. Never. No matter what you do to me, I will never sell my soul."

As he took a deep breath, he slipped two fingers past my swollen folds, driving them deep inside in a tempered fashion. Then he had the audacity to curl the tips, the shift in the angle providing more pleasure than any other man had given me.

"We shall see what you're capable of, little bird." He added a third finger, thrusting harder. When he swirled his thumb around my already aching clit, I almost lost it. Some men had no clue about pleasing a woman. He was practiced, prepared to take his time to force me into orgasming.

No fucking way.

I forced myself to glare at him, even managing to keep a smile on my face as he continued tormenting me, his actions becoming more savage when I didn't do as he wanted. However, the man was good, bringing me to the very edge of ecstasy then pulling back, playing the game much better than I was able to do.

"You continue to fight me. Soon, you will learn to beg me for pleasure."

"Never," I whispered, no longer recognizing the hollow tone of my voice.

"And when you do, I'll take you like you deserve to be taken, brutally and often, filling you with my seed."

When I tried to look away, he issued a low but very authoritative hiss. He continued finger fucking me, leaving me aching all over, my body involuntarily rocking against his hand only seconds later. Panting, I dragged my tongue across my lips, my throat starting to close from the anxiety of trying to hold back.

"That's it. Release for me."

I held my breath, refusing to give in. Refusing to… the climax swept through me so unexpectedly that I tossed my head against the window, doing everything I could to hold back a scream of pleasure.

He whispered several sentences in Russian. It didn't matter what he was telling me, or the words he was using. It was the inflection of his voice that added fuel to the fire. A second orgasm came out of nowhere, one so powerful that I bucked hard against his hand, panting like some crazed schoolgirl experiencing the joy for the first time. Every sound I made echoed, and I could no longer feel my arms or legs, the rapture that incredible.

"Oh… My…" I heard a laugh as it bubbled to the surface and a wave of embarrassment rolled over every inch of my skin creating goosebumps. I was as humiliated as I'd ever been, no longer bothering to try to focus. He'd already taken a small part of me just to make certain I knew he could at any time.

"Good girl. I'm pleased," he whispered after I stopped shaking.

When he removed his hand from my wrist, I reacted without thinking, cracking him hard across the face. My action even shocked me, enough so I didn't move quickly enough. When I attempted to do it again, he snagged my hand, smashing it against the glass.

"That's not something good girls do, Walker. That's going to cost you." He flipped me around so quickly I thought I'd fall, pushing me hard against the window. Then he grabbed my hair with one hand as he used the other to push the tip of his cock just inside my aching pussy.

There was no stopping my cry of disbelief. He was huge, my muscles straining immediately to accept just how large he really was.

"Please, you're so big," I struggled to say, slapping my hands against the glass.

He said nothing as he slowly pushed another few inches. When he finally thrust the remainder inside, my entire body shook violently. I couldn't believe the way my pussy clamped around his shaft, managing to pull him in even deeper.

"So damn tight," he growled and grabbed my hip, yanking me further away from the glass, forcing me to arch my back.

The sensations were all over the place, but within seconds, there was nothing but extreme pleasure as he started fucking me in earnest.

I could see his reflection in the glass, the strain on his face as he rocketed into me. Every sound he made was guttural, every breath he took labored. Within seconds, my hot breath had fogged the window, but it still felt like I was on public display, the entire city watching me being fucked by a brutal killer.

His actions more forceful, he pushed me onto my toes, my face crowded close to the glass. He kept his hand woven around my long strands of hair, fucking me long and hard. I was exhausted from battling with him as well as the intense fear, finally shutting down all efforts to try to fight him. It was no use. But I would find a way to escape his clutches. Somehow.

I closed my eyes, trying to pretend I was somewhere else.

With someone else.

Other than a horrible poor excuse for a human being.

But the dazzling sensations prevented my mind from free flowing, keeping me very present in the moment, enough so that when he pulled all the way out, I almost begged him to continue. A slight laugh pulsed from my throat, the sound dry and bitter. I pressed my face against the glass, taking several raspy breaths.

He yanked me another few inches away from the window, pressing down on the small of my back. "Your first lesson in obedience, Walker. I assure you that there will be many others. Now, I'm going to fuck you in the ass."

What?

I smashed my hands against the glass, trying to find the will to fight him once again, but he was just too strong for me. He was quick with his actions, placing the tip of his cock against my puckered hole. Then he grabbed my hips with both hands, digging his fingers into me as he pushed several inches inside, past the tight ring of muscle.

"Oh. Shit." I hung my head, my nails involuntarily scratching down the glass. Blinking furiously, just trying to focus on anything became arduous, pain washing up over my shoulders as my ass muscles constricted. He didn't waste any time, thrusting the rest deep inside. I was thrown against the window by the force he used, trying to concentrate on anything but the burning anguish.

The sounds erupting from his throat reminded me of some barbarian, a hunter catching his prey. While he remained crushed against me for a full ten seconds, I knew it was short lived. When he pulled out, leaving only the tip inside, I undulated my hips, shocked at the tingling sensations rushing through me.

But as I'd done since he'd walked into the door, my actions failed. He plunged even harder, his heavy body smashing against me, leaving my heart thudding and my legs no longer working. When he repeated the move, all I could do was pant.

"That's it. Take all of me," he growled, keeping me bent over as he drove into me like a crazed beast.

His rhythm seemed perfect, one coming after the other. Then his actions became rougher, pounding into me so forcefully, my entire body was jarred.

"Uh. Uh. Uh. Uh. Uh." The agony shifted, turning into another moment of sheer pleasure, pushing several more buttons on my road to ecstasy.

He pounded into me hard and fast, stripping away any rational thoughts. While another wave of incredible sensations rocketed through me, I could tell he was close to coming. A series of ragged pants left my throat, the only thing I could concentrate on the sound of his skin slapping against mine. I was lost in another haze, every sound I made unrecognizable.

When his body stiffened, a snarky smile crossed my face. At least he was almost finished.

His cock throbbed even more than before, the bellow he issued a sound I would never forget. His fingers digging into my skin, there was no doubt he erupted deep inside.

A single bead of perspiration trickled down the side of my face. As it slid across my nose, finally dripping onto the floor, all I could see were bloodstains.

"I'm going to fuck you every day, taking you in every way I desire," he huffed, his breathing just as rapid as mine. Yet as he continued to play me with filthy thoughts, filling my mind with all the ways he planned on ravaging me, I managed to shift to that alternate location in my mind, my conviction strengthening.

The bastard would never break me down the way he wanted. I would never *need* him, nor would I allow my bizarre desire to cloud what was really happening.

He was a monster.

And I was his pawn.

* * *

He'd bound my wrists in front of me, tying a thick piece of cloth around my eyes before shoving me into a vehicle. Wherever he was taking me, it was obvious he didn't want me to identify the location or anything that might help me ascertain where I was being held. Every muscle in my body ached, so tense my teeth chattered. I felt his looming presence as he eased into the driver's seat, the rumble of the engine adding to the churning sensations in my stomach.

"Where are you taking me?" I asked, fearful of the answer.

"Somewhere secure and secluded where we can talk."

Talk. What in the hell did he think I was supposed to tell him?

"I don't have anything else to say to you."

I hated when he laughed at me, as if I was hiding something important. "Oh, you will talk, Walker. We're going to have a long conversation about the man who formerly owned the condominium you live in."

I sucked in my breath, my heart racing. This was about Samuel after all. I'd never even met the man, but it would seem his gift of signing over the condominium had already changed my life. I'd done my homework before accepting the incredible, terrifying present, grilli man's attorney on four occasions. Then I'd done a search of Samuel, finding nothing of any concern. He'd been listed as an accountant for... shit. If I had to guess, I'd say the firm was a front for the mafia. The horror was only increasing.

"I already told you. I don't know him."

Another laugh vibrated throughout the vehicle. "At some point, you will tell me the truth."

"And if I don't, let me guess. You're going to punish me."

"You're finally beginning to understand. That's good."

Exhaustion had clouded my mind to the point I could barely stay awake. I had nothing further to say to him, although every little detail Samuel's attorney had mentioned during our initial meeting filtered into my mind. Nothing had seemed sinister, although the fact I didn't know the man who had provided an expensive piece of real estate was unusual. Maybe I'd wanted to get closer to my father in some crazy way since I knew nothing about him. My mother had laughed at first, until she'd realized I was serious.

Then her face had turned ghastly white.

I should have listened to her, ignoring the gift and moving on with my life. As I slumped into the seat, the tension remaining, I eased my head against the glass. Wherever he was taking me, I had a feeling I'd never return.

"He was just a family friend, but I never met him. My mother acted as if the man was horrible, scourge of the earth." I laughed, as if any of this was funny. Maybe my nerves had finally gotten the best of me. "I found out he was an attorney but nothing more."

I wasn't surprised he remained completely quiet, probably finding it difficult not to pull the car over, punishing me for lying to him. At this point, I didn't care. I was so tired that nothing mattered.

"I received a letter in the mail three months ago from an attorney I'd never heard of. I ignored it because of my work schedule for almost a solid week. Then I got this strange phone call, a message. The male voice on the other end of the line said nothing more than it was important that I ignore what I might have heard about Samuel. How could I have heard a thing? I lived in New York. He lived in Chicago. Against my better judgment, I ignored my inner voice. How stupid of me but I wanted this job at the hospital I'm currently employed at. I know, weak. Right?" Yawning, a cold chill shifted down my spine, but this time it was from my body shutting down, fear the great equalizer. I wasn't going to tell him about my father. He didn't deserve to dig deeper into my family. Nope. No fucking way.

The fact the bastard remained quiet was starting to piss me off.

"I had no idea who the person was who called, but as I would guess the caller expected, I opened the mail, stunned at the brochure about the condo and a request for a meeting with this attorney. I figured what did I have to lose?" My laugh was dry, the sound bitter. I continued rattling on, finally closing my aching eyes. "No one else was there, except for one pompous, opinionated attorney. I'll never forget the way he looked at me, as if I wasn't worthy for what I was about to receive."

At least my captor finally laughed.

"When the jerk confirmed Samuel had transferred a glorious condominium for me in the heart of Chicago, I burst into laughter. Then I headed for the door, certain the meeting was nothing more than a bad joke. But it turned out... to be... true." I yawned again, a series of nervous tics floating from my mouth to my legs. I wasn't certain how much longer I could stay awake. Maybe I'd never awaken again since I wasn't the person the gorgeous, buff, rough and tumble man sitting next to me had expected.

"And nothing else. No details?" he asked.

"No details. I didn't bother answering him at the time. In fact, I made the attorney answer a barrage of my questions over several days before I even considered the offer."

"But you took it."

"Yes, I did."

My entire body continued to shake, my mind racing as to why the jerk was asking me these questions. I had nothing to hide.

"You know my name, Mr. Killer. Why don't you tell me yours?"

"You don't need to know," he muttered.

"It's not about need, asshole. It's about what I deserve. After finding a headless dead man in my apartment, a maintenance guy who never did a damn thing to anyone else in his life, I deserve to know who you are. For being grilled by a stupid detective, who is vying for a promotion but will never get it because of the way he dresses alone, I deserve to know who you are. And finally, and much more important," I managed, although I wasn't certain my words were making any sense, "since I was accosted, spanked, and fucked by a stranger, although I admit one that is just about the most gorgeous man I've ever seen even though that's not the point, then taken as his hostage without any reason given... I. Fucking. Deserve. Period. The... end." My eyelids were so heavy, my mind shifting into a blur.

I gave him one more look then... Then...

CHAPTER 7

*M*aksim

"Maksim Calderon," I huffed, tightening my grip around the steering wheel. I hadn't intended on giving her my name at any point. There was no reason to do so considering she meant nothing to me, nor did I want to personalize the situation. However, just hearing the angst in her voice, the words that came easily given how tired she was, I couldn't seem to avoid telling her the truth.

Whether or not I believed her story wasn't the point, at least not now, although her statement held an air of sincerity. It was possible Samuel had a good reason for giving Walker such an expensive gift, but none of the reasons I'd thought of were plausible. Even if she was special to him in some personal way, in doing so, the man had to know he'd place a target on her back. Unless Samuel thought he'd gotten away with the theft.

In my line of work, I'd seen corporate moguls fold given the pressure of extortion. I'd witnessed grown men begging for their lives in creative manners. And I'd seen fathers giving up their daughters in exchange for paying their dues. Nothing fazed or surprised me any longer. But… there was always a reason a powerful man made the decisions he did. Desperation. Greed. Subterfuge. Nothing was ever done without consideration made to the consequences.

Either Walker wasn't who she claimed to be, or she was more valuable than she had any idea of. That made her capture and subsequent interrogation even more vital to the organization.

"What was the reason given for the gift you received? Did this attorney tell you?" I asked, the exit off the interstate less than a mile away. When she said nothing, I snarled. Then I heard a sweet and fascinating noise.

She was snoring lightly, the sound more like a delicate little purr of a kitten. I chuckled under my breath, turning up the heat in the Mercedes since I'd noticed goosebumps on her arms.

I certainly wasn't going to get anywhere with her tonight. At least I could check out her story. Perhaps finding both the identity and the location of Samuel's attorney might begin unraveling what had become a ridiculous mystery. The former accountant had crossed the kind of line there was no chance of recovery from. The fact he'd been murdered, but not by Ivan or a member of the organization meant he'd crossed more than one person in his life.

Why would he dare put anybody he cared about in such a precarious position? There was a story behind all of this, one dark and ugly.

That is, if Walker was telling the truth.

A slight blip of my phone indicated a text, not something Ivan or my Capos used in everyday communication. At this point, I chose to ignore it. I wasn't in the mood for any additional bullshit.

As I slowed the Mercedes, making the turn onto the off ramp, I second guessed my decision to take her to my home. I'd never had another female in the house, and I certainly had never brought someone considered a problem that needed to be handled anywhere close. There were locations in which to handle business, and not just the playhouse I'd created. I tapped my index finger on the steering wheel, glancing in the rearview mirror. There was no other choice, although I was following my gut and not my usual method of protocol.

If there was a single remote chance Walker was telling the truth, that could mean others would be coming after her, believing she was holding onto the money. If so, then they could believe they would make a power grab by abducting her. I rubbed my finger across my lips, contemplating the best way of ensuring she was telling me the truth.

It would take very creative measures in order to break her both mentally and physically. She was a tough girl, refusing to give in even though she'd witnessed the aftermath of a horrific crime.

When I finally pulled up to the house, shifting the gear into park, I yanked my phone into my hand, snarling before seeing the identity of the texter. Then I smiled, shaking my head, the series of emojis always giving me a smile. I closed my eyes, allowing both wonderful and nasty memories to slide into my mind. I hadn't allowed myself to go down memory lane for years, the pain too intense. Why now?

Walker.

Her presence had unlocked a portion of my soul. Damn it. I fisted my hand, staring down at the screen for a full ten seconds before looking away. This was the last thing I needed tonight. I would answer the text tomorrow. There was still business to take care of.

A quick glance at my watch was enough to add another layer of despair. It was almost eleven. The text was far too late. That meant another bad night, one of dozens of them.

After climbing out of the vehicle, I glanced toward the darkened sky, the moon hidden behind thick, ominous clouds. Something didn't feel right. Hell, the entire situation reeked. My instincts were almost never wrong. If I was right, then we were being played.

Only Walker could tell me, even if she believed she didn't know.

The lovely woman didn't budge when I cut the engine or opened her door. Her head was lolled, her breathing even. I found it hard to believe she'd fallen asleep after all she'd been through, but exhaustion could do crazy things to a person. After brushing hair from under the blindfold, I gathered her into my arms, pulling her against my chest and kicking the door to the vehicle closed.

As I headed inside, my footsteps echoed on the expensive tile hardwood floor. I walked up the stairs, heading toward the guestroom, reminding myself that even given her level of exhaustion, Walker could be a master story-teller, lying perfectly. Women were damn good at doing that.

The door to the guestroom was open, although I wasn't certain how long I would or could keep her here. This was my home, not a place for the rough interrogation I'd be forced to use. But for tonight, I would allow her some comfort, even though I refused to trust her.

After yanking the covers down to the middle of the bed, I eased her down, turning on the small light on the night-stand. The room was sparse, mostly because I didn't give a shit about having a single guest. At least there was a bed, a table, and a lamp. That's all she needed at this point. I removed her shoes, sliding her legs under the covers then tugging off her mask. She seemed so damn peaceful in her slumber, her rosy lips pursed, slight murmurs coming from her throat.

her for a few minutes, my cock aching as much ~~before~~. I could fuck her all over again, even while she slept. That made me a very bad man. Hissing, I looked away, realizing I had no lock on the door. Trusting her wasn't an option. I pulled the covers up to her chest then headed for my room, opening the hidden compartment I'd had added to the basic design of the house.

The vault was secure and hidden, the eight-by-eight space holding weapons, cash, and body armor. I grabbed a pair of handcuffs, quickly returning to the guestroom. She was still sleeping peacefully, her eyes rolling back and forth under her long eyelashes. I pulled the switchblade form my pocket, carefully cutting the rope I'd used to tie her. Then I lifted one arm, securing her wrist to the headboard.

She wasn't going anywhere.

At least not without my permission.

I kept my heated gaze in her direction, laughing softly hearing her soft murmurs. Even in her sleep, she was gorgeous, her skin shimmering in the dim light. I had to push down my attraction to her or I'd fall into a deep hole that I'd find difficult to climb out of.

Rule number one in the Novikov syndicate: Never get friendly with prisoners or enemies. That only led to questioning methods and decisions, which could lead to death.

Rule number two was even worse, but one I'd adopted without question. Kill without hesitation, but not before issuing a painful last few breaths.

I left the light on to give her some sense of normalcy, even though by all rights I should strip her bare, leaving her lying on a mattress with no covers for warmth. Exhaling, I moved toward the door, closing it. I might allow her a few creature comforts, but she needed to be cut off from the rest of the world until I unlocked all her secrets.

As I moved down the stairs, I continued to piece together what little I'd been told about the situation. Samuel Rossi had worked with Ivan for almost six years. During that time, he'd never crossed a line or broken a rule. From what I'd been told, he was an expert numbers guy, the best money launderer in the business. In some circles, including with law enforcement, he'd been able to make Ivan's various corporations look squeaky clean, using the recent real estate developments as a lucrative prop. Why would he risk the Russian's wrath by stealing from the man?

There were two possibilities in my mind. Samuel had been threatened or he'd been playing Ivan all along. The latter would have taken a complicated plan, Samuel's acting abilities put to the test. Possible, but not likely.

I wasn't going to answer any questions tonight. But tomorrow I'd begin interrogating Walker. For the rest of the night, I planned on finding out everything I could about her background and past. The more I knew, the easier it would be to break down her defenses.

The moment I headed into my living room, the sound of my phone interrupted my thoughts, raising my hackles given the lateness of the hour. Even Ivan kept a regular schedule, enjoying time spent with his family almost every night.

I glared at the screen, not necessarily surprised at seeing Kane's number. He served under my regime in charge of the Diamond Club, one of our most profitable legitimate businesses in the Midwest, our revenues exceeding three hundred fifty million last year alone. He was considered a tough taskmaster, enjoying the perks of running such a lucrative and successful business.

"Kane. Are there issues?"

He huffed before answering. "You might say that. I think you need to get down here. My gut tells me we're about to have a problem."

The man was just as brutal as I was. He also didn't need either my permission or my help in handling intolerable customers. He had his own soldiers, men that always flowed through the casino, tossing out anyone who created a problem. That meant there was more serious trouble, another rival organization causing a more challenging issue.

"Then get rid of them."

"I can't. The guest is a damn prince," he huffed.

Fucking great.

"I'm on my way." I didn't waste any time, heading out the door as I called my Capo. "Brick. Get down to the Diamond. We might have trouble. Dispatch a dozen soldiers."

"On my way, boss. I'll take care of it."

Even given the lateness of the hour, I still had difficulty with traffic, the location surrounding the entertainment mecca always crowded no matter the time of day. Ivan's business expertise in setting up an entire entertainment complex complete with two massive hotels, several restaurants, a small but luxurious shopping center, and four dance clubs had expanded our wealth. Between the powerful politicians and the various celebrities crossing through our doors, the Diamond Club was considered the premier club within several states.

I eased my weapon into my jacket before exiting the Mercedes, scanning the parking lot before heading toward the back entrance. There were no obvious signs of trouble, but that meant nothing given the massive size of the facility as well as hundreds of private rooms.

What infuriated me was the fact there were very few soldiers within eyesight as I walked in. My hackles raised, I took long strides through toward the hostess stand, drawing the attention of one of the girls.

"Yes, Mr. Calderon?"

"Where's Kane?"

"The Presidential Suite."

"Regular or a private party?"

She seemed nervous. "Private."

All our employees were well trained, able to sniff out trouble before it brewed.

I nodded, tapping on the counter before making my way through the crowd, heading toward the bank of elevators. The Presidential Suite consisted of an entire floor within the main building, the area complete with its own kitchen and separate employee entrance. The price tag for admittance was five thousand dollars. A private party cost well over a quarter million. To rent the entire floor, including all the lavish accompaniments started at one million and went up from there depending on the services.

It had only been rented out four times before.

What the hell was a damn prince doing here?

While guests were screened for weapons and other contraband before being allowed admittance, that didn't mean an employee couldn't have been bought off by some group of assholes who wanted to take the Novikov organization down a peg or two. That's what always troubled me the most. Good employees were damn hard to come by.

I placed my hand on the console of the private elevator, antsy given the few seconds it took for the computer to scan my palm print. By the time the thick metal door opened, I'd already unbuttoned my jacket, preparing for the possibility of trouble.

Before I even stepped off the tin can, my intuition unfortunately came to fruition as several gunshots were fired.

I shifted to the corner and out of sight, snarling as the door finally opened. The sound of two additional shots allowed me to grasp where the battle was taking place. Then I heard several female screams. I bolted down the corridor, my Sig now in both hands.

One of my soldiers was already down, blood splattered on the front of his shirt from a chest wound. Several people came running out of the main ballroom, both employees and what appeared to be customers alike. I pushed my way through them as another round of gunfire peppered into the air.

Shoving several people aside, I pushed my way in through the door, immediately noticing some asshole in a damn ski mask of all freaking things. With one shot to his head, the man went down. I turned in a full circle, noticing there were at least four men down, but from what I could tell, not a single guest had been injured.

The entire scene had obviously been staged. Goddamn it.

"Get out of here," I called to the remainder of the guests as I headed toward the back. Out of the corner of my eye, I noticed another son of a bitch in a mask attempting to flee the scene. What in the fuck was going on? I wasted no time, lunging toward the shithead, managing to tackle him to the floor. A hard punch was thrown, the hit to my jaw brutal enough that stars swept in front of my eyes.

I slammed my fist just under his neck, almost with enough force to crush his windpipe. He wheezed, struggling to shove the barrel of his gun against my chest. We continued fighting, pitching and rolling as he did everything in his power to get off a shot. With a savage jab to his throat followed by a punch to his gut, I slammed his body against the floor, smashing the hand holding his gun several times.

After the weapon slipped from his fingers, I pitched it away, ripping off his mask then pointing the barrel of my gun against his cheek. "I suggest you stop fighting me."

He took scattered breaths as he stared into my eyes, and goddamn it, the son of a bitch had a twinkle in his. I shifted my gaze toward the gun he'd carried. His choice of a Walther PP meant the attack had been planned by a highly organized and well-connected group. Who that was remained to be seen, but by the assassin's attire, it was likely he and the other hired guns had blended in with the guests, his tuxedo more expensive than the suit I'd worn.

The assassin coughed several times, forced to take shallow breaths.

I snapped my hand around his throat, keeping him in place, the weight of my full straddle keeping him in place. "Who the fuck are you?" I demanded, taking another quick scan of the area. The open door to the kitchen meant the service elevator had been used. Either an employee had been forced to allow the assailants entrance or had granted it. I would find out one way or the other.

The fucker had the nerve to laugh.

I added pressure, enjoying the way his face contorted.

"You have three seconds, asshole. There won't be a fourth."

"You've... been warned," he finally stated. There was no accent, his indiscriminate looks unable to give me any indication of who the hell he was working for, but if I had to guess, I'd say he was a hired assassin, not simply a soldier from another mafia family or a random attacker. He and the other men had been sent with a specific task in mine.

"Three. Two. One." I fired a single shot, my rage increasing. After wiping blood from my face, I stood, surveying the ugly scene. Kane appeared with Brick flanking his side, both men obviously forced to engage in the attack.

I stormed toward them, constantly shifting my gaze from one side of the room to the other. "What in the fuck just happened here?"

Kane snarled, inching closer. "A private party. A Saudi prince, their entire enclave taking up a good portion of the hotel. The man is dead. So are several of his body-guards. Someone decided to send us a message."

A message.

While the Novikov family had several enemies on both sides of the law, an attack this brazen meant war.

"Who and how the hell did the assassins get past security?"

"Someone from the inside provided assistance, if not more than one," Brick answered.

"Then we need to hunt them down. How many got away?" I moved around them, heading into the kitchen. Several employees had been shot, but at least there were few survivors. I crouched down, turning one of the waiters onto his back, pressing my fingers against the side of his neck. His pulse was weak. Damn it. This wouldn't look good happening on my watch.

"I counted six in masks. I killed one of them, but several rushed in, took a few random shots and left." Kane's answer was clipped, his breathing labored.

"You were obviously tipped off. Why not throw them out?" I turned my attention toward Kane.

"One of the prince's men alerted me that there were uninvited guests after he returned to the ballroom. That's when I called you. I'd already dispatched extra security, but as soon as my men entered the room, all hell broke loose." Kane took several deep breaths, staring down at one of the slaughtered employees.

I'd always followed my gut, my instincts almost never wrong. Something didn't add up. "Brick. Make certain our guests are comfortable and block off the floor. No one enters without my approval. Also check on how many require medical attention. Kane. I want the roster of every employee who had access to this floor. Someone fucked with us, and I need to know who and why."

Kane shifted even closer, staring me in the eyes. "What are you thinking?"

"This was nothing more than a message being sent, a blatant statement that our security isn't as tight as it should be." I snapped my head in his direction. "And I blame you for that."

While his rage surfaced, his eyes flaring, he backed down quickly, lowering his head and nodding. "You're right. I fucked up."

"Yeah, you did. You've been loose in your security attempts. Hear me, Kane." I towered over the man by several inches, which I didn't mind using. He'd been a favorite of Ivan's, working with him for two years longer than I'd been allowed into the fold. From what I'd seen, he'd become a loose cannon, enjoying his notoriety to the detriment of business. "When all this is over, you will face punishment. Now, seal off the area. If one word leaks to the press, before we're ready I'll cut out your tongue. Do you understand?"

He bristled, but knew better than to challenge me, especially when I was this angry. "Don't worry, Maksim. I'll shut it down. What about the men?"

"I assure you that I will get them medical attention. Make certain you have them taken to a one of the suites."

"Not a problem."

The problem would be when I contacted Ivan. I moved away from Kane, yanking the phone into my fingers. The last thing I needed at this point was a war on our hands. Things had been quiet in the streets, business running smoothly, even with the odd recent rumors. Whatever the hell had happened tonight was only the beginning. Kane had somehow managed to play into their hands. At this point, I couldn't trust anyone but those closest to me.

"You're calling very late, Maksim. Have you found the required information from the son of a bitch who has the money?" Ivan asked.

"That's taking a back seat at this point. The Diamond Club was just hit, several of our men killed, others injured." I wasn't prepared to tell him Walker was a woman, at least not until I had solid information to provide.

He cursed in Russian. "How bad?"

"Bad enough and I think we have a problem. As you suspected, someone is attempting to move into our territory, but given they hired outside of their organization to send us a message, I don't have anything solid."

"Fuck. One of my shitass little informants tried to warn me something was brewing just last night," Ivan huffed. "I mentioned it to Vadim, but I've heard nothing else. What did Kane say?"

I took a deep breath, shifting my head in the man's direction. Maybe I was too close to the edge, but the man was acting cagey. "That he has no idea how this happened."

"And your thoughts?"

"Someone from the inside."

Ivan cursed in Russian again. "Find whoever it is."

"I plan on it," I snarled.

"And Maksim? This was on Kane's watch. He needs a harsh reminder that this kind of thing can never happen again."

Sighing, while I knew that what Ivan was suggesting was necessary, I had more important things on my mind. "I'll take care of it after getting help for my men and securing the situation."

"Understood. What do you need, more support?"

"Maybe, but right now I need to concentrate on saving our men. You're in direct contact with Dr. Booker. Is he available?" My anger only continued to increase as I walked from one room to another. The hit had been kept to the party room where only a portion of the guests had been, others gambling at the private tables or enjoying one of the two dancefloors. However, the assassins had been tipped off that the prince was holding court in the playhouse. They knew damn good and well Kane would have additional soldiers assigned to the room.

Ivan snickered. "Dr. Booker will always be available."

"Good. Then I need him ASAP."

"Done. Whoever is to blame, you will find them, Maksim. I placed my trust in you for a reason. Find the fuckers."

It was interesting how he'd just bypassed Vadim.

"Don't worry, Ivan. I plan on it."

"I'll call you when the doctor is on the way. I want names as well as action by the end of the day tomorrow. As far as Walker Sutherland, I want his head on a silver platter. Get me the location of my money."

"And you'll have it," I stated, hissing under my breath.

"I knew I could count on you. You're like a son to me, Maksim, a true leader. From what I can tell, you'll be the one running the organization."

I wondered if Vadim had already heard the news. I wasn't in the mood to be in the middle of a family squabble.

After Ivan ended the call, I wasted no time going through the two assassins' pockets, finding nothing that would indicate who they were working for. I knew the game better than most. Their tuxedos were from the same manufacturer, whatever store they'd purchased them from likely paid in cash. They'd cased the casino, taking their time to learn the layout as well as how best to infiltrate the operation.

How long had this been planned?

After checking on the conditions of my fallen men, the fact I'd lost three, four others in various conditions pushed my rage to an entirely different level. When I found those responsible, they would learn to pray, begging the devil himself for death rather than face my wrath. I did what I could to make them comfortable. Fortunately, none of the bullet wounds seemed life threatening.

"Breathe, Adam. You're going to be just fine," I told him, finishing tying the tourniquet. "What did you see?"

"It happened pretty quick, boss. I'd just walked into the room and six guys started shooting."

Exhaling, I glanced around the room. "That's what I heard."

"They didn't identify themselves. That's for certain," Adam struggled to say.

"Just rest. The doctor will be here soon."

I stood, moving toward the door main door, glancing down the hallway. All seemed clear.

Less than five minutes later, Ivan called.

"The doctor is MIA," he snapped. "The little weasel left town without telling me, but you can't take them to the hospital."

Ivan had used the same former surgeon for years, insisting on his loyalty to the family. While he'd handled several crucial operations in the past few years, I'd never trusted the man. Then again, trusting anyone in this business was a dangerous concept.

"We won't have to, Ivan. I have someone in mind who can help us."

"You trust him?"

"Yeah, I do." I damn well better be able to trust her.

He hesitated, which had always been in Ivan's nature. "Alright. If he does a good job, I want to talk to him."

"I'll make that happen." I shoved the phone into my pocket. It was time to find out for certain whether the lovely Walker was lying to me. If she was, I would no longer allow her any leeway.

The kind of punishment she would face would shatter her tough resolve.

And I'd be the only man who could end her suffering.

CHAPTER 8

 *alker*

Angry shadows.

The second I'd popped open my eyes, I'd seen them in the darkened space, my mind so screwed I was certain I saw several pairs of eyes.

All of them staring at me with demented hunger gnawing at their systems.

Every inch of my body ached and when I tried to roll over in order to hide my face from the demons, the shock of realizing I'd been tethered to the bed was almost as horrifying at the images rushing into my brain. Ugly, vile flashbacks that I couldn't stop. The bastard had locked me in a room. Where the hell had he taken me?

Shivering, I glanced at the handcuff shackling me to the bed, wiggling it furiously. As the metal snapped against the wood, I resisted a whimper.

Think. Breathe. Control.

I did my best, concentrating on where I'd been taken, the shadows finally fading. From what I could tell, I was in a bedroom inside of a house somewhere. Wait a minute. That didn't make any sense. Wouldn't the man who'd ripped me away from my life dump me in a hole somewhere, a cage maybe? Swallowing, I turned my head, studying the limited furnishings. There certainly wasn't anything special about the room itself or the furnishings. A large bed, a nightstand, and a lamp. There was nothing more. The door was closed, no other sound that I could hear but my ragged breathing.

After taking several deep breaths in order to calm my nerves, I managed to ease into a sitting position, kicking away the covers. My head ached from continuing exhaustion and the fear keeping me on edge. What was mystery man going to do with me?

Ultimately, the answer would mean death. Whether or not he was obsessed with me right now wouldn't matter for long. Men like him threw women away. I realized the asshole had removed my shoes before putting me to bed. Why bother? Why not just dump me on a mattress?

I yanked at the handcuff, doing little more than chafing my wrist. There was no way to break it free, the post the cuff was attached to made of steel. I was wasting my time.

When my eyes fell on the single drawer in the nightstand, I bit my lower lip before reaching for the handle. Who knew? Maybe I'd get lucky and there'd be a weapon inside, something I could use against the man. I should have known he'd never be that stupid to leave me with anything remotely dangerous to him. The drawer was completely empty.

A blind covered the two windows, but I could clearly see it was still dark outside. I hadn't been asleep for very long, just enough to make me groggy.

Slumping forward, I placed my head into my hand, fighting rage and sorrow, anxiety and a bout of oncoming depression. I forced my thoughts to return to Samuel's attorney and various conversations. There'd been no additional information, just a single business transaction, although he'd left a letter addressed to my mother, which she'd refused to take.

I'd decided to take it with me, determined to read it at a later point. Unfortunately, I had no idea if I'd tossed it during the move or if I'd accidentally left it at my mother's house. At this point, everything was foggy.

I fell back onto the covers, staring at the ceiling. Answers wouldn't come easy if at all. The second I closed my eyes, I heard the door being opened and jerked up, my heart racing. When he walked through the door, I was shaken all over again just seeing his hulking frame. As he walked closer, the vibrations I'd felt earlier strummed through me all over again.

He swept his eyes over me before pulling a key as well as the blindfold I'd been forced to wear earlier from his pocket. Every move methodical, he unlocked the single handcuff, leaving the other one locked around the head-board. In an unexpected move, he crouched down in front of me, taking and holding a deep breath. When he expelled the hot air, I looked away.

The bastard grabbed my chin, forcing me to look him in the eyes.

"You have one chance to tell me the truth. I'll understand if you lied to me before. But you will not lie to me again. Understood?" His gravelly voice sounded more strained than before. With the man being this close, I could see what appeared to be specks of blood on his face. Then I realized he'd changed shirts. He'd been out killing someone else. My stomach churned at the thought.

"What do you want? You won't even tell me who you are."

His eyes held the cold, hard stare of a monster, but his expression softened. "Maksim. That's all you need to know."

"Well, Maksim. I can't say I'm happy to meet you."

He leaned forward, allowing me to catch the scent of peppermint. "Are you a nurse or were you lying to me?"

Why the hell did he want to know? Besides, he should have checked my credentials by now. That meant something had occurred while I was sleeping. My first inclination was to lie to him right now, but I had the distinct feeling he would know. Then what small amount of trust I might gain would be lost, tossed away. "Yes. I'm a trauma nurse. I work in the emergency room most of the time."

"Are you good?"

"I guess. Why?"

"Then you're coming with me." He wasted no additional time placing the mask around my eyes then shoving my tennis shoes onto my feet. "I don't think I need to remind you of this, but I will. If you try and run away or get anyone's attention, the kind of punishment you'll face will be worse than death."

"Okay. Where are we going?" It felt weird for him to be tying my shoes, the silly action only adding to the jitters coursing up and down my body.

"To save some lives." He jerked me to my feet, dragging me along behind him.

What? Whoa. This was crazy.

The blindfold blocked out every millimeter of light and as he pulled me down a set of stairs, I tried to remember climbing them. I couldn't. Had he carried me up to the bedroom?

I could feel a blast of cold air, which meant we were going outside. When he shoved me into a vehicle, I could barely think clearly. As he'd done before, he said nothing as he started the engine, the powerful set of vibrations matching the chattering of my teeth.

"Who am I trying to help?" I asked, unable to stand the silence.

"It doesn't matter."

"Obviously, it does to you. Is there any medical equipment wherever we're going, a first aid kit? Something?" He seemed thrown by my question, the sound of his breathing changing.

"I'll make certain you have what you need."

Huffing, I fought every urge to rip off the mask. "Listen to me, Maksim. From the look on your face earlier, I could tell that whatever happened troubled the hell out of you. If this isn't a basic cut or light burn, then you're going to need to tell me what I'll be dealing with."

He exhaled.

Was he kidding me? I wasn't a miracle worker. I turned toward him, fisting my hand, furious I couldn't look the asshole in the eyes. "Goddamn it. I can't help you if I'm not given the right information. I'm not God."

"Gunshots. Multiple gunshots."

Fuck.

I took several deep breaths, furious with him, angry with myself. "These people need a hospital."

"That's not possible."

"What is wrong with you? You're trying to save them, yet you won't take them to the one place that can help?"

Another moment of silence kicked in.

"My men were attacked inside one of the family businesses."

The family. I doubted he was talking about his brothers and sisters. Mafia. Of course. With a Russian name and accent, he was Bratva. I'd read enough, seen enough on television over the years. "How severe are the injuries?"

"Two are minor, shoulder wounds but both have bullets lodged. Another with a leg injury. The fourth has lost a significant amount of blood, although I managed to get it stopped before I left, the tourniquet stopping the flow. His heart rate was elevated and he was in a significant amount of pain, but he was completely conscious before I left."

"It sounds like you know something about medicine. If you do, then you understand the important of having the right supplies. Clean towels and bandages, sterile knives and antiseptic. Painkillers would be preferable but aspirin. Anything."

He snorted. "Yes, I know more than I give a shit about. It was shoved down my throat for two years."

My God. The man was more complicated than I'd realized.

"You studied medicine. Didn't you?"

"How astute of you, Walker. It no longer matters."

"From lifesaver to murderer. I bet your parents are proud of you." I couldn't help myself, the words tumbling out of my mouth before I could stop them.

When he snapped his hand around my thigh, I knew just how angry I'd made him.

"I will stop at a drugstore where you will get everything you need, but you need to make it quick and stay quiet. Do. You. Understand?"

"Yes. Of course." I could tell by the difference in his voice to shut the hell up. I'd seen the outline of his gun when he'd walked into the room. I also knew exactly what he was capable of. I took several deep breaths, concentrating on any sounds around me. "Depending on how much blood this man has lost then he might need a transfusion. I doubt you'll know his blood type."

"He was conscious when I left, Walker. However, I'm his blood type. I'm a universal donor."

I wasn't certain if he was trying to impress me by offering to roll up his sleeve. It honestly made me even sicker to my stomach.

Only minutes later, I could tell we were slowing down. Then he made a turn. After he cut the engine, I felt his presence drawing closer and held my breath. He untied the blindfold, giving me a stern look before climbing out. After blinking several times so I could focus once again, I glanced up and down the street perpendicular to where he'd parked. He'd stopped at a Walgreens store in a neighborhood I certainly didn't recognize. Thank God it was open twenty-four hours.

He kept his hand on the small of my back as I grabbed a basket, moving past the only person I noticed inside. While the woman eyed us carefully, I had a feeling she'd do so for anyone walking in this time of night. I remained quiet as I headed for the medical supplies, tossing everything I could think of into the basket. With the way he'd described the injuries, the men have a fighting chance, but I wouldn't have another opportunity to get what I needed. I still felt sick inside, but not being tied like an animal was giving me a sense of purpose. Plus, maybe I'd learn more about my captor.

"The syringes are too small to be effective."

"What about the pharmacist?" he asked.

"That will draw attention and we don't have a prescription. You better hope your man did stop bleeding."

He gave me a strange look, as if he realized another person connected to him could die because of the business he was in, although what the hell did I know?

As we walked to the register, I could tell he was concentrating on the front window, staring out at the street.

"That'll be two hundred seventy-two dollars and fifteen cents," the woman said.

As usual, he remained quiet, yanking out his wallet and tossing his credit card. What he didn't know was that I had better than twenty-twenty eyesight. Before the woman was able to pick up the platinum card, I was able to read his full name.

Maksim Calderon.

The name sounded vaguely familiar, but I had no idea from where.

He continued to stare outside, forcing my gaze to follow. There was a vehicle on the main road, literally crawling by the front of the drugstore. When he moved in front of me to sign the receipt, I sensed he was attempting to protect me. The dichotomy of this man was far too confusing.

As we moved toward the door, he hesitated, leaning over and whispering in my ear since the store clerk was likely watching. "Be a good girl and climb into the vehicle without wasting any time. Then crouch down. Do you understand?"

"Yes, of course I do." I did what he asked, unable to take my eyes off the road. As soon as Maksim stepped off the sidewalk, the car sped away. When he climbed inside, he pulled his weapon into his lap.

"We might have company," he said gruffly. "And not the kind that's going to save you, Walker. The kind that will eat you alive."

"What's going on?"

"Business." He sped out of the parking lot, driving more erratically than he had before, slowing only after he'd checked the rearview mirror several times. Then he drifted into the quiet mode from before, saying nothing as he drove onto the interstate.

"You can sit up now," he instructed, growling under his breath.

I slipped onto the seat, able to tell how tense he remained. Whatever had happened kept him on edge.

Ten minutes later, I knew exactly where we were going. A casino. I could see it in the distance, the bright neon lights lighting up the sky even as the morning light began lifting over the horizon. I'd never been, but I'd heard about it from other nurses at the hospital.

The Diamond Club was swanky, expensive, and star studded.

It was also owned by the Novikov crime syndicate. I should have put two and two together except that Jack Springer wasn't in the mob.

Or was he?

Was the building a front, owned by Ivan Novikov?

I shrank against the seat, my throat starting to close.

He drove around back to a private parking area, only waiting a few seconds to allow me to grab the two bags of medical items before pushing me toward a huge steel door. Once inside, I realized it was the service entrance.

He moved through the brightly lit area, obviously knowing the place inside and out.

There were dozens of people from various jobs moving from one room to another, the scent of food filling the airspace. He continued walking, turning corners as he headed for whatever our destination was inside the massive facility. Had his men really been shot inside? Weren't gangland style wars only seen in the movies? But the fact people were still going about their everyday business meant they were either not aware of whatever had gone on or were used to gunfights.

Everyone gave him a nod of respect as the gorgeous man walked me through the kitchen, all taking a moment to stop what they were doing and if I didn't know any better, they were paying homage to the man. Jesus. Did everyone think he was a damn celebrity? It was almost six in the morning and the casino was still this busy? It was crazy.

I glanced down at my jeans and sneakers, realizing I didn't fit in with the fancy attire I knew was required. He caught my look and shook his head, pushing his palm against one of the swinging doors and into a hallway. He remained in front of me as he scanned the corridor. What was he looking for?

Whoever had attacked his men, I realized just how angry and unsettled he was when he cursed several times under his breath.

"Do you own this place?" I asked after at least four other employees greeted him warmly.

He didn't bother answering me as he led me through to a bank of elevators. Then he pushed me against the wall as he pressed the button. "Don't ask too many questions, Walker. This isn't a social visit. That's something for you to keep in mind."

"I know that better than you do, Maksim. I'm your prisoner. Remember?" I stared at him defiantly, even though I felt even smaller standing in front of him than I had before.

Lifting my chin with a single finger, he stared into my eyes. "I believe you are who you say you are, Walker, but don't push me. I'm not the kind of man you want to fuck with."

"If you're trying to scare me, don't bother. I'm already so terrified I can no longer feel my legs." The doors opened and he looked away, but I could tell he remained tense.

"Mr. Calderon," the two young men exiting the same steel box said, absolute respect in their voices.

"Gentlemen," Maksim said as he led me inside, backing me into the rear.

He narrowed his eyes, pressing one hand against the elevator wall. For a few seconds, I thought he was going to kiss me, but not like before. I could swear there was a real person behind his stunning blue eyes. He remained hovering over me for a few seconds then pulled away, turning toward the doors.

"Whatever happens, you will not allow my men to die." His statement was a threat without question.

I closed my eyes, concentrating on how fast my heart was beating, a lump forming in my throat.

"And as I told you, I'm not God. I will do everything in my power to help your men, but I won't be held responsible for the fact so much time has gone by or that they were gunned down because of the profession they chose."

"Sometimes, a profession chooses you for reasons you might not be able to understand."

Why I found his words profound, I would never know. I shook my head, holding my breath when the elevator pinged. He turned his head to glare at me, taking long strides into another corridor, expecting me to follow.

A man approached and I was able to see an outline of his weapon even though he was wearing a suit jacket.

"Everything is under control," he said as he stared at me, his eyebrows lifting as he eased his slow and steady gaze down the length of me. "Interesting change in the doctor."

Maksim grabbed me by the arm, leading us down the hall. We were in the hotel portion of the casino, and everything was very quiet, maybe too much so.

"I don't have time to explain, Brick, but I've been assured that Ms. Sutherland can help us. She's a registered nurse with the local hospital." Maksim's answer was clipped, without emotion. "Any trouble?"

"Nothing new," Brick told him, still giving me quick glances, his expression one of amusement. It was obvious the man didn't know who I was.

"They're resting comfortably. No appearances from the police." Brick moved ahead of us, unlocking one of the doors. "I tried to think of some things that the doctor might need."

"Is Kane tending to the Saudi prince's family?" Maksim pushed me inside, anger remaining in his voice.

Saudi prince? I glanced around the room, amazed at just how well some people lived. The expansive room was at least fifteen hundred square feet, the posh surroundings accentuated by a baby grand piano and gorgeous art adorning the walls. There was a significant amount of money to be made in the business of gambling.

"Yeah, he's trying to. I only hope we don't have some international incident. At least the prince's consorts believe he was the target."

Maksim sighed. "We won't be able to keep the press away from long."

"They've already been notified," Brick told him quietly. "If I had to guess by who, I'd say a guest from the prince's party."

"Then we need to make this quick. Send some men out on the street. I had a creeper following me to the drugstore."

A creeper. I almost laughed, more because of my increased nerves than anything else.

"Look, while I get you need to discuss... business," I interrupted, "if there's a man whose lost a lot of blood, time isn't a luxury we have." I glared from one to the other, anticipating backlash.

Brick nodded, backing away, but I could clearly see the smirk on his face, oh so amused by a woman standing up to the big man on campus.

"They're right through there. Let me know if you need anything, Ms. Sutherland. I'm certain there's a first aid kit somewhere."

Maksim pushed me toward the door, turning the handle. "They aren't your friends, nor will they help you, Walker. Talk to them only when necessary."

"I get it. They're loyal to you." What the hell was he worried I'd say?

"I think you're beginning to understand."

"More than you know. What we don't have is a knife."

"What?" he barked.

"If bullets are lodged, I need a damn sterile knife."

Maksim exhaled, pulling out a pocketknife. All he had to do was give me a harsh look. Nodding, I accepted the olive branch of trust, realizing my life might depend on returning it without making an attempt to kill him. "We need to sterilize this."

"Alcohol will do the trick."

I held my breath as he opened the door, expecting a warzone. I was pleasantly surprised as well as sickened that all four men seemed to be comfortable, the bullet wounds they'd suffered obviously not bothering them to any degree. While all four turned their heads in my direction, none of them greeted me. It was likely some protocol used by crime syndicates.

He pushed me further into the room and I pulled away from him, heading immediately toward the bar located in the corner of the room, beckoning me to follow. My hand shaking, I held out the blade as he poured vodka over the steel, his eyes never leaving mine. Then he headed toward the man who'd been shot in the leg.

"Hi. I'm a nurse. I do know what I'm doing. I'm going to examine your leg. If we're lucky and the bullet went straight through and the bleeding has stopped, then you should be fine." My God. I sounded like I had the first semester of nursing school.

The guy lifted both eyebrows, managing to grin through what had to be significant pain. "Help yourself, doll. It isn't every day a beautiful woman spends time on the floor in front of me." His laugh brought about a vicious cough and there was no doubt he'd riled Maksim. I could feel the man's hot breath cascading across the side of my neck.

As I peeled away the portion of a tablecloth that Maksim had used, I realized his quick thinking likely saved the man's life. After retrieving the bullet, I'd need to give him stitches with a needle meant for little more than sewing. But I was a nurse; I had an oath to follow as well as my conscience. The four men needed my help and that's what I was going to provide.

I stared at the knife for a few seconds, wondering how many times it had been used for something other than saving lives. Then I got to work.

In the hotel room, time had no meaning. While Maksim didn't bother me, the other men ignoring my work altogether, watching some sports channel, they did some shop talk, enough to know they had no idea who'd attacked them, killing several of their men. That's why Maksim was so tense. It would seem they weren't used to being the victims in the world of organized crime.

I had no idea how long I'd been working, but the sun was fairly high in the sky. However, I managed to extract the two lodged bullets, cleaning up the man's leg and providing stitches I hoped would hold. After I'd finished, I finally moved away, stumbling toward one of the large windows on the other side of the room. I needed a hot shower and a change of clothes, their blood managing to splatter all over my shirt.

Maksim approached from behind me, his reflection appearing huge in the refracted light. I could feel his penetrating stare, could almost read his mind. He wasn't certain whether to kill me or fuck me. When he remained quiet like he usually did, I pressed my forehead against the glass.

I fingered the sheath of the pocketknife before lifting it into the air. He took his time before taking it, his touch affecting me just like it had before. I shuddered, sucking in air to keep from issuing a single sound.

He sighed and I watched as he pocketed the knife, his eyes never leaving me.

"What about the Saudi prince?" I asked.

"He's dead."

"And you'll be blamed?"

Maksim snickered. "They're under the impression the prince was the target."

"But you know better."

"Let's just say I'm used to being threatened."

He said the words so lightly as if it happened all the time. How could he live that way? An awkward tension settled between us, which continued to heighten my anxiety.

"Were you serious about giving your blood?" I wasn't certain whether my question mattered, but maybe I was trying to find some ounce of decency in him.

"Yes, Walker. Without hesitation. I live and die by those men who are loyal and would give their lives."

"God. I could never understand that. I might do it for family, but no one else."

Sighing, he crowded closer until the electricity sparked between us all over again. "That's what you don't understand. We are a family."

"A murderous one." Now I was the one who sighed. "I guess I should apologize. I'm jumpy and exhausted." I'd put together some of the pieces, hearing enough chatter. This really was a nightmare.

"You're right, Walker. In our line of work, we've had to do unimaginable things but is it any different than a doctor being forced to choose one life over another? Haven't you been forced to make decisions that haunt you to this day?"

I swung around to face him. "They're not the same thing at all, Maksim. Nurses and doctors take a Hippocratic Oath to save lives whenever possible. Do deaths haunt us? Absolutely, because we're human. We make mistakes just like anyone else. We do have to make choices in order to try and save more lives. But it's because we care about people. We have humanity. You had that opportunity to find that and you turned your back on it. You threw away the opportunity of a lifetime. Now, you take lives as if they don't mean anything to anyone else. What about their families? What about their children, mothers, and fathers? What about growing old with the person they love the most? Doesn't that mean anything to you?"

When he crowded even closer, I realized my voice had risen. I was certain I'd pay for that little infraction. He planted his hands on either side of me, making certain I wasn't able to go anywhere.

"We all make choices, Walker, ones that we loathe and those that we regret. You're right. I chose to throw away a career that had been shoved down my throat. Bratva is in my blood, an honor that is highly respected in order to keep the peace."

"What peace, Maksim? We're not at war in this country."

He laughed, lowering his head and whispering so only I could hear. "You're very privileged, aren't you, Walker? Let me guess, you went to the finest schools, your tuition paid by Mommy and Daddy. You never had to work a day in your life until after you graduated. You were given cars as presents, a huge allowance. Or am I completely wrong and you have or had a sugar daddy on the side paying for everything in exchange for your body whenever and however the man wanted?"

"You son of a bitch," I hissed, my chest rising and falling. The second I tried to raise my arm to slap him, he gripped my fingers, twisting and squeezing until I bit back a scream of pain.

"Yes, I am. As far as your statement regarding wars, as astute as you seem to be, you've ignored everything around you. All you have to do is turn on a television station or read the internet news. I'm certain you have an iPad you carry with you everywhere you go. What about satellite radio in that fancy doctor's car of yours? If you haven't heard about the violent crimes occurring in this country by those you would probably consider innocent, then you're not as savvy as you think you are. Men and women are murdered every day for a loaf of bread or a television that can be sold for drugs."

"Yet, you sell those drugs. Don't you?" I countered. "You're to blame like everyone else."

He huffed, lifting his head, his jaw clenching. "As I said, Walker. Everyone must make choices in their lives. Perhaps you're correct in that we are partially to blame, but there is one major difference. We follow a code of honor. We would easily die for our own people."

"What do you think that makes you, Maksim, a better person?"

"No. That's what makes me human."

CHAPTER 9

$\mathcal{M}$ aksim

Walker had remained silent after leaving the hotel. I glanced over at her tense form as she crowded against the passenger door and sighed. Things were getting out of control.

Power.

I'd craved power for as long as I could remember. I'd ascertained early on that being the one in control meant doors opened with ease, people unwilling to go against me. I'd learned that from my father, his often offensive and curt mannerisms giving him the label of being one nasty doctor. He had everyone fooled. While he and I never really got along, he adored my mother, treating her like a queen. He was like Jekyll and Hyde with it came to spending time with her.

He'd given me far too many lectures on life, making selections carefully, most of which I'd tuned out. However, there was one piece of advice I'd listened to, finding even the way he'd delivered the information fascinating.

"Love is difficult, often heartbreaking, but when you find the single woman that can thaw the ice in your heart, then you will learn to do everything in your power to make her happy, including at the expense of your own. But in doing so, you'll find the greatest peace you've ever known."

There was no reason I'd thought about his words at this moment. It seemed inappropriate as hell. Walker meant nothing to me. Granted, she was a beautiful woman and I'd enjoyed taking her, but there wasn't a woman alive who could crack the shield of ice I'd placed around my heart and soul. Not that I wanted it to happen. While Ivan had gotten married and had given birth to Vadim, still taking time to be with his wife every night, I sensed he remained unhappy. Maybe because he'd been forced into an arranged marriage or perhaps it was because he'd had a single child. I didn't ask. I didn't care.

But he'd made certain to tell me never to get involved and fall in love because it would only end badly. That had been the single piece of advice coming from my uncle since I'd knocked on his door over eight years before, telling him in no uncertain terms that I wanted to be a part of the organization. Hell, I'd demanded it much to the man's amusement.

"What happens now?" Walker asked, breaking me out my ridiculous rambling of memories.

"We talk. If you give me the answers I'm searching for, then I might let you go." I didn't need to look in her direction to know her eyes were open wide behind her mask. To her credit, she had yet to try to remove it, but I had no doubt she was planning some act of retaliation or escape.

"And what if I don't?"

"Then I'll be forced to use different tactics in the way I pose the questions." She could have used the knife expertly, killing one of my men and making it look like an accident, but she hadn't. I wasn't certain whether to give her praise or laugh at her trust in mankind.

She laughed softly. "You're really going to hurt me, Maksim? Are you going to cut off a finger or maybe your method of torture is more like waterboarding? Am I getting warm?"

I'd yet to meet a man who was left alive who'd challenged me to this degree. No one had that kind of audacity, yet she didn't care about pushing any buttons. Either she had a death wish or she didn't believe that her life hung in the balance. "You've been reading too many books, Walker. I'm not the Chinese military, and this isn't Sicily, although you will find my methods very unpleasant."

"And if I tell you that I've already given you the full truth? What would you say?"

I turned down the driveway to the house before answering. "Then I'd say you need to dig much deeper, Walker, or it's going to be a very long day." As I pulled the car in front of the house, cutting off the engine, I stared out the driver's side window, angry with myself for being hesitant with her. What if she was telling me the truth? I had to investigate the possibility.

The second I heard a noise, I knew exactly what the little bird had done.

She'd fled my car, racing toward the dense trees surrounding the house.

"Goddamn it," I hissed, shaking my head as I jumped out onto the aggregate. I was shocked that she'd gotten as far as she had, her long legs flying.

Then she completely disappeared in the trees.

What the hell?

While I continued to admire her spunk, I'd grown weary of her behavior. She was acting as if this was all a game, able to end it whenever she decided. No more interruptions. It was time to deal with what she knew, even though my tactics would obviously need to be harsh.

I'd purchased an estate in a more secluded location on purpose, the old barn transformed into the playhouse. There was no one around for over two miles, which added to both the security as well as the privacy. A man could scream for hours, and no one would hear.

She'd managed to get a decent enough head start that I only caught glimpses of her long hair flying in the light breeze. She'd ripped away the blindfold, but she had no clue where she'd been taken. However, I knew she would keep trying to escape until she was caught, or was overcome by exhaustion.

When I lost sight of her completely, I stopped and listened. If she honestly thought I wouldn't be able to hear her trudging through the dense terrain, she'd misjudged my tracking capabilities. She was moving in a diagonal direction, heading in the direction of the playhouse. I chuckled under my breath before trailing behind.

The single yelp she made indicated I'd gotten closer. Even with her running shoes, the forest would remain a tough deterrent. I stopped a few seconds later, lifting my head. The call of several birds meant she'd interrupted their slumber.

"There's nowhere for you to run, Walker. I suggest you show yourself."

As expected, she remained quiet, probably hiding behind a tree and hoping that I'd head in the wrong direction. As I studied the ground beneath me, I was able to see a few footsteps in the dirt because of the recent rains. I moved silently through the trees, scanning from one side to the other. A single crack of a broken limb under my foot gave my location away.

I heard a rustle of trees and bolted in her direction, jumping over several fallen limbs as I zigged and zagged to keep up with her. A smile crossed my face when I saw her just up ahead. She obviously heard me coming, tossing her head over her shoulder. Even from the distance, I could see her expression of terror.

Within seconds, I'd closed the distance, only a few yards left between us.

"Get away from me," she screamed, the sound dissipating almost immediately.

"Come to me, Walker. I won't ask you again."

"Fuck you."

She sprinted to the right, moving even closer to the playhouse. Snickering, I took my time, knowing exactly what she was headed for, the patch of briars thick and thorny.

Walker yelped and I took off running. When I was able to grab her arm, yanking her against my chest, she let off a bloodcurdling scream. I shoved her against a tree, staring down at her as I contemplated what the hell I was going to do with her.

The little vixen fought me with every ounce of energy she had left, issuing a barrage of solid punches and hard kicks. I finally lost my patience with her, wrapping my hand around her throat and squeezing until I could tell she had difficulty breathing.

Her eyes opened wide, but she hissed, pushing her fists against me. "Get. Off. Me."

Exhaling, I glanced from right to left, finally locking my eyes with hers. "I don't think you understand what you're facing."

"And I don't care."

"Really? You don't care?"

I gave her a few seconds to rethink her ridiculous statement. Finally, a good portion of the venom vanished from her face, her mouth twisting and quivering as she clawed at my jacket.

"Please," she whispered, no longer struggling.

"I trusted you to follow my orders. My mistake, and one I won't make again. You'll have to earn my trust before I'll allow you any additional privileges. As of right now, you have none."

"What... do you... want?"

"The truth, Walker. Now, tell me. Who is Samuel Rossi to you? Your lover? Your sugar daddy? Or were the two of you working together in his infiltration of our organization?"

There wasn't just shock in her eyes as what I was insinuating. There was disgust.

"You're crazy. You're sick!" she managed, even though I kept my tight hold around her throat.

I cocked my head, inching closer. Even after everything she'd been through, her spunk remained. I took a deep breath, my balls tightening from the richness of her natural scent. Goddamn, the woman drove me nuts, keeping me on edge as well as fully aroused. Fighting my desires was becoming impossible. "Why? Tell me why what I said bothered you so damn much."

She pushed one fist against me then the other, finally grabbing and yanking my jacket, pulling me in even closer. "Because he was a friend of my father's."

Father. What in the hell? That just added to the mystery even more.

I'd done another search of the internet, and nowhere had I found a connection between Samuel and Walker, but I knew when a person was lying to me. She was telling the truth, at least as far as she knew it. I loosened my hold but kept her pinned against the tree.

"You're lying to me," I insisted.

"I'm not lying. My mother confirmed Samuel knew my father."

"And who the hell is your father?"

"I... I don't know. I've never met him, but he ran out on my mother. They're both bad men, at least that's what it seems like."

Was that possible? If so, what she'd just told me was an interesting twist. That would give a plausible reason why Samuel had willed her the condominium since it would appear given my search that he had no living relatives. However, why would the man put her in harm's way given the amount of money he'd extorted from the syndicate? And was her father a player here? Almost nothing added up.

"That's a good story, Walker. Nice try."

"Oh! I hate you. Why would I lie? I didn't know the man. As I already told you, I received a letter in the mail from the man's attorney. Believe it or not, I was given the condo as a gift, which was a dream come true, or so I thought."

"What was his attorney's name?"

Now she seemed confused, her eyes glassing over. "I… I can't remember."

I slammed her against the tree, knocking the wind out of her. "You've never met two men who were important in your life, and you can't remember the name of the attorney. You're a smart girl. Imagine how that sounds to a man like me. I think you need to fill in the blanks, Walker, if you want me to believe you."

When I noticed the single tear slipping past her long eyelashes, something snapped inside of me. I'd lost all the humanity and joy of life that I'd once had. I'd been indoctrinated into becoming a killer and nothing more. Just like my mother had warned me. Inhaling, I knew I'd reached a point with her that she would either break, telling me everything she knew, or no matter the kind of treatment I gave her, she would never be able to provide any other decent information.

"Ryland something…" she said, wiggling in my hold.

"Go on." The first name was familiar, but from where?

"I can't. I don't remember! I…" She closed her eyes briefly then spouted off a name.

A name I'd heard before.

"Ryland Showalter."

I reared back, sneering as the name pushed back and forth in my mind. Yeah, I'd heard the name before and in direct connection with Samuel. Still, if the woman was clever enough, the story could have been fabricated. I needed time to verify.

As I studied her eyes, the brutal savage in me continued to come alive, hungering for her like I'd done the first time I'd laid eyes on her. She was like kryptonite to me, an addiction I couldn't seem to get enough of.

"What money could he owe you? He was an accountant for some small corporation," she said absently, still trying to process what I'd told her.

I chuckled. "Who told you that?"

"I looked him up before I accepted the gift. I'm not stupid." She looked away, her brow furrowing.

"Did you mother tell you anything about him?"

"Not really. She said he was a horrible man and that I'd be a fool to accept anything from him." Her eyes clouded over as she continued remembering.

"Then your mother was correct. Samuel served as the chief accountant for the Novikov crime syndicate for years. He laundered money, handled acts of extortion, and was even involved in several acts of… punishment." For some reason, I'd decided to sugarcoat a portion of Samuel's life from her. She was obviously disturbed, her heart rate increasing.

"Then why in God's name would he leave me his condo? Why?"

"That's a damn good question and one you're going to help provide the answers to. As far as Samuel, he was damn good at his job, able to parlay the family fortune into billions of dollars. His expertise was sought after by other organizations, but he insisted on staying with Ivan."

"Then what the hell did he do?" She was becoming overwrought. Maybe it was time for her to understand her benefactor wasn't the man she thought him to be.

I tilted my head, almost regretting the smile that crossed my face. "He absconded with millions of dollars, Walker. In addition, he left with some valuable information." That wasn't something Ivan had told me. I'd found it out from my Capo. I knew it was an embarrassment for Ivan, something he took personally. Samuel knew enough that if another organization was involved, they could blackmail some of our customers and powerful people we kept under our thumb.

She didn't respond, her face showing no emotion. Then she looked away. I could tell she was fighting to keep from becoming emotional. "Why did he leave me the condo? Why? Did he think I wouldn't find out? Was he gloating? It doesn't make any sense to me."

For some reason, I had a feeling her mother hadn't shared important details with her own daughter. Her father was a player in all of this. I made mental note to find out her mother's maiden name. That might lead to finding at least a few answers. "Let's assume you're telling me the truth. Did Ryland provide anything else? Anything?"

"Nothing. A letter addressed to my mother, which she refused to take, and I haven't read."

A letter. I knew Samuel far better than almost anyone with the exception of Ivan. They'd been friends, which had made his discovery so burdensome. The Samuel I knew was a man who did nothing without a reason. He abhorred disorganization, preferred keeping to himself, and had a penchant for making cash grow. No. he hadn't given Walker the condo out of his good-natured heart. He'd done so for a specific reason.

One that I would find no matter how long it took or what boulder I had to turn over. I shifted my gaze in her direction, taking several deep breaths. Ignoring the odd circumstances wasn't in my best interest.

"If I find out you're lying, I won't be able to save you."

"You mean from your boss?" she threw out at me. "Is this all about taking orders from a horrible, dangerous man?"

I took a deep breath, trying to curtail my anger. She didn't deserve my wrath, at least for her words.

She'd been paying close attention, gleaning as much information as possible. She wasn't just bold as well as enticing, she knew better than to remain the victim. Good for her. I laughed, my fully aroused cock pushing hard against my trousers. I said nothing, which seemed to amuse the hell out of her.

"You work for Ivan Novikov. Right? You're just one of his flunkies, a man who will eventually be killed or captured by law enforcement. Isn't that right?" When I didn't answer her right away, she shook her head. "I just moved to Chicago. I'm certain a man of your... intelligence can determine that easily by talking to all the little people you bully into supplying you with information. That's what you do, right? You purchase or blackmail people into doing your biddings."

"What do you think you know, little bird?" There wasn't a cell in my body that wasn't on fire, all because she refused to cooperate. That was a clear sign that she continued to think she had the upper hand.

She looked away, her hands clenching. "I know what I see on television. Novikov's clan runs the underground of Chicago. He's considered one of the most dangerous men in the country. How sad you chose to work for a man like him."

There was no reason for her words to rile me on any level. She was tossing balls into the air, hoping she'd frustrate me enough that I'd let her go. When I backed away from her, releasing my hold, she seemed shocked as hell.

"You might find it interesting that you and I have something in common, my sweet little baby bird."

"You and I have nothing in common. You're a vicious criminal and I'm a law-abiding nurse."

I laughed, the sound bitter as hell. "You've never broken the rules? Not once in your life?"

"I obey the laws," she insisted.

"You've never cheated on an exam or run a red light fearful that you would be late to an important meeting?" I could tell I was making her uncomfortable. The truth always hurt. "And you've never had to question a decision you made with regard to a patient, perhaps cutting corners or telling a white lie to their family?"

"What made you so damn cold and hard, Maksim? Is this all about money? Is that what's most important to you? I don't give a damn about money. All I need is enough to get by. That's another reason we will never, ever have anything in common."

As I placed one hand on the trunk of the tree next to her head then the other, leaning over until our lips were almost touching, there was no doubt we were both drawn by the connection we shared. Her lower lip trembled, and her hardened nipples were easy to see through the thin material of her shirt. "That's where you're wrong. Ivan Novikov is my uncle, a man I didn't know until I was twenty years old. My mother refused to admit that she had a brother, a man she called a monster."

In her eyes, I could tell she remained confused, although she was doing everything that she could to put the pieces together.

"You grew up in the United States. Didn't you?" she asked. God, I loved the sultry tone of her voice, my body reacting instantly. I was so aroused that I knew there was no chance of denying my needs.

"As I said, you're very astute."

"Maybe your mother or your father encouraged you to go to medical school, but you only wanted the criminal life. I don't expect any answers from you. You can't even be honest with yourself. Can you?"

I sucked in another breath, trying to keep from engaging, but the way she was staring into my eyes, searching for whatever truth she could find continued to infuriate me. I'd never allowed anyone to get under my skin.

Not my father.

Not my instructors.

And certainly not Ivan.

Damn her for finding the ability to peel back the layers surrounding me.

"If you're his nephew then…" She shifted her gaze away, obviously realizing that I was more powerful than she'd assumed.

I gripped her chin, forcing her to look at me once again. "Yes, you are correct. I'm an heir to his throne, at least a portion of his massive holdings. That makes me one of those powerful men you've seen on television, ruthless men who will stop at nothing to get what they want. Now that you better understand, perhaps you'll finally comprehend your circumstances. You disobeyed me for the last time, Walker. I'll be happy to feed into your burning need for answers."

"The use of terror tactics doesn't look good on you, Maksim," she hissed through clenched teeth. "I honestly thought you were a man of character and fortitude, refusing to succumb to whatever need for violence you have buried deep inside of you."

She had an innate way of pushing my anger to an entirely different level than any man ever had. I was forced to take a deep breath before continuing.

"So you know. My father is a surgeon of the highest esteem, a man not to be questioned. Everyone in his highly revered field respects the hell out of him, even if he's nothing more than a brutal dictator, which is exactly the way he treated his only son, demanding I become just like him. When I told the pompous asshole what I wanted out of my life, he backhanded me. When I defied him completely, he cut me out of his precious world, therefore my mother's as well. While I grew up an American boy with hopes and dreams of a different life, as a man, I became Bratva, finding more power and acceptance than you could fathom. We are done with the question-and-answer period for now, but there will be many more inquiries that you will be required to answer. But right now, you're going to be punished severely for attempting to escape."

Her rebellious attitude returned, her mouth twisting as she arched her back until our lips were little more than centimeters apart. I could lose all control with her right here and right now, which appealed to me more than it should.

Fucking her was a necessity to calm the beast dwelling within, but only after she was thoroughly punished.

When she opened her hand, pressing it against my chest, she dared to kiss me, her lips brushing back and forth across mine. The flare of electricity turned into a raging fire within seconds.

As her soft moans filtered into my ears, she darted her tongue across the seam of my mouth, wiggling her hips against me until the friction was almost too much to bear. My god, the things I could do to her.

And I would.

"Mmm…" she whispered, pressing her lips against mine in an effort to dissuade or confuse me. And still, I found her impossible to resist.

red her mouth, thrusting my tongue past her lips,
ing every inch. She still tasted like the perfect
combination of sweet and tangy, pushing my adrenaline
level to the stratosphere.

She continued grinding back and forth, every sound she
made seductive. The feisty woman knew what she was
doing, but she had no idea who she was dealing with even
now. I allowed the moment of heated passion to continue,
digging my fingers into her jaw as I dominated her
tongue. I had to admit, I could kiss her for hours, which
was unusual for me, but I would never be able to get
enough of her.

When she slid her hand down my chest, cupping my
crotch, I bristled. The feel was far too good, shoving me to
that very moment of losing all control. After another few
seconds, I pushed away, shaking my head.

"Nice try. I'll give you credit, Walker. You were taught
well how to dissuade your enemies. However, that doesn't
change a thing. Undress." I backed away by a few steps,
watching as her expression changed once again, becoming
hard and bitter. Then her eyes misted over, which was a
perfect indication that she was playing me.

"Here? Why?"

I laughed then tugged out the pocketknife she'd used on
my men. When I held it into the light, she issued a single
disgruntled moan.

"Because you and I are cutting a switch together."

"You're out of your mind."

"Noted," I said, laughing. "Undress."

Walker glared at me, blinking several times. Then she shifted her gaze back and forth as if someone could be watching us. I kept a smile on my face, my mouth watering to see her voluptuous body once again. When she hesitated, I cocked my head, allowing my expression to show her just how serious I was. My statement wasn't a request.

It was a demand.

"I hate you," she muttered.

"So you've said."

Her mouth twitching, she moved away from the tree, her facial expressions highlighting a mixture of emotions. This wasn't the last time she would try to escape my wrath.

When she turned around, her body shaking as she kicked off her shoes, I reached down to my aching cock, shifting its position in order to try to get some relief. I'd never felt so possessive about a woman in my life, my needs to both protect as well as require her full surrender only increasing.

Walker darted a single look in my direction before ripping her shirt over her head, holding it in front of her for a full five seconds before dropping it onto the ground. The fact it was speckled with blood remained in the back of my mind for some crazy reason. She fumbled with the lacy bra she'd chosen, muttering under her breath before easing her arms around her back to unfasten the clasp.

I moved to the side, doing what I could to control my breathing.

A single growl erupted from my throat when she finally bared her breasts. The shimmer of sunlight through the trees highlighted her rosy nipples, keeping my blood pressure high. I squeezed the knife in my hand, fingering the ornamentation as she finished undressing, pressing her body against the tree when she was fully naked. I could tell her breathing was ragged and the way her long hair filtered across a portion of her face was sexy as hell. My captive was vulnerable, the way she looked adding credence to her innocent plea.

However, my training reminded me that every action she'd taken and every word out of her mouth could be nothing more than a ploy.

"Come with me," I said after basking in her beauty for a few precious seconds.

"You really are a bastard. Whatever happened to you, I'm certain your parents are ashamed."

This time, her words didn't bother me.

But she was right.

I took her by the arm, leading her carefully through a bank of trees toward a shrub I knew would provide exactly what I was looking for. She didn't fight utter a single word until I'd located the bush.

"Why don't you select a branch for me?"

She shot a hateful look in my direction, closing her eyes briefly. "This is the thanks I get for helping you?"

"This is the punishment you're going to receive for attempting escape. It's a simple matter of consequences."

"Then pick whichever one you want, asshole. I don't care any longer. You're going to do whatever you want to me. Why should I bother engaging with that process?"

"Fine. So be it." I moved closer to the shrub, fingering several of the limbs before selecting the perfect branch. She watched me intently as I made a quick cut, then narrowed her eyes as I scraped the leaves and a portion of the bark away. When I snapped my wrist, testing its durability, she jumped, her body shivering.

I stared at the switch, turning it back and forth in my hand. She was right in that I'd sold my soul to the devil the day I'd decided to join the Bratva. Until this moment, I'd never second guessed doing so. Why now? I almost laughed from the quick answer in my head.

She'd truly dug out a portion of my soul, trying to change my ways. Little did she know that it was impossible. No one could drag me from the depths of darkness I'd not only fallen into but enjoyed on an everyday basis.

But... something deep within my psyche remained troubled, the unanswered questions nagging at my mind.

Even as I held the thick twig in my hand, a part of me hated what I was doing. She was like a beautiful flower, a gorgeous woman who didn't deserve to fall into my hands. As she tried to regain her defiance and hatred against me, even though she was more vulnerable than ever, I closed my eyes, another statement Ivan had made rushing into my mind.

"I've found that women thrive having a dominant man in their lives. That's the only way they are able to flourish in their meager lives. They'll thank you for it one day and in the meantime, you'll enjoy how docile and compliant they become, serving your every need. Never forget they are possessions to be enjoyed and nothing more. If you allow them to weasel their way into your heart, then you no longer have the capability of leading."

I'd ignored the comment, disgusted at the time. Now I stood with a switch in my hand, prepared to subdue her with punishment. While she sorely needed a reminder that her freedom had been stripped away, I questioned the reasons as well as the methods needed.

Ivan's words were in direct conflict to those of my father. I'd never thought about the difference before this, but I felt as if I'd reached a fork in a road, even more so than before. Whatever choice I made, it would stand for the rest of my life. Who was I kidding? I wasn't like my father. I'd never been.

"Stand facing the tree. Wrap your arms around the trunk," I instructed.

"I hate you." This time her three repetitive words had a resounding effect on me, even though they shouldn't.

"It's to be expected."

Walker laughed, then obeyed me, fisting her hands before hugging the tree. Her breathing remained ragged, but in yet another act of defiance, she straightened her spine, spreading her legs apart.

Goddamn it, I could barely think straight, my needs over-powering my ability to process what I was about to do. The wind was strong enough it carried the scent of her unwanted desire straight across my nose. All I could think about was driving my cock into her mouth.

Her pussy.

Her tight little asshole.

What in the hell had I turned into?

As I approached, I fingered the thin reed, taking deep breaths in order to focus. I eased her long strands of hair away from her shoulders, running my fingers down the length of her spine, slowly sliding them to the crack of her ass. While she flinched, rising onto her toes, she remained in position.

Like a good little girl.

A part of me, the portion buried deep inside under a thick layer of chains remained on edge, but my hunger outweighed everything else. I'd considered myself a sadistic man my entire adult life, unable to find solace or satisfaction in what others considered a normal relationship. Providing discipline had become a way of life, finding women who not only tolerated but also craved a firm hand.

This woman, this gorgeous vibrant girl had awakened something else inside of me. But this was my life, and I had no other choices. I slid my hand between her legs, cupping her bare pussy, allowing myself to finger her clit for a few seconds. She was wet and hot, my intimate touch forcing a single moan from her mouth.

I took two steps away, taking a deep breath before snapping my wrist. The moment the branch sliced across her bottom, I was almost euphoric. When she allowed a muffled whimper, I raked my hand through my hair, my needs becoming insatiable. The whoosh through the crisp air was invigorating, my pulse increasing. When I switched her several times in rapid succession, she jerked away from the tree, throwing her back her head.

"Asshole. I'm not lying to you!"

"That's beside the point, Walker. You broke the rules."

"You abducted me."

After tightening my grip on the switch, I cracked it across her bottom four times then against the tops of her thighs twice.

"Oh. Oh! That hurts," she managed, her entire body shaking, her words barely a whisper. She kicked out her leg involuntarily then slammed her foot against the ground, wiggling back and forth.

I brushed my hand from one side of her buttocks to the other, enjoying the building heat as well as the crimson color floating across her skin. I had difficulty focusing as I snapped my wrist several more times, making certain I covered every inch of her bottom.

She threw a look over her shoulder, snarling as her eyes narrowed. "One day I will kill you."

"That would go against everything you are as a human being."

"As if I care. You don't own me."

Her words had a profound effect on me, rattling and collapsing the rest of my resolve. "You're wrong, Walker. In my line of work, I take what I want without reservation. Whoever you were no longer matters. At this point, your former life doesn't exist. If you ask me why, I'm happy to tell you. You're mine. You belong to me."

Saying the words was more profound than I could have imagined. It felt right, damn good in my system. I wanted her and as I'd already told her, I took what I wanted.

There could be no additional second guessing. There would be no turning back.

"Never," she whispered.

I closed my eyes for a few seconds before switching her a few additional times, finally unable to hold back my needs.

After dropping the switch, I moved closer, pulling her into my arms. "I can't wait to be inside of you, Walker. Fucking you. Using you. Over and over again."

Reaching out, when I pulled her against my chest, cupping the side of her face as I lowered my head, I realized I'd made the choice. I'd chosen the path of least resistance, even if a small part of me continued to try to reclaim what might be left of my soul.

Power.

Money.

Influence.

That's all I'd ever wanted.

I'd found it, exceling in every aspect of how I handled business for my family's organization, relishing in the perks that being in command of a portion of an empire had afforded me. There'd been no questioning my decisions, no sense of personal retribution.

And I'd been happy.

Or so I'd thought.

Until Walker had dropped into my life.

CHAPTER 10

 *alker*

Choices.

Everyone made thousands of them in their lives, some meaning nothing while others altered our future. I'd always wondered what it would be like to have a time machine, finding out how my life would have been if I'd made other decisions. During the heated exchange, I'd seen something in Maksim's eyes that indicated what I'd accused him of had been right.

At least to some degree.

He truly was a brutal man.

But there'd also been something else, a fleeting moment where I'd seen someone else buried deep inside of him, a man who just might surprise me.

However amazing that moment of self-doubt had seemed, a tortured man questioning his past, he'd shifted into the cold, dark bastard I'd faced in my doorway what seemed like a lifetime ago. Why did I continue to want to try reconnecting to the powerful and intriguing man who'd sparked something deep inside?

Maybe I didn't know what the hell I was thinking. Falling for my abductor was absurd in any language. He was a criminal after all, which meant he could be a consummate liar.

To hear that he was related to the mob kingpin was horrifying and that should have squelched whatever sick connection I'd felt with the man.

But it hadn't.

The moment he dragged me forward against the explosive heat of his chest, I'd found it difficult to breathe.

As he pulled me onto my toes, sliding one hand under my aching bottom, I couldn't seem to stop shaking. Sadly, the reason I was trembling had little to do with the pain I'd endured while being spanked like some wayward child. I remained electrified from his touch, which infuriated me even more than before.

A snarl curled across his upper lip as he held me, his eyes darting back and forth. What the hell was he searching for? His chest heaved as he lowered his head ever so slowly until I longed for the softness of his lips shoved against mine, until his rugged fragrance spilled into every cell, knocking me sideways.

Until all I could think about was having his cock shoved deep inside of me.

Blinking didn't help.

Shutting down my thoughts couldn't save me.

Pretending I wasn't aroused was next to impossible.

My nipples were hard as diamonds.

The scent of my feminine wiles stronger than ever.

And my skin was shimmering from the electrified sensations shooting through me.

"*Krasivaya zhenshchina*," he muttered as he breathed from one side of my face to the other. "Beautiful woman," he repeated as he brushed his lips across mine.

I closed my eyes, allowing his words to linger in the forefront of my mind. I longed to be anywhere but here, enjoying an amazing moment with a man I cared about.

You could care about him.

No. That was bullshit. No way.

When I let off a single involuntary moan, he took that as a sign of excitement, capturing my lips as a lover would do, slowly opening and closing my mouth. Tingling, I gripped his arms, kneading his solid muscles as he pushed his tongue just inside, taking his time exploring as I started to shiver, his guttural sounds only adding to the intense yearning pooling inside of me.

The kiss reeked of passion, a man taking his time to savor every moment, but within seconds, his brutal nature took over. He dominated my tongue, growling as the passion became more fervent, his hips grinding against mine.

He slammed me against the tree, using the hard surface as leverage. I was electrified, my desire so intense that even the savagery of his actions didn't bother me. I wanted more.

Craved more.

The draw to him left me dizzy, my desires vivid and terrifying. When he yanked first one hand over my head then the other, wrapping his fingers around both wrists and stretching me to my full height, I opened my legs in response. Even as a wave of embarrassment brought a red-hot flush across every inch my naked skin, the dirty, sinful act only continued to add current to my arousal.

Maksim raked his fingers down my side, swirling the tip of a single finger around my nipple before sliding it further down. I bucked against him, arching my back when he tickled my belly button. Then he continued his torment, slipping his entire hand between my legs, fingering my clit as the kiss continued.

There was nothing I could do to stop him, although only a small percentage of me wanted to any longer. He had me under some kind of crazy spell, all rational thoughts shoved aside.

When he broke the kiss, pulling away by only a few inches, I took several shallow breaths, his taste still lingering in my mouth. I could tell his hunger was only increasing, his pupils dilated, the color much darker than usual.

As he cocked his head, he slipped several fingers past my swollen folds, a slight smile crossing his face. "Fucking you will be a pleasure."

"One you don't deserve."

"Maybe you're right, my little bird, but that no longer matters." He was so damn possessive in everything he did.

His words.

His actions.

The way he fucked me.

And his hunger was all off the charts, the man losing his patience. As he tore at his belt buckle, he issued a low and husky string of growls and nipped my lower lip, sucking on my tender tissue. I rocked hard against him, struggling with the tight hold he had on my arms. In truth, I wanted to feel him, sliding my hands underneath his shirt, able to touch his muscular chest. My mind was clouded with the ridiculous need to wrap my fingers around his cock, masturbating him until my hand was covered in strings of hot cum.

But he had other things in mind.

As soon as he freed his shaft, he positioned the tip against my pussy lips, hesitating only long enough to shove his hand against the bark of the tree. Then he impaled me, driving so deep and so hard that he pitched me against the tree. I wrapped my legs around his, still fighting him as he pulled out, plunging into me again.

And again.

As he developed a brutal rhythm, his thrusts becoming more relentless, I lolled my head. My throat was tight, my heart racing. A part of me wanted to scream but my instinct told me there was no one close enough to hear my cries. I'd taken a quick glimpse of his house before racing into the forest. He lived in the freaking middle of nowhere. Even blindfolded, I'd been able to tell that easily. There'd been no stoplights for miles before he'd made a turn. It had been open road and little else.

No noise.

No traffic of any kind.

No safety net.

I was on my own. Even if Jessie had discovered I was missing, hunting down the detective in charge of the murder investigation, I hadn't been gone long enough for anyone to take my disappearance seriously. They might have thought I'd left my condo on purpose, unable to handle the fact a murder had occurred in the middle of my living room.

My… living room.

My benefactor's expensive, lush condo.

A man who I didn't know and probably didn't want to either even if he was still alive. Was it true what Maksim had told me? Had he been engaged with the Russian mob? Had my father? Everything was jumbled together.

Maksim muttered something else in Russian, drawing my attention once again. The feel of having his thick cock buried so deep inside me was breathtaking, my body on fire. I couldn't seem to take my eyes off his and the way he was looking at me was a clear indication that he believed I belonged to him.

Did all mafia assholes think they could take what they wanted without asking? Was that some perk or code of honor? I almost laughed at my thoughts but shut them down entirely as another sweeping wave of vibrations shoved me closer to a mind-blowing orgasm.

"I will fuck you when and how I want to," he whispered in my ear.

"Uh-huh."

He rose onto the balls of his feet, driving so brutally that my back was scraped against the roughness of the tree. But I didn't care. His eyes narrowed as he continued his barbaric actions, the same damn smile remaining on his face. He knew exactly what he was doing to me, how wet and tight I was, my pussy muscles clamping down against the thick invasion.

I tossed my head back and forth as an orgasm rushed closer and closer. I shouldn't give him the satisfaction of knowing what he was doing to me, but I couldn't control my body's reaction to him any longer.

"Oh… Mmm…"

"You're so wet. So tight. Come for me, Walker. Slicken my cock with your sweet juice."

His commanding words were too intensely delicious to ignore. I'd never felt so filthy in my entire life, but being in the middle of a forest, surrendering to a man who intended me harm was a crazy, sick kind of aphrodisiac. Within seconds, the electricity bursting through me doubled, a powerful climax sweeping through me like a tidal wave.

"Yes. Yes. Yes!"

He chuckled, the sound seductive and erotic, his hot breath lingering against my skin. Even the sound of his voice was so warm and inviting, pulling me into a moment of ecstasy.

One orgasm blew me away, but when another erupted from the darkest place inside of me, the rapture was unlike anything I'd ever experienced before. I lifted my head, but as I opened my mouth on a scream, I was shocked that it was silent. It was as if the man had stolen that from me.

Maksim refused to stop, fucking me like some crazed beast. I couldn't stop shaking, exhausted from the amazing moment of raw bliss. Blinking furiously, I tried to focus, struggling to breathe as his actions intensified. I could tell by the strain on his face that he was doing everything in his power to hold back, elongating the moment.

A laugh bubbled up from my throat as I squeezed my muscles, breaking his concentration and his practiced resolve. Within seconds, his entire body was shaking violently, his guttural sounds no longer human. After several additional savage thrusts, he threw his head back and roared.

And all I could think about was what was going to happen next. I'd defied him. I'd escaped. I'd run.

But at least he had a reason to keep me alive.

Finding the money.

The letter. My instinct told me that the mysterious man had left a clue in the note my mother had refused to read. If only I could get my hands on it then maybe I could use it to bargain for my life. Why couldn't I remember where the hell it was? I closed my eyes, fighting the craziness of the moment, my skin still tingling.

When he finally pulled away, his demeanor changed once again, the cold, brutal killer returning. Damn it. Why did he continue changing, acting as if I was nothing but a thing?

Does it matter? Really? Why do you care?

"What happens now?" I asked as he tugged his pants over his hips, yanking on the zipper.

He leaned in, lowering his head, this time studying me as if I was nothing more than an object. "Now, I put you in a place you won't be able to escape from as I determine whether or not you're lying to me. As I said before, if you are, then nothing will prevent me from handling business in a way you won't find pleasant."

"You mean you're going to torture me for more information before you kill me. Right?"

"If necessary."

"Because you're some compliant soldier to a horrible man." I could tell I'd pushed another button when he slammed his hand against the tree with enough force I jumped.

"Because that's the way things must be handled in my world, Walker. When people disrespect our organization, they receive swift punishment. I suggest you make certain you haven't left anything out before we get to our destination. I won't ask you again. Your fate is in your hands."

With that, he grabbed my clothes from the ground before tossing me over his shoulder as if I weighed nothing.

I didn't bother struggling. It was no use. Where the hell would I go completely naked, barefoot, and with no clue where I was?

Straight to hell.

I was shocked he carried me several hundred yards through the dense forest, acting as if I weighed nothing. I could tell the terrain changed, a small clearing appearing out of nowhere, although I couldn't see anything.

At least at first.

As I lifted my head, I blinked several times to understand what I was seeing. A barn. In the middle of nowhere?

After he approached the building, he pressed in a code then pushed a door open, flicking a switch a few seconds later. After he dropped me to my feet, I backed away, almost tumbling to the floor, the wood rough under my bare feet.

"Look around you, little bird. There is nowhere for you to run."

Swallowing, I took a few seconds to collect myself before I obeyed his command.

When I did, another wave of absolute horror killed every thought of the attraction to the man I'd had earlier. The location was nothing but a torture chamber.

Just like I'd suspected he was capable of.

I could no longer feel my legs as I stared at the inside, the rustic look of the exterior nothing like the pristine facility inside. There were two steel tables positioned underneath a massive fluorescent fixture, several metal cabinets flanking two walls. I could only imagine what was kept behind the doors.

There were also several wooden chairs, all of them with some form of shackles attached to the legs and arms. While they were terrifying, a clear indication of how Maksim handled his enemies, what petrified me the most was the steel cage located off to one corner, a padlock hanging open. Why did I have the distinct feeling the metal box had been used on several occasions?

After shuddering, I forced myself to look away, ignoring the visions clawing at my mind. While there were several windows, bars covering them, preventing anyone from escaping, at least there was some limited light.

My stomach lurched, my throat threatening to close. I was lightheaded but remained just as enraged as I was terrified. *Bastard!*

"What do you see, Walker?" he asked as he stroked the back of my head.

"Do you really expect me to answer that?" I jerked away, only to have him grab me by the arm, yanking me around to face him.

"When I ask you a question, you will answer me." He cupped the side of my face, rubbing his thumb back and forth across my cheek. The warmth of his hand was just as inviting as it had been before, but nothing about the man was redeemable. Yet I had to keep reminding myself that he'd sold his soul long before.

I pressed my hand against his chest, staring into his eyes. "I see the reason you're going straight to hell."

My answer amused him, the smile he gave me showing off dimples I hadn't noticed before. He thought trying to scare me was entertaining. My God. How could I have thought anything about the asshole other than he was a real living and breathing monster?

"Of that I have no doubt." He jerked me into the center of the room, his heavy boots thudding against the wooden floor. The sound echoed in my ears, matching the fast beats of my heart. When he led me toward the cage, I did what I could to jerk out of his hold. "Don't fight me, Walker. This is as much for your protection as it is to keep you in line. You won't be in here long."

"My protection? Am I supposed to believe you care about me now? The only person I should be protected from is you."

Maksim took a deep breath before opening the cage door. Then his grip lessened even as he forced me to face him once again. "If you're telling me the truth, Walker, which remains to be seen, there is a possibility that I'm not the only one who is aware of who you are in relation to this man you claim you don't know."

"Are you trying to tell me that someone else could be after me? Or is this just another scare tactic to keep me obedient?"

"I have no reason to lie to you as seem to continue doing with me."

e last time, I'm not lying to you. If I'd known about ...at my father's friend did for a living, I would never have accepted his generosity. That much I assure you."

We were at another impasse, his hold on me tightening.

His expression hardened before he pointed toward the cage. "Get inside. If you're a good girl and don't cause any trouble, I'll release you when I return."

"What about my clothes?"

He looked over his shoulder at where he'd dumped them, his nostrils flaring. "Given your level of disobedience, you'll need to earn what few privileges I allow you. Get. Inside."

I shuddered as I dropped to my knees, able to feel the rapid beating of my heart in my throat. As I crawled inside, I fought the increasing fear, doing everything I could to fight back against the tears already stinging my cheeks. I failed, forced to wipe them away furiously as I crawled into the back of the metal box, hugging my knees. At least I managed to keep my hard glare pinned on the man as he closed the door, snagging the lock into place. When it was snapped shut, I fisted my hands, pulling my knees even tighter against my chest.

He stood over me for at least a couple of minutes before crouching down, peering at me like I was an animal in a cage.

"No food. No water?"

"I won't be gone that long."

When I looked away, he exhaled, grumbling under his breath as he walked away from the tight confines. He returned seconds later with a bottle of water, unlocking the cage long enough to ease his hand inside. Venomous thoughts rushed into my mind but there was no sense in attempting to fight him at this point. It would result in a far worse level of punishment. As I grabbed the bottle, our fingers touched and I yanked my hand away, the electricity between us far too strong. As the water tumbled to the cage floor, he remained silent, watching as I rolled into the corner.

"Do you have a copy of the transfer deed at your condo?"

"Yes."

"Where?"

I didn't want to tell him a damn thing, but if it meant proving that I wasn't lying, I would do almost anything. "It's in my nightstand."

He remained unblinking for a few seconds then nodded. "Good. The letter?"

"I honestly don't know. It could be there, or I might have left it in one of the boxes I've yet to unpack. For all I know, I dropped it at my mother's house. You see, it wasn't important at the time." Although it should have been. There were answers inside, most of which I guess I'd pushed aside for fear of learning the truth.

While he chuckled, the same unfeeling expression remained. "Let's hope for your sake that it's there and able to provide certain explanations."

"I know. If not, I'm doomed. Right?"

The bastard returned to his silent mode, positioning the lock as he'd done before then rising to his feet. This time, the way he was peering down at me left me aching inside. The man was filled with so much emotion. I looked away on purpose, tired of trying to give him the benefit of the doubt.

Without any further hesitation, he moved toward the entrance, ready to turn off the light. When he stopped short, I could see his shoulders heaving before he shifted his head to look back. "One of my men will stand guard until my return. Let's just hope for your sake that you're telling me the truth."

When he snapped off the light before allowing the afternoon sun inside, I had to bite my lower lip to keep from crying out, reminding myself that I was nothing but a possession to him. I would remain strong and the first chance I had I would gut the man. The thought not only allowed me to smile but also gave me courage as well.

Yet when he closed the door, leaving me in near darkness, I was unable to stop the tears.

Maybe he'd broken me after all.

CHAPTER 11

$\mathcal{M}$ aksim

"Get to the playhouse and remain there until I return," I barked into the phone, furious with my actions. I hadn't intended on locking her in the cage, but she'd pushed me too far.

"Will do, Maksim. You put the girl in there?" Brick asked, which for some reason riled me even if he had every right to know who he was preventing from any attempt at escape.

"For now. I have some things I need to handle."

"Just so you know, Maksim, word on the street is getting bad."

"Meaning what?"

"Meaning that it seems like whoever is putting the squeeze against us has put the fear of God into some people. I had some issues with getting product out this morning. A few gave me some crap."

"And?"

"I took care of it," Brick said, laughing under his breath.

"Don't cause too many waves right now until we know what we're dealing with."

"That will make you look weak. I don't think you want that."

At that moment, I didn't like his condescending tone, but I let it go, realizing that given the number of unanswered questions, anything was likely to piss me off at this point. "What about the assholes who were following me last night?"

"No one's talking. I put a hard push on my usual sources. I swear to God. It's like they were terrified, ready to accept my wrath. I've never seen anything like it, Maksim."

This shit was getting out of hand. "Then you need to bring down the hammer harder. I don't give a shit what you need to do, Brick. Find the fuckers. Use all available soldiers." There was no doubt the instances were connected. This was like a net being cast, pulling in the larger fish while destroying the weaker, smaller ones. That would leave the streets swept clean enough for the unknown entity to avoid tactical difficulties.

"Does that mean you want me to take them away from watching over the Diamond Club?"

"They won't hit that twice, Brick. That's not the way these assholes work. As I said, do whatever is necessary. However, get here as soon as you can, Brick. I'll return in a couple of hours."

There was another slight hesitation, as if the man was questioning my tactics. I was at the end of my rope with regard to patience.

"Sure thing, boss."

After ending the call and tossing the phone into the seat, I rubbed my eyes as I thought about everything that had transpired. There were dozens of organizations that liked to talk big, but only a handful with the resources to infiltrate a territory our size. Was it possible that Chamberlain's buddies had figured out about Gregor's demise, using our methods of handling business to extend their own warning? All they had to do was talk to the right people on the street and the rumors would fly.

My gut told me this was bigger than their organization. Besides, I couldn't imagine they'd have the balls to challenge us, especially after learning of Gregor's disappearance.

The best thing I could do was confirm everything both Ivan and Walker had told me from the ground up.

My first stop, a meeting with Kane.

I stormed into the club, bypassing the hostess, barely scanning the area before heading toward the man's office. I walked inside without knocking, not surprised when he ignored me at first, taking his time finishing up a call. I made myself at home, moving toward his lavish bar, the ornate piece taking up an entire wall. As I listened in on the conversation, I made myself a drink, chuckling as I noticed that every brand of liquor was top shelf. The man certainly thought highly of himself.

I'd already learned that he was enjoying a few more perks than his appointed job allowed him. That pissed me off almost as much as his lack of attention to detail. That would change or I'd hire someone else.

After pouring a small portion of Glen Fiddich, I swirled the liquid in the crystal tumbler, marveling at the colorations in the light created by one of the half dozen wall sconces. While the call seemed like nothing special, a typical discussion with one of the vendors, I sensed Kane was on edge. I could tell by the tension in his voice.

When the call was ended, it took him almost six seconds before he acknowledged my presence.

"Maksim. I wasn't expecting you."

I took my time as well, enjoying the taste of something other than my usual. "Did you find whoever was working with our assassins?" I remained where I was, not bothering to turn around.

184

Kane cleared his throat, flanking my side a few seconds later. "I believe so. I had to make a few phone calls, but one of our newer waiters seems to have a hefty bank account, a recent large deposit certainly not coming from his paycheck or tips."

"Name?"

"Rusty Zimmer." He took his time selecting a beverage of choice, obviously not worried that it was still early in the day.

"Is he working today?" I asked, taking another sip.

"Let me check."

Somehow, I would have thought Kane would know the kid's schedule like the back of his hand. Sighing, I placed the glass on the surface of the bar, flexing my fingers before turning around.

Kane was barely scanning the computer screen, finally darting a look in my direction after he realized I was watching him. "Yeah, he's working. His shift just started. Usually works the casino floor, but we needed extra help given the size of the prince's party."

"Any ramifications from the man's death?"

"Nothing we can't handle. You know there are always fingers pointed." He laughed and I could swear it was nervously.

I didn't bother hesitating, taking long strides in his direction and slamming him against the wall, instantly retrieving my weapon and pushing the barrel against his throat.

"What the fuck, Maksim?" Kane snapped one hand around my wrist but didn't try to get away.

"Need I remind you who you work for, Kane?"

"I... I don't understand."

"I think you do. This casino and every person who works inside the various buildings is under your control, as is everything that goes on here. I expect you to be on top of your game at all times, not drinking expensive liquor and fucking the staff. Do you understand what I'm telling you?"

A single bead of sweat trickled down one side of his face. "Yes. Yes, sir, I do."

I squeezed his neck until he choked then let him go, lifting my head to stare into his eyes. While he was arrogant as fuck, bordering on incompetent, he wasn't working with anyone else. That much I could tell.

"You're certain this Rusty Zimmer is the problem?"

"Yes, sir."

"Okay, then you can go ahead and eliminate his file from the employment records. As of today, he's terminated."

He knew exactly what I was saying. While I could tell that my statement troubled him more than usual, he said nothing to try to change my mind. "Any idea about the assassins?"

I slipped my weapon into my jacket, shaking my head. "Not yet, but I assure you we will hunt down whoever is responsible." I moved toward the door, refusing to waste any additional time. "One more thing, Kane. If anything like that ever happens again, you'll be the next of the list of unemployed. Understood?"

"Without question, Mr. Calderon."

As I walked out, heading for the bank of elevators, I only hoped that Kane had provided the correct information. I would hate to interrupt an innocent man's life.

As I headed toward the casino, I stopped by the hostess stand, asking if the lovely young woman had seen Rusty.

Today, he was working in the Royal Flush, one of the smaller, more private casinos. As I walked into the room, given he was the only male working, I moved toward him quickly.

"Let's take a walk, Rusty."

He opened his eyes wide, easing the tray of drinks onto the surface of the bar. At least the asshole kept his mouth shut as I pulled him down the employee corridor to one of the exterior doors. When I pushed it open, ushering him outside, he seemed stricken.

"I'm not going to mince words, Rusty. It would seem you're working for someone who doesn't like the

Novikov organization very much. I need to know who you've been talking to."

Almost immediately, he lost all the color in his face, shaking as he darted his head back and forth.

I closed the distance, towering over him. "No one is going to get you out of this but yourself, Rusty. I'm not a patient man, so I suggest you start talking. Who paid you to sabotage that party?"

"I don't know what you mean," Rusty whispered.

I placed the barrel against his cheek, giving him a hard look. "Tsk. Tsk. Rusty. You know exactly who I am and what I'm capable of. I suggest you start talking or this won't be your lucky day."

It took him less than five seconds before he started talking. While he seemed scared shitless, at least it appeared he was more worried about what I would do to him versus the other party.

However, the kid knew shit.

He'd been sent an anonymous note that he ignored then a threat, finally finding two of his tires slashed when he didn't respond a second time.

"I swear to God. That's all they wanted was for me to leave the back door unlocked. Nothing more. I'm not lying to you. I wouldn't do that. I just… I mean…"

I placed my hand on his shoulder, exhaling. The fuckers were good, refusing to own up to who they were and the reason for their ridiculous actions.

"Please don't kill me, Mr. Calderon. I know I should have come to you but I just… I was scared and I…"

By all rights I should terminate him permanently, but I knew the kid was telling the truth. "Today is your lucky day after all. You get to live; however, you will no longer be working for the Novikov family. I suggest you get out of town for a while as well. Can you do that for me, Rusty?"

"Yes. Yes, sir. I'll leave tonight, sir. Thank you, sir."

"Get out of here."

He didn't waste any time in racing away from me, looking over his shoulder only once. I thought about what little he'd told me and hissed. Without anyone doing any talking, the search meant nothing.

I returned my Sig to my pocket, shifting my thoughts to Jasmine. I'd been away from her for far too long.

Jack Springer's apartment was in a less fashionable area of Chicago. Other than the man working in the South Loop condo, I hadn't been able to locate any connection between the maintenance man and Rossi.

The area was a shithole in comparison to the high dollar place of residence Samuel had purchased a few years before. Up to that point, he'd insisted on living modestly. It was always fascinating what absconding with money could do to a person.

When I walked inside, I could tell the apartment had been gone over with a fine-tooth comb by members of the police force. I wondered what the hell I could find that might be helpful. After thirty minutes of searching, I had my answer even though it was laced with additional questions, although my gut was working overtime, already forming a scenario. Sadly, only a portion of it made any sense.

I also found a stash of weapons in what appeared to be a secret compartment in the man's closet. The location was such that I didn't think the police had found it. If they had, they certainly didn't see it as important. I thought about the photograph I'd found, my curiosity increasing even more.

After pocketing the limited information, I headed for Walker's condo, making certain no one was around as I used her keys to unlock the door.

As soon as I walked inside, I noticed a business card had been slipped under the door. Detective Miles Declan. I ran my finger across the card before pocketing it in my jacket. She was wanted for additional questions. That meant her disappearance would soon come to light. If Vadim had left any evidence, the police would soon be knocking on our doors.

I headed for her bedroom, flicking on the light. I stood just inside, scanning the area. She'd left the bed unmade, the purple comforter a surprising find for some reason. She was so rough and tumble that a reminder she was all woman allowed a knot to form in my stomach.

Exhaling, I moved toward the nightstand, finding several business papers including the deed of transfer exactly where she said it would be. As I read the contents, I took a deep breath. Nothing about any of this was making sense to me.

The gift.

The maintenance man.

Samuel's disloyalty.

There had to be a missing connection and I had a feeling I knew what that was.

What I could confirm is that the beautiful woman was telling the truth, at least about the gift. As far as whether she was in on the missing funds could be another story, but I was beginning to doubt she was anything but a hapless victim. If so, I was absolutely correct in that her life could be in danger.

At minimum, she was a valuable piece of the puzzle.

I did a careful search of every box I could find in her home. There was no letter to be found. However, that didn't mean it wasn't in another location that she simply couldn't remember given the stress she was under. Or at her mother's house. That posed a problem given the woman lived in New York.

Before leaving her place, I checked for any hidden safes or other possibilities where Samuel had stashed the cash. The man wasn't that stupid. He'd converted the cash into something else entirely or had used a different name in establishing an offshore account.

As I was prepared to leave, I stared at the small suitcase in her closet.

I liked the girl, more than I should. My feelings weren't just about physical attraction or the incredible electricity we shared.

"You're going to be just fine," I whispered, rage boiling inside of me.

She reached for my hand, her lower lip quivering. "I'm scared, Maksim."

"I know but everything is going to be okay."

"Promise?"

"Have I ever lied to you?"

Fuck. Fuck!

Why the hell had another memory popped into my mind? I rubbed my jaw, the damn answer the same as the last time.

Walker.

She'd gotten under my skin, which was the last thing I needed. Still, I couldn't seem to get her out of my mind or to shove my desire away. She'd been the only beautiful creature in recent years who'd managed to spark my attention as well as my hunger.

Hissing, I grabbed the suitcase, tossing in a few of her items. She certainly didn't deserve to be treated like an animal, which is exactly what I'd done to her. However, I also couldn't allow her to return to her normal life. Was there something in between? Not that I knew of. After placing her case into the trunk, I headed for Ivan's house, several of the aspects regarding the entire situation still bothering me. Namely, why would Samuel consider putting Walker in the crosshairs if he was such a good friend of her father's?

Unless that had been his plan all along. Was Walker being used as a scapegoat?

Or as a luscious treat dangling on a fishhook?

When the housekeeper opened the door, she knew exactly why I'd come, pointing toward the living room. As I walked inside, I wasn't surprised to find the man with several different newspapers spread out on the sofa and coffee table. Ivan loathed reading on the internet, keeping multiple subscriptions to those who continued sending them out in newsprint format. From New York to Los Angeles, Miami to Boston, he made certain he kept well informed as to who was making headlines in the larger cities.

Including past enemies, one of them coming to mind.

When I walked in, he removed his reading glasses, tossing them aside. The man was as vain as they came, refusing to allow anyone to see anything he called a weakness.

"Maksim. How are you? Join me for a drink?" he asked, already heading for what was likely his third alcoholic beverage of the afternoon.

"Unfortunately, this isn't a social call." I walked further into the room, shaking my head as I noticed he'd circled several of the articles.

"Business, eh? You work too much, but I appreciate that about you. Hopefully, you've come to give me the information I've been waiting for."

As I reached for a group of papers, I turned my head in his direction. "May I?"

"Of course. Shove them aside. There's nothing going on in New York, which is good news." He laughed and took a gulp of his drink before returning to his perch on his favorite leather chair.

I pulled the pages into my hand, scanning the headline. The crime stats in the Big Apple were increasing, the control of the crime syndicate in charge taking a toll on residents in every borough. However, the fact the Marciano syndicate was making headlines meant they were planning something, expansion or war. I knew all about Ivan's past dealings with them, his hatred of the organization even though he did everything he could to hide it. I tossed the papers aside, remaining on the edge of the chair.

"First things first. Did you handle Kane?" he asked.

"Yes. He's aware this is his last warning and no, he has no new information on the assassins. It would appear it was a message and nothing else."

"Kane is a worthless asshole. I knew I shouldn't have hired him. You told me that yourself."

"He's good at what he does."

"Yeah, well, you know how to handle him."

I waited until he finished grousing before addressing the real reason for my visit. "Walker Sutherland is a woman." How interesting. He didn't seem surprised by my piece of news.

Ivan took a sip of his drink then crossed his legs. "I wondered how long it would take for you to tell me that piece of information."

"Who told you?"

"Does it matter?"

To me it did. That meant someone in my employ had mentioned Walker had been brought to help our soldiers, which was likely against the rules. At this point, I didn't give a shit, except for the fact my trust had been betrayed. The only person that came to mind was Brick. Why? "She claims that she didn't know Samuel before the huge gift was dropped in her lap. She also never met the man, his attorney handling the business transaction."

He didn't respond at first. Then he smiled, chuckling under his breath. "While interesting, I'm not certain I care. You believe her? You know how easily women can lie."

"I have a deed of sale with zero dollars as the price indicating she might be telling the truth."

"Interesting, although he could have left the condominium to her because she was his mistress."

His response surprised me. "That's not like the man I knew, Ivan. Samuel still wore his wedding ring after all the years his wife has been dead. He adored her. I just can't see it."

"Women can drive a man to do crazy things. Is she beautiful? From what I heard she is."

I was forced to suck in my breath to keep my response respectful.

"As I said, I don't buy that. What's interesting is that if what she's told me is true then Samuel put Walker in danger. There must be a reason." I wasn't certain he bought my response by the way he was looking at me. I thought about the photograph, a part of me wanting to keep it to myself.

"I have no doubt there is, or Samuel was playing a game, providing a decoy," he mused, half laughing. The fact it had taken him almost a month to realize Samuel had purchased a condominium in an upscale neighborhood far removed from his own meant Samuel had tried to make sure no one found out about his purchase or the gift. Or the man didn't give a shit either way.

"You honestly believe the deed was forged?"

"Anything is possible, my boy, especially when money is no object."

I glanced down at the newspapers, trying to shove aside my personal feelings. He was right. There wasn't a document that couldn't be forged but I still believed she was telling me the truth. However, the Marciano name continued to bother me. I grabbed the *New York Times*, holding it out. "Do you think there's a chance this is about what happened a few years ago with the Marciano family?"

Ivan barely glanced at the paper. "I highly doubt it. They learned their lesson then."

"They are much more powerful today, Ivan. You're well aware of that. You read the papers." The most powerful crime syndicate in New York had set their sights on Chicago, making a move several years before I had joined the organization. While I'd heard stories from older soldiers, Ivan had never expounded on what had occurred. However, I'd always known there'd been more to the story and the coincidence was far too strong.

"Let it go, Maksim. Leave the past in the past."

The man knew how to infuriate me with his arrogance. "If this has something to do with an act of revenge, then you need to look into Samuel's past. What exactly do you know about his background?"

"An interesting question to pose to me now, Maksim." He appeared angered but nodded once. "I checked out his background. His references checked out. As you well know, that was years ago."

"I'm curious. Where was he from?"

Ivan snorted. "Upstate New York as far as I can remember. The man is dead. Why do you need to know?"

New York. I glanced down at the story he'd been reading as well as thinking about where Walker was from. While there were far too many details that didn't make sense, I had a feeling the only answers would be found by paying New York a visit. "Because I have no doubt in my mind that Samuel is one of the keys to all of this. I think the man lied to you. I think he was someone else altogether. You need to honestly ask yourself about whether or not this is an act of retaliation."

"After all these years? That wouldn't make sense."

"Who did you kill, Ivan?"

He took his time sipping on his damn drink. Then he leaned forward. "I think you've already learned that it's often necessary to remove a cancerous portion of an organization."

"True."

I was surprised he seemed uncomfortable. "Tony Marciano made the mistake of attempting to take a portion of Chicago. I simply couldn't allow that to happen."

He killed the firstborn son of a rival organization. Exhaling, I closed my eyes.

"As I said. That was years ago, Maksim. Let it go."

I wasn't certain I would be able to do that. The entire situation smelled of revenge. "Remember that sometimes revenge is best served cold when the other party least expects it."

As he narrowed his eyes, I could see his mind churning. "You have a very good mind, Maksim. I'll find out if Samuel had anything to do with that organization. If so, then we know who we need to strike."

"Just be careful, Ivan." I tossed the paper, but my gut told me I was right.

He waved it off, muttering in Russian under his breath. The man truly thought he had more power than God.

"Something about this doesn't smell right," I continued. I thought about what I'd found out about Samuel. There was absolutely no reason for me to hide what I'd discovered in Jack's apartment, but the fact Jack Springer, Gregor Chamberlain, and Samuel Rossi had been in the Marine Corps together meant they'd remained close. My thought on coincidences continued to flash in the back of my mind. I wanted to do some additional research before I mentioned anything to Ivan. What I thought I might find I wasn't certain, but their relationship held a part of the mystery.

If I had to guess, I'd say they'd been involved in several business propositions together. But that wasn't it entirely. The situation gnawed at me.

Ivan took another gulp of his drink, the clinking ice cubes drawing my attention, his gaze piercing. "Bottom line is that I couldn't give a shit who she is or whether or not she was provided an expensive gift because she's a nice piece of ass. That goddamn condo was purchased with my money. If she doesn't know anything, then the issue needs to be eliminated."

While his statement was something I'd expected; my emotions around his harsh words weren't. My stomach churned, my blood pressure rising. I refused to kill her just because she'd been yanked into the middle of something she hadn't expected. Hissing, I looked away, realizing my nerves were on edge.

Her image flashed into my mind, my heart immediately racing from the thought of never seeing her again. That just couldn't happen. Goddamn it, she wasn't to blame. I trusted my instinct and it was screaming that she was a victim in all of this.

"Is there a problem, Maksim? I've never known you to hesitate like this before."

"The problem is…" I sucked in my breath, calculating the best answer I could provide to buy some time. "There is no problem, Ivan. Quite frankly, I believe she has more to tell me, including where the whereabouts of the rest of the money could be."

He stared at me with his hard, cold eyes, typical of him when he didn't believe some asshole's attempt at lying. "Very well. Interrogate her. Use her. Fuck her for all I care. Just finish this off soon."

I nodded, although my rage was reaching a boiling point. "Do you have any idea what the hell happened at the Diamond Club?"

"Nothing concrete. Yet. Although I have my suspicions."

Why did I have a feeling he wasn't in the mood to provide that information? If I didn't know better, I'd say Ivan was hiding something significant. There was nothing more ugly in this world than being shoved into a vacuum. There was nothing worthwhile I wanted to say at this point.

If this was all about revenge, then Walker was being played. Why? What could the Marciano family possibly gain by using her in the middle of what they were planning?

"Incidentally, the reason I'm allowing Ms. Sutherland a reprieve is the fact she kept our men alive and nothing else. How sad that Dr. Booker met his maker a few years too early." He grinned, once again leaning back against the sofa. "I'll be on the search for a new doctor to serve our needs. If you have any ideas of who that might be, please do let me know."

As I stood, I had a feeling Ivan was also nervous about the recent events, unable to wrap his arms around what was happening. That usually meant he went on a rampage, killing anyone who might be an issue. With the detective determined to find answer for Mr. Springer's murder, that could pose a problem.

"I have work to do," I said, immediately heading for the door.

"Just remember that Ms. Sutherland is nothing to us. Nothing. While I understand your need to find someone else to fill that black void you'd had for years, she's not the one to do it. Get rid of her. I suggest you remember you're poised to take over at least half of my organization after I retire. I know that's what you've wanted for years."

His implied threats disguised as promises always pissed me off. End her life or else. I fisted my hand, holding my tongue. Until I discovered real answers, riling him any more than the circumstances already had wasn't in my best interest.

"Don't worry, Ivan. I couldn't care less about being involved with anyone. Women are meant to feast and fuck and nothing more."

He laughed, giving me a nod of respect. "You are one hard man, Maksim. Just another thing I adore about you."

As I headed for the door, I realized that whatever was really going on had been for years. Samuel had a reason for betraying the Novikov family. No matter what I needed to do, I was determined to find out if it had anything to do with the assassination of Tony Marciano.

Even if I had difficult choices to make.

CHAPTER 12

"*But that afternoon he asked himself, with his infinite capacity for illusion, if such pitiless indifference might not be a subterfuge for hiding the torments of love.*"

—*Gabriel Garcia Marquez*

Maksim

The term subterfuge had various meanings in the back of my mind. One thing I'd come to realize is that I couldn't handle betrayal of any kind. The fact that Brick had told Ivan about Walker's true identity infuriated me to the point all I could think about was inflicting harsh punishment. While I'd understood from the beginning that my Capo had been loyal to Ivan for years, not only serving under the man's leadership but being nurtured from nothing more than a grunt to a man garnering respect, that didn't change the fact he'd made a mistake.

Maybe our friendship was nothing but a farce.

What I was forced to realize is that my quest to find the truth could mean that I was headed into treacherous waters, no longer able to count on Ivan or the majority of my soldiers to have my back. No one was going to go against the Bratva leader under any circumstances. His request to have her life ended had likely been turned into an edict. If I didn't kill her, someone else would.

As I jumped into my car, I took a few seconds before starting the engine. Far too many things continued to trouble me. Finding the truth could disturb the makeup of the organization, which my instinct told me was the case. If so, then whatever choices I was forced to make could mean the end of my career.

Huffing, I turned over the engine, slamming the gear into drive. As soon as I rolled down the driveway, the sound of my phone pinging did little to calm my rage. "Brick," I answered, roaring onto the street. I was ready to launch into him when I heard his heavy breathing. It sounded like he was outside.

"You need to get here as soon as possible!" he yelled, which was totally unlike his usual calm demeanor.

"What the fuck are you talking about?"

"I heard shots in the distance and went to investigate. Your house looks like a shooting gallery."

His answer floored the fuck out of me. Who the hell would be so damn brazen? "And Walker?"

"So far, no one has found the playhouse," he answered, his heavy breathing indicating he'd been running. "But there had to be a half dozen of the fuckers from the looks of it."

"Then get her out the hell out of there."

"Where the fuck am I supposed to go? I can't tell if the assholes are still here."

"Get to the park."

"You're serious?" he asked, taking gasping breaks. He was definitely outside by the noise in the background.

I'd used a certain park on two occasions. One for a drop-off. The second for a particularly nasty elimination. "Do as I say. I'll meet you there in twenty minutes."

"Okay, boss. Whatever you say."

His hesitation was voiced in his tone, another aspect that angered me. However, at this point, I wasn't going to make any rash judgments. One thing remained very clear in my mind.

Not only had I been compromised but whoever was responsible had been given help.

Now, all I could concentrate on was getting Walker to safety. Whether or not she was the intended mark, or if I was didn't matter at this point. Our lives were intertwined by circumstances if nothing else.

Yet the term of 'subterfuge' continued to rattle my mind.

So did other thoughts, the adoration I felt for her agonizing.

As I sped down the road, my anger only continued to increase exponentially. I would hunt down the fuckers involved, and they would pay dearly. I floored the accelerator, ignoring the speed limit, racing around curves. Everything in the back of my mind told me that if I didn't get to her quickly, she would be dead.

That wasn't going to happen.

Fuck. Fuck. *Fuck!*

The park in question was rarely used, especially this time of year. Brick knew exactly where to go. As I swung into the location, slowing in order to scan the perimeter, my nerves remained on edge. Seconds later, I noticed his SUV, Brick standing by the driver's door. He seemed antsy, shifting from foot to foot as he continually scanned the area. His behavior only intensified my concern. Was it possible the man I was supposed to trust with my life had sold me out?

I rolled beside his vehicle, stopping short and immediately jumping out. Brick offered a single nod, but I could tell he had something on his mind.

"Were you followed?" I snarled, pressing my hand on the glass as I stole a look inside, realizing I was breathing a sigh of relief just seeing the fact she was still alive. As I yanked my weapon into my hand, I checked and snapped the ammunition clip in place. I had enough bullets to take out whoever was necessary.

"Not that I could tell but I heard a few additional shots as I was getting the hell out of there. I called for reinforcements," Brick stated, giving me a curious look.

"Good. Hunt the bastards down."

He nodded, shifting his gaze toward the passenger side of his SUV. "She didn't fight me, but she's scared."

"That I can understand. Walk me through what happened," I demanded.

"I have no fucking idea. I heard gunshots and when I reached the house, the front door was still open. All I had to do was walk in. Thousands of rounds were used. It was crazy," he breathed as he raked his hand through his hair. "What the hell is going on?"

"I think whoever is playing games is about to make an appearance. Anything else disturbed?"

He snorted. "Not that I could tell. I admit it to you, Maksim. I got the hell out of the place pretty fast."

Exhaling, I shifted my attention to the interior of the SUV. "Was she hurt?"

"No. She's fine. Asked a lot of questions though. What are you going to do?"

"Locate a secure place to take her."

"Do you want me to find you one, boss?" he asked. Why did I feel like his question had a far too eager tone?

"No. I'll figure something out. What I need you to do is get with the other men. I need quick and detailed information on who the fuckers were. Gun them down but not without extracting information. Do you understand me?"

When he shot Walker a look through the glass, I was forced to yank back my still increasing rage. "Sure. I'll have the guys search all the usual spots."

"It's possible they're going to make another significant hit, Brick. Cover all the casinos, the warehouses and put our corporate clients on notice but do it carefully. Whatever happens, I want information by tonight. Do you hear me?"

He could tell by my tone that I refused to accept anything less. "Yes, boss. You'll have something." When he started to walk away, I moved in front of him.

"Brick. You and I are going to have a chat about what I expect out of my closest men."

Exhaling, he nodded only once, realizing now wasn't the best time for him to be arguing with me.

I narrowed my eyes, studying him for a few seconds before moving around to the passenger seat. When I opened the door, Walker seemed shocked I was standing in front of her.

"Are you alright?" I asked as I gathered her into my arms.

She threw her eyes in Brick's direction, doing her best to shove me away. "I'm fine. What the hell is going on? I heard gunfire. I thought… Anyway, what is happening?"

At least my Capo had allowed her to dress. "We need to leave. I'll explain later."

"Why?"

"As I said, we'll talk later. Let's go." As I pulled her by the hand, leading her away from the SUV, the goosebumps raised on the back of my neck. I'd always been damn good at knowing when an attack was going to occur and right now, I had no doubt my location had been compromised. In my mind, there were two ways that could have happened. One was being followed. Two was Brick.

While I loathed what I was thinking, I couldn't ignore anything, including my instincts.

"Listen to me. Get in my car and get as far onto the floor as possible. Do you understand?" I dragged her away from the SUV, moving toward my car as I continually scanned the area.

"Now you're scaring me."

"Good. You need to be scared." After opening the passenger door, I heard a series of sounds.

"We have incoming," Brick snarked.

I shoved her inside, slamming the door then moving to the end of the car, crouching down on the ground, my weapon in both hands.

Within five seconds, two vehicles came roaring down the gravel path.

Pop! Pop! Pop! Pop!

As the gunfire peppered in our direction, I got off several shots before racing toward the other side of my Mercedes.

Ping. Ping. Ping. Ping. Ping. Ping.

At least three bullets slammed into the area just behind the driver's door. Goddamn it. I shifted, emptying the entire clip, cutting down the first asshole who'd exited the huge black truck before peppering enough gunfire both windshields were shattered. As one of the drivers slumped over the steering wheel, I reached for another round of ammunition, snapping it in place, prepared to fire again.

Pop! Pop! Pop!

The assholes refused to stop.

"What the fuck?" Brick yelled, dropping and rolling before getting off several shots.

"Get the fuck out of here," I yelled before jumping onto the driver's seat. The fuckers likely thought they had us boxed in, but I knew the park like the back of my hand. I'd been here hundreds of times, the peaceful location providing tranquility when nothing and no one else had been able to do so.

Out of the rearview mirror I was able to see that Brick had followed my orders, still able to get off several shots before following behind me. I slammed my foot down on the accelerator, the rear fishtailing as I shot off through the trees, able to find the second exit within seconds.

I took a quick glance at Walker as she hunkered on the floor, her breathing ragged but she was a hell of lot calmer than I would have expected.

"We'll get out of this," I snarled.

"Then what?"

"Then we go somewhere safe."

"There's nowhere safe around you."

* * *

Walker

Fear and confusion.

That's exactly what I was feeling, uncertain of what the hell was going on. My captor had been shot at, almost killed? A powerful mafia man? Nothing really made any sense and it hadn't since I'd opened my door, finding a body inside.

I leaned against the door of Maksim's incredibly expensive car, shivering even though the heat was on full blast. He'd said almost nothing since we'd left, driving north for over an hour. I'd grown weary of asking him any questions, realizing that he was going to tell me nothing until we'd reached our destination.

However, he continued to glance into the rearview mirror every few minutes, taking side roads whenever he had the chance.

When I noticed a sign, I almost laughed. I'd heard of the place, a little vacation spot a lot of the nurses had gone to.

Union Pier. From what I could tell, the small town was settled with hundreds of pretty little cottages nestled against Lake Michigan. His choice was curious, but if I had to venture a guess, I'd say he was disturbed as hell at what had happened less than two hours before.

He finally pulled into a small driveway, immediately heading for the little garage located behind the bungalow, slowing down and shoving the gear into park and grabbing a set of keys from the glove compartment. "Stay right here, Walker. I mean it."

I had no energy to run from him at this point.

After climbing out, he shoved one of the keys into a lock, scanning the area before opening the garage door. Returning, he wasted no time in moving the car inside.

"Stay close to me until we get inside," he growled, quickly exiting and opening the trunk. Then he moved to my side. When he opened my door, I noticed he had his weapon in one hand, keeping it low but his hold was firm. In his other he held one of my little suitcases. What the hell had he taken from my room?

"What did you bring?" I asked.

"Things I'd thought you'd want, Walker. Just stay quiet right now."

He lowered the garage door, locking it then ushering me toward the back porch, sliding another key into the lock. As soon as we were inside, he pressed his index finger across his lips, shaking his head. He dropped the suitcase beside me, now holding his weapon in both hands.

He didn't need to tell me to stay exactly where I was until he checked the premises. Only two minutes later he returned, taking a deep breath.

"We should be safe for now."

Safe.

He'd used the word enough times I knew he meant from whoever the assholes were who'd been shooting at us. Someone was waging a war with his great empire.

I stood exactly where I was, shivering from the air temperature as well as what the hell was going on. This was crazy, just another layer to the nightmare.

"Will you tell me what's going on now?"

"Why don't I start a fire first? The kitchen is through there. See what you can find as far as provisions."

"Provisions?"

He didn't bother answering me, moving toward the stone fireplace and grabbing wood that was already positioned on the hearth. I stood watching him for a full minute before willing my feet to follow his orders. As I turned on the light in the small kitchen, I realized that this was indeed a vacation home for someone. I had to admit, it seemed like a strange choice for a man like Maksim.

I rubbed my hands before blowing on them, finally curious as to what I'd find. After opening several cabinets, I realized that the place had been well stocked, but mostly with cans and other food items that wouldn't go bad. I hated to admit that I was glad to see several bottles of wine. At this point, I could use a drink.

At least we could find something to eat, even though I wasn't in the least bit hungry. However, I did grab a bottle of water from the refrigerator, moving quietly into the living room, studying Maksim as he sat on the hearth, staring at the fire. I wasn't certain why I gave a damn that he was troubled, but I did. Still, I knew if I engaged in a conversation, he'd grill me again, determined that I was hiding juicy details from him when he was the one keeping ugly secrets.

I moved away, heading down the short hallway, finding two rooms and a single bathroom. When I walked into what appeared to be a master bedroom, I couldn't keep myself from snooping. There were feminine touches everywhere, which continued to add to my curiosity. I also noticed a single picture on the nightstand and nowhere else. After glancing over my shoulder, I moved closer, gingerly picking it up in my hand.

The photograph couldn't have been taken that long ago,

the older couple standing behind a young girl on a swing. They had to be her grandparents. The find only added a layer of perplexity to the entire situation.

Seconds later, I felt his presence, the bolts of electricity shooting through me creating a wave of vibrations. I put the picture back in its place before turning around, unable to read the expression on his face.

He glanced all the way down the length of my legs, the look of hunger from before returning, but there was more —an unreadable emotion.

"I didn't mean to snoop. I just…" I had no idea what the hell I wanted to say.

"Friends of mine own this place. They mostly use it in the summer months. This will be an efficient and safe location to stay for a couple of days until I figure out my next steps. However, keep in mind that you are never to leave this house under any circumstances unless I'm by your side. I don't want to be forced to tell you this more than once."

With that, he disappeared. No other explanation and no admonishing words for looking at the picture.

He had to know I'd trail after him, refusing to allow him to get away with telling me nothing. Before I headed out of the hallway, I glanced into the second bedroom. A kid's room. Pink adorned the walls, the furniture meant for a toddler. There was even a rocking chair in the corner. "Talk to me, Maksim. Who was shooting at us? Why do we need to stay here? Don't you have an army of men who can protect you?"

After giving me another hard look, he walked into the kitchen.

What the hell was he doing? I followed him, folding my arms as he grabbed a bottle of some liquor from one of the bottom cabinets. He'd certainly been here before. He had keys, for God's sake.

"Maksim. Please."

"What is your full name, Walker?"

"What?" The question confused me.

He shot me a look over his shoulder, lifting a single eyebrow. "Your full name. Walker is an unusual name for a woman."

Christ, the man was infuriating. "That's my middle name. My mother had a favorite author or something. My first name is Rafaella, but I haven't gone by that since I was a child. Why does it matter?"

"Everything matters at this point. Would you like a drink?"

Laughing, I walked further into the room, shaking my head as I tried to figure out what to say to him. "Why the hell not? I'm cooped up with a brutal killer in an adorable little cabin on the lake. Why not have a drink with him like we're buddies."

"We'll never be buddies, as you told me before." He pulled down a rocks glass and a crystal stem, finding a wine opener without having to search.

I couldn't seem to take my eyes off him as he opened the wine, taking his time to pour just the right amount.

"Let me see if I can figure you out," I said quietly. "You were on your way to becoming a doctor but decided that a savage lifestyle better suited you, so you dropped out. Still, it's obvious you're well educated and not just with regard to whatever time you spent in college. You speak fluent Russian but you're American through and through. You know how to open a bottle of wine and you have what appears to be very nice normal people who allow you to have a set of keys to their place. You dress nicely, not like some thug, and your decorating style is comfortable and serene. Who the hell are you really, Maksim?"

He finally lifted his head, bringing both glasses closer. When he handed me the stem, he made certain our fingers didn't touch, but dear God, his eyes penetrated every inch of darkness I had inside, filling me with the kind of energy and desire that didn't make any sense.

"I didn't drop out of Harvard, Walker. I changed majors from medicine to business. And yes, that pissed off my mother and father, the man I barely knew basically disowning me. My mother escaped the brutality of Russia, falling in love with my father when she was in college. That's why I speak fluent Russian, although I also know several other languages. I appreciate the finer things in life, including excellent wines and good food. Yes, I have

218

friends that have nothing to do with my lifestyle, including the couple who own this location. Is there anything else you would like to know at this point?"

"I feel like I should say I'm sorry, but I can't. You're just a man who threatened and kidnapped me." His credentials were impressive, which added to the confusion about why he'd sacrificed his life to become a criminal.

A wry smile curled across his lip as he inched closer. "Is that really all I am to you?"

I took a purposeful step away, still struggling to find the right words. "Who were the men chasing us?"

"The truth is, I'm not certain, but I think it has everything to do with you."

"There you go again. I'm nothing but a nurse trying to better herself."

"We need to talk, Rafaella. Let's go by the fire."

"Don't call me that. I don't like the name."

"The name suits you much better. It's beautiful, just like the woman."

While there was more emotion in his voice than I was used to, I still shuddered from the uncertainty of what I was facing. Maybe he'd taken me up here to dump my body in the lake where no one would find me after the long winter.

"Another curiosity, Maksim. You have all these men who work for you. You must have somewhere you can go where they'll protect you with their lives if necessary. Right? Why bring me here?"

As he walked closer, my muscles tensed. He stood in front of me for a full five seconds, narrowing his eyes as his nostrils flared. Damn it, the man had a way of getting to me no matter how hard I tried to shield myself.

"Trust is earned, Walker. I'm certain you can understand that. When it's challenged more than once, I become very cautious. It's necessary at this point to limit my exposure."

"Someone betrayed you, or at least that's what you're trying to figure out."

His smile was almost like a reward for digging past his armor a bit more. "Be careful searching too closely. You might not like what you find."

After sliding his knuckle across my cheek, he walked into the other room. Exhaling, I took a sip of the wine, trying to calm my nerves before following him. I moved to the chair, doing everything I could to keep my distance from him while he returned to the hearth, remaining far too close to me in my opinion.

"Samuel was friends with the man who was killed in your condo."

"Jack? Really?"

"They served in the marines together and while I haven't had a chance to look into their background, I'd say they were in a specialized combat unit together. The weapons I found in Jack's apartment indicate my findings are correct."

"That's why he had a gun with him when he came to my place. But why did he feel the need?"

"I'd venture a guess that he was asked by Samuel to look after you if anything happened to him."

I'd never been more confused in my life. I took a sip of wine, hating the fact my hands continued to shake. "That still doesn't answer why."

"No, it doesn't. Let's see if this helps." When he pulled out a picture, handing it to me, I wasn't certain what he wanted me to say.

There were four men, only one I vaguely recognized that could be Jack. "Who are they?"

"The man on the right is Samuel. The man on the left is someone I recently did some business with. Unfortunately for Samuel, he was working with that man behind our backs, trying to take another portion of our business."

"And you killed him too. Didn't you?"

He narrowed his eyes, glancing toward the fire. "I won't sugarcoat what I do, Walker. I deal with business in a way that works for our organization."

PIPER STONE

"At least you told me the truth. This is Jack but I don't know who the other man is. I swear to you that I don't."

Maksim leaned forward, staring me in the eyes. "I think that's your father."

"What?" I glanced at the photograph again, blinking several times. While the picture was older, it was in very good condition and clearer than I would have expected.

"If you look closely, you can see a resemblance."

"No. That's crazy. That's…" He was right. The same nose. The same forehead.

"Is it? You said you didn't know your father."

"No. My mother barely mentioned him. I don't even know his name. I have her last name on my birth certificate."

"You mother didn't offer a single story to you, a reason the two of them aren't together? She didn't keep a picture or anything for you? That seems crazy to me, Walker."

I tried to think about anything she'd told me, but nothing came to mind. "Look, my mother worked two jobs to try and give me the best life. She must have had her reasons why she hated him the way she did. In a single moment of weakness, she told me that he ran out of her and nothing more. There are always reasons for why people do certain things, Maksim. Isn't that what you've already told me about yourself?" I could tell my glare was just as vicious as I'd seen on him earlier.

"Touché."

"Jesus," I muttered. "What would it mean anyway if this was my father? Who gives a damn?"

He chuckled in his usual dark way, taking a sip of his drink. "The reason could be your father's background or his family ties. If so, that's why you were left the condo."

"His fucked-up payment for leaving me as a child?"

"Perhaps."

Goddamn it. He was so calm when I wanted to scream.

"Let's just say I buy it, Maksim, far too much of this weird mystery doesn't make any sense. The condo cost what, two million dollars?"

"Over three million."

I exhaled, trying to breathe normally. "Samuel stole money from the Novikov syndicate to purchase me a condo. That's insane."

"Exactly. But we need to find out the reason. Because of the various attacks, you might be the target of the assholes who destroyed my home and attempted to kill us." He laughed again as he brought the glass to his lips.

"Maybe there's something in the letter. Did you find it?"

"Nope."

"Then maybe my mother kept it. She has more answers than I do. I guess I could call her."

Maksim exhaled then lifted his eyebrows. "It may come to having a long discussion with your mother, but not tonight."

"I won't let you hurt her. If that's what you intend on doing, then you'll have to go through me. She's been through enough in her life." I realized I hadn't talked to her in over two weeks, which wasn't like me.

"How admirable. I have no intentions of doing so unless I don't get what I want."

"What if that can't be supplied?"

"Then I'll do what's necessary in order to determine who is intent on destroying my world."

"But you couldn't care less about mine." I knew that pushing his buttons wasn't in my best interest, but after everything I'd been through, I doubted he'd suddenly change, becoming my hero.

He shook his head, snorting as if what I'd just said was hysterical. "What I care about is finding the truth. I would think at this point that's exactly what you'd want as well. It's obvious that you were lied to your entire life. Doesn't that make you angry?"

I continued to shiver, no longer able to think clearly about anything. "I don't know what you want me to say. That I'm pissed off my mother hid my father's identity all these years? You bet, but I figured she had a valid reason. Now, I know she did. That I'm curious why Samuel would give me the kind of gift that could get me killed? Without a doubt. Even worse, what if those men are after me, their intentions to eliminate some crazy connection to my father? Would you do anything about it or stand by and watch as I'm murdered in front of your eyes?" Why did I bother asking? I knew exactly what the answer would be.

"What I can tell you is that I am the only man who can keep you alive. You don't know what kind of monsters they truly are, Walker."

"Worse than you?"

For the first time, I could tell something I said bothered him and in turn, I was taken aback.

"They are the kind of men who won't think twice about hurting that gorgeous body of yours for hours and in ways that even in your worst nightmare you couldn't understand. However, I will make you this single promise. If the bastards attempt to take what belongs to me, I will kill every one of them in my effort to protect you. And if that means dying in the process, I have no issue allowing that to happen."

His admittance and his promise shocked me more than I wanted to believe. A lump formed in my throat, my heart racing. *What belongs to him.* I was still that possession, yet in my warped mind, I found his words comforting instead of horrifying. Every cell was alive, every nerve ending on fire as another disgusting, but incredible wave of desire rushed through me. My mouth suddenly dry, I found myself leaning even closer, intoxicated by his masculine scent.

"Why? I don't mean anything to you." Even the words sounded hollow, but he didn't care about me.

"Maybe you do, Walker. Maybe you've awakened something inside of me that has been dead for so long. Even worse, maybe I don't want to ever lose the feeling." He clamped his hand so tightly around his glass, I thought he would crush it between his fingers.

My heart continued hammering, my pulse skyrocketing.

When he lifted his gaze, there was so much trauma behind his eyes. What in the hell had he been through to make him disrupt his entire life? For a few amazing seconds, it was as if the two of us were connected, our souls and our hearts, able to bypass the brutality and the fear. I wasn't certain what continued to draw me to him, but at this moment, as crazy as I knew it was, I needed to touch him.

I craved being close to him.

A slight growl erupted from whatever darkness existed inside of him, the sound creating a trickle of pussy juice against my lace panties. When he polished off his drink, allowing the glass to fall to the floor, I could tell the man was going to devour me. But still, he took his time, removing his weapon, making certain the safety was on before sliding it all the way across the hearth and directly in front of me.

"Come to me," he whispered, his chest rising and falling.

I shot the weapon a single glance, a small part of me saying I should try to make a lunge for his weapon, tying him up then taking his car somewhere safe.

But that wasn't going to happen, and he knew it.

After putting my wineglass on the table, I found myself sliding onto the floor, creeping closer. His eyes never left me as I inched closer, but I could tell by his ragged breathing that he was struggling with how he felt about me. I was crazy, certifiably, but I wanted him.

No, I needed him just like he'd mentioned before, a crazy foretelling that I couldn't understand but also couldn't deny.

God help me.

I was falling hard and fast for a man who didn't deserve anything but my rage and hatred.

Instead of my love.

CHAPTER 13

 *alker*

Passion.

I'd longed for it my entire life, dreaming of finding the perfect man to enjoy long walks in the woods or quiet evenings in front of the fire. Never in my wildest imagination had I thought I'd find myself thinking those things once again with a man like Maksim, but as the thoughts filtered through my mind, he cupped my face, pulling me closer.

His eyes had changed color, no longer the stunning blue that had attracted me in the first place. Tonight, they were as obsidian as his soul, but that only added to the extreme excitement as well as the danger.

Only this time, the peril consisted of losing my heart altogether.

As he lowered his head, he took his time rubbing his thumbs back and forth, tingling my skin even more than before. This wasn't about fucking me like the bastard had done before. This was about exploration, indulging in a filthy sin we should have forbidden ourselves.

My beating heart echoed into my ears, creating a vacuum all around us. It was as if we were locked in a period of time, neither one of us able to escape our passions. A series of stars floated in front of my eyes as his actions became rough, his finger sliding back and forth across my lips brutally. Then he lowered his head, taking several deep breaths before whispering words that fueled my fire.

"You mean more to me than you should, Rafaella. Much more." As he captured my mouth, he shifted to the floor, wrapping one hand around the back of my neck. His hold was just as possessive as the man himself, but as he stroked my skin, I could finally experience the tender side of him, the one he'd shut away.

The one he felt guilty showing.

I had no reason to think that way, but I knew it by instinct alone. The man had shut himself off from the world of emotion to keep from feeling anything. And I'd awakened a sleeping beast.

Moaning into the kiss, I slid my arms around his neck, caressing his skin before tangling my fingers in his hair. It felt far too good to be in his arms, his touch igniting the woman I'd buried inside.

We were like two moths coming too close to the flame. We would be consumed, lost in a sea of violence and power. He pulled me tightly against him, rolling his fingers down to cup my bottom. The feel of his hard cock pressed against my stomach added to my increasing arousal, my nipples aching to the point of anguish.

And this was just the beginning.

The kiss roared of passion, his tongue dominating mine. He growled several times, the sound floating between us just like the series of moans I continued to issue. I was no longer the woman I'd once been, able to distinguish what was good for me and not. While somewhere inside I knew that being with him would destroy my entire world, at this moment that didn't seem to matter.

His body exploded with heat, and I could feel his rapid heartbeat against my chest. As I undulated against him, he squeezed my buttocks, the action only drawing me even closer. He swept his tongue back and forth in my mouth, exploring every dark crevice, but I was already craving more.

When he finally broke the kiss, he nipped my bottom lip, allowing several low and husky growls to slide past his luscious lips. He dipped me into an arch, fisting my hair and yanking on my head to expose my neck.

Panting, I stared up at the ceiling as he licked just under my jaw, moving to circle the tip around my pulse of life. Then he bit down on my skin, raking his teeth back and forth. The man was so intense, every sound he made savage. I closed my eyes, enjoying the sparkling light flowing across my field of vision. The moment he finally had his fill, unable to hold back his needs any longer, he pushed me away, ripping my shirt over my head and tossing it aside.

"I can't wait to be inside of you," he muttered, a smile crossing his rugged face.

I yanked at his shirt, almost ripping the buttons in my effort to free him of the tight confines. He chuckled under his breath, finally grabbing the shirt by the shoulders, jerking himself free. When I placed both palms on his chest, he let off a heated animalistic roar, the sound keeping quivers dancing along every part of my body.

When he cupped my breasts, flicking his fingers back and forth across the thin lace covering my nipples, I could tell his patience was waning. I struggled to release the hooks, allowing him to drag the thin lace and satin away. He did so, but not without pulling it under his nose, taking a deep whiff of my scent.

The man was a true carnivore, incapable of putting his hunger on hold. My breathing even more ragged, I kneaded his chest muscles with one hand as I slid the other ever so slowly down to his pelvis, dragging a single finger down the front of his zipper.

"Be careful teasing me, little bird," he managed, dropping his head and engulfing my nipple.

"Oh. Yes." The heat and wetness from his mouth seared every nerve ending and the way he swirled his tongue around my hard pebble created more wetness between my legs.

"Mmm…" he muttered as he slid his lips to my other breast, repeating the delicious move.

I found it next to impossible to concentrate as I stroked his cock, rubbing my hand up and down, but I could tell I was driving him crazy with the friction. After a few seconds, I fumbled with his button and zipper, finally able to slide my hand inside. Dear God, the man was on fire, the temperature of his skin sending a shockwave of torrid heat up the entire length of my arm.

Maksim bit down on my nipple, the explosion of pain mixing with the joy of touching him. The sensations were all over the place, my legs shaking like leaves.

Seconds later, he pushed me away again, his upper lip curling and every sound more savage than before. "I refuse to wait any longer."

As we ripped at each other's clothes, I shut down what was left of the rational part of my mind. Tonight I was going to enjoy my descent straight into hell. The thought almost made me laugh even as I dragged my tongue across my lips, my mouth watering from the sight of pre-cum glistening on his engorged cockhead. His shaft was throbbing, the tip a deep purple, his balls swollen. Without hesitation, I eased my hand between his legs, cupping and squeezing his testicles.

His body began to shake, his eyes now half closed. He remained on his knees, allowing me to roll his balls between my fingers. I kept my eyes on his face, enjoying the myriad expressions, all of them dominating as hell. When he finally lowered his head, the smile was now just as dark as the man.

"Suck me."

His command was not to be denied.

But I couldn't help continuing to toy with him as I lowered my head, blowing across his sensitive slit then darting my tongue through the beads of cum.

I loved the way his chest continued to heave, every muscle in his body tense.

He laughed softly, snagging my hair with his fisted hand, holding me in place. "You heard what I said."

"Maybe," I purred and swirled my tongue around his cockhead several times, finally wrapping my hand around the base of his shaft. As I stroked up and down, twisting my hand, he rocked his hips forward. I took my time licking up one side then down the other, allowing my fingers to meet my lips. The taste of him was tangy, his cock so large I knew I'd have difficulty fitting it inside my mouth.

"You're driving me crazy," he muttered as he twisted my hair at the scalp, holding me firmly in place.

I remained quiet, darting my tongue around first one testicle then the other. When I finally took one into my mouth, he threw his head back and bellowed like a wounded animal.

"Fuck. My God." Panting, he continued shaking as I moved to his other ball, savoring the taste as the scent of his testosterone filled my nostrils, mixing with the exotic fragrance of his lingering aftershave.

I was lightheaded, pussy juice trickling down the insides of both thighs. Goosebumps prickled almost every inch of my skin and the second he ran the fingers of his other hand down my spine, leaning over and smacking my bottom several times, I couldn't hold back several ragged whimpers.

"Open that hot mouth of yours and take all of me. Every. Single. Inch."

As soon as I'd released his balls, licking along the under-side of his cock then engulfing the head into my mouth, he jutted his hips forward a second time, forcing several inches inside. My jaw muscles ached as they accepted the thick intrusion. When I took him down another inch, swirling my tongue back and forth, I struggled to keep my breathing even.

Maksim pressed on my head, pushing me all the way down. "I said all of me." Every growl he made was more savage than the one before. As the tip hit the back of my throat, I did everything I could to keep from gagging. He held me in place for several seconds then released his hold on my hair, cupping both sides of my face.

As he took control, sliding his cock in and out, I tried to relax my throat. The force he used rocked my body, my pussy clenching and releasing several times. I was so aroused, so wet and hot that all I could think of was having his cock thrust deep inside.

He shifted into a perfect rhythm, face fucking me for several minutes, his face becoming strained as he tried to maintain control. I wanted nothing more than to suck him dry, licking up every drop of his cream. When I dared to squeeze his balls again, I could tell he'd almost lost it. With several husky guttural sounds, he pushed me away, taking several strangled deep breaths.

"You are one bad, bad girl."

"Uh-huh." I backed away, but he snagged my arm, chuckling as he yanked me closer. "Tell me in Russian."

"*Plokhaya devochka*. Whether I say it in Russian or English, it will always be true." Now he was teasing me, pushing me down onto the rug. As he leaned over, he raked the rough pads of his fingers on his open hand down my chest, darting his eyes toward me every few seconds. Then he rolled his knuckles around one nipple then the other. "But you will be controlled. If you stay a very good girl, you're going to learn all about the joys of pleasure. Imagine the things I can teach you."

His words were a cathartic draw, pulling me further and further into the sweet darkness of his warped and seductive mind. I could no longer feel my toes, yet his touch kept various flames fully ignited.

"No man can control me. Haven't you figured that out yet?" My words were rattled, hushed from the building excitement. I couldn't seem to stop shaking and when he trailed his hand down my pussy, the touch so light I could barely feel anything, I jerked up from the soft pelt.

"I assure you, little bird, you will learn that following my every command is in your best interest." His words weren't meant as a threat this time, more as an enticement.

"Or what?" I whispered, unprepared for the way he twisted my hips, capturing both legs with one of his massive arms before bringing his hand down several times against my bottom. "Ouch!"

He kept his firm hold, relentless in teaching me a lesson, one hard smack coming after another. I couldn't believe the way my body reacted, the pain barely recognizable as pleasure took over, keeping me tingling all over.

I pressed my hand and my face against the rug, staring at the fire as he spanked me long and hard, not for the fact I'd misbehaved. This was all about a reminder that he would always be in charge. Or maybe he was simply trying to tell me not to consider getting too close to him.

When he finally flipped me back over, I was forced several deep breaths, sliding into an entirely d....᠊ kind of headspace. He slipped his fingers in between the slick folds of my pussy, fingering me gently, casually, yet the slightest touch at this point was pushing me toward euphoria.

"Do you see how wet you are, little bird?" he mused, taking his time and rolling the tip of his finger around my clit.

"I'm not... wet." All I could do was laugh at my ridiculous attempt at lying to him.

"Hmmm... It would seem you haven't learned your lesson yet." He pinched my nipple between his thumb and forefinger, twisting roughly until I cried out.

"Lord. Oh. Oh!"

"Now, tell me, *malen'kaya ptitsa*, do you hunger for me?"

"Maybe."

His deep laugh was followed by a wave of hot breath cascading across my stomach. Then he moved his hand to my other breast, pinching and plucking my hardened bud.

"Do you want to reconsider? If you tell me the truth, I'm going to tongue fuck that tight little pussy of yours."

His tone was so alluring, keeping me on the very edge of nirvana and he knew it. As if to seal the deal, he lowered his head, tormenting me with his mouth, driving his tongue just inside. I couldn't breathe, certainly had no ability to think clearly and all I could think about was shouting out to the world exactly what I wanted. "Ummm…" When he leaned back, I almost screamed, begging him to continue.

"Let's try one more time but this time a different command," he mused. "Tell me what you want."

"Please…"

He smacked my pussy lips with two fingers, jarring me out of the sweet lull of depravity.

"Please lick me." My God, my voice sounded so weak.

"More. I want to hear you tell me in no uncertain terms what you need, my sweet and beautiful little bird."

I couldn't take the pressure of the building desire or the tension strangling every muscle in my body. "Lick me. Eat me. Then fuck me. Yes. Yes! That's what I want."

"Then that's exactly what you're going to get."

As he'd done before, he gathered my thighs into his arms, lifting me off the floor before lowering his head and burying his face in my pussy.

"Oh. My. God." I was shocked how the shift in the angle pushed me almost immediately into pure nirvana. I tossed my head back and forth, my breath skipping as he licked up and down. As the utter bliss continued to build, I slapped my hands on the rug, trying to control my breathing. I was letting go with him completely, accepting the kind of insanely delicious rapture that I'd only read about.

Every guttural sound he made was so expressive, as if this was the only thing he'd ever wanted, feasting like a starving animal. I could tell the sounds I made were just as animalistic, but the way he was licking me kept me spiraling above myself, trying to hold onto the extreme pleasure for as long as possible.

No man had ever licked me with such ferocity before, the way he alternated between slow and easy licking, then increasing the speed of his tongue until I was pushed into a frenzy was incredible, but when he sucked on my already sensitive clit, I was blown away.

There was no possibility of holding back a climax for very long. I was elated then crazed, yelping then moaning and the man refused to stop. Finally, I was wrung out and unable to keep the rush of vibrations from turning into something else.

As the first climax rushed up from my curled toes, I pushed hard against the floor, lifting my body even higher.

Several growls slipped past his lips as he licked me even faster, lapping up every drop of my cream.

"Oh. Oh. Oh. Oh!" I couldn't keep my screams and cries silent until I finally slapped my hand over my mouth. I had no idea if others could hear us in our aggressive passion. Several emotions rolled through me just as the single orgasm turned into an incredible wave, sucking all the energy out of me until I felt the pressure of a finger pushed against my asshole. "No, I..."

It was too late. When he shoved the long digit inside, thrusting past my tight ring of muscle, my entire body spasmed. This time, the climax hammered all throughout my system, slamming every muscle as it rolled through me. I'd never experienced such raw sensations but as his continued his brutal actions, I was driven straight into pure ecstasy.

My panting and whimpering echoed in my ears as he pumped like a crazed man, adding a second finger then a third as he assaulted my tight little asshole, preparing it to accept his big fat cock. I couldn't keep from smiling, all the fight plunged out of me. I was exhausted yet elated, on edge yet peaceful. Everything was one incredible, delicious blur.

I was barely cognizant when he eased my legs to the floor. All I could do was concentrate on my breathing, but there was no way to ignore his presence, the larger-than-life man peering down at me. I blinked several times, reaching for him. He studied me intently as I brushed the tips of my fingers down his chest, marveling in his muscles, so carved and perfect. I had so many things I wanted to say to him, so many questions to ask, but I didn't want this moment to end.

When I ran my finger along the side of his cock, his body tensed all over again, but he remained where he was, almost as if he was enjoying the view.

I rubbed the inside of my leg against his, biting back a cry as he slowly looked down at my action, an amused look on his face. What was he waiting for? I wanted his cock inside, throbbing as he fucked me long and hard. When I finally didn't accept the wait any longer, wrapping my hand around his shaft and tugging, he finally let out the softest growl of all, but it was also the most possessive.

"I was waiting for you to decide," he said as he lowered down, pulling first one leg around his hips then the other.

"Decide?"

"Whether or not you were going to reach for my gun."

I opened then closed my mouth, finally twisting my lips since I had no idea what to say to him. Maybe I should.

But I wouldn't.

A part of me already belonged to him.

As I dug my fingers into the skin on his chest, he positioned his cock against my pussy. After giving me an explosive look, he pushed inside. Only this time, he didn't seem to be in such a hurry to require me to conform, using sex as a tool highlighting his power. This was so much more, deeper and very personal.

We kept our eyes locked on each other as he lowered down, placing his forearms on either side of me. I wrapped my feet together, kneading his chest as the sensations immediately built, the electricity we shared combustible. With one final thrust, he was fully seated inside, his body still shaking as it had before.

"You feel so damn good," he muttered then pulled almost all the way out, plunging into me again.

I bucked hard against him, wrapping my fingers around his forearms. The feel of having him inside was unlike anything I'd ever experienced. His cock throbbed, expanding as my muscles clamped down, pulling him in even deeper.

Time seemed to stand still as he fucked me, driving in and out so many times I lost count. His eyes were still twinkling, the light of the fire creating an incredible golden hue around him almost like a halo. That was the funniest thing of all. The brutal killer with a golden halo.

As the amazing sensations continued, I arched my back, lifting my head until our lips finally touched. The second I darted my tongue around his mouth, he responded by sucking on my bottom lip.

Then he rolled me over unexpectedly, forcing me to ride him. The smile on his face was just as devilish as before and when he eased both his arms behind his head, I could tell this was a moment of offering me trust.

Trust to take what I wanted.

Trust not to fight him in any way.

And the ultimate trust in not reaching for his weapon.

Perhaps he didn't know what I was made of.

As I started to rock, clamping my knees against his sides, he narrowed his eyes, allowing his gaze to fall to my breasts. Then he lost his moment of self-control, teasing my nipples, at least until I threw my head down, keeping our lips just a few centimeters apart. Maybe that was the moment I realized just how strong my feelings were for him. I closed my eyes, pressing my lips against his, continuing to rock against him.

This time, the kiss was gentle, a subtle reminder of the passion we were sharing.

"Ride me harder, little bird."

I laughed, his command breaking the strange tension that had developed between us. Then I did as I was told, riding him like a wild stallion. I adored the way his body reacted, his breathing just as ragged as mine. I should have known he had other surprises in store for me. When he lifted me away from him completely, turning me around to face the other direction, I laughed nervously.

But when he pressed his hand against the small of my back, pushing me forward then placing the tip of his cock against my dark hole, I snapped my hands around his massive thighs, raking my nails across his skin.

I continued tensing, taking shallow breaths.

"Breathe for me. I'm fucking this tight ass of yours."

When he slipped the tip inside, I threw my head back, the pain almost instant. But as he continued sliding in an inch at a time, the anguish quickly morphed, the sensations nothing but pleasurable.

He gripped my hips, holding me in place as he brought me up and down several times. The angle was incredible, tingling my muscles. I dug my knees into him, easing forward then doing what I could to take control. As I lifted my hips, slamming down against him, he smacked my bottom several times.

I could hear his heavy breathing, could tell he wasn't going to be able to hold out for long.

"You're so damn tight."

As I threw my head over my shoulder, I was mesmerized by the look in his eyes. So dominating. So possessive.

I bucked hard and fast, enjoying the incredible ride for a few more seconds.

Then I squeezed my muscles and within seconds, his grip on my hips tightened, his breathing even more ragged. As his cock began to throb, I closed my eyes, saying a silent prayer that my ugly monster would become my prince.

Then as he filled me with his seed, reality slipped back in, wrapping around me like a suffocating blanket.

This wasn't real life, nor was he the man of my dreams. This was nothing more than a passing of time, waiting until a plan was developed.

Then the viper would strike.

And all that I'd worked for would be lost.

CHAPTER 14

*M*aksim

"Obman," I whispered in the glow of the firelight, the word remaining in the forefront of my mind. Deception.

I continued to have a nagging feeling that someone very close to me had deceived me. Betrayal was something to be feared in my world. Loyalty was vital, more so than heavy artillery, money, or even power. With the secrets kept both professionally and personally, any act of treachery could mean death or even worse.

As I stared into the fire, one hand leaning on the mantel, the other wrapped around my third glass of whiskey, I continued to think about the list of men who had the opportunity to betray me. While a few of my soldiers had learned about some aspects of my personal life, including with regard to my past, only a handful knew enough to cause any issues in my life that way.

However, regarding business, that was something else entirely.

I'd learned from Ivan early on that some men could be bought far too easily, cutting all ties with the family for the simple reason of obtaining a few additional dollars in their pockets. I'd seen it in action, men turning their backs with no regard to the consequences. Hell, I'd been forced to deal with a soldier as well as an informant recently, both men dishonoring the Novikov family.

In the end, they'd realized their mistakes, but not before it was too late for anything other than retribution.

Unfortunately, the only person who knew that I'd asked Brick to meet us at the park was my Capo himself. However, that was far too easy, and Brick wasn't that stupid. He'd certainly know I'd questioned what the hell had happened immediately. Maybe he was being used as a scapegoat, but that also seemed farfetched.

What I knew for certain is that someone wanted me out of the way. What I didn't know is whether the intent was capturing Walker or killing her. I realized my grip on the glass had tightened, my anger reaching another insanely high level. We certainly couldn't stay here for longer than a day or two.

Then what?

An ache formed in my heart, one that I wasn't used to. I'd enjoyed every minute of being with Walker, although I really did prefer her given name. Rafaella was beautiful. It was also Italian. What I hadn't told the woman I was far too engaged with was that I had an inkling of why she was so important, although none of it could make any sense without corroborating information. That certainly wasn't going to come easily if at all. If her mother held the key, that might make things dicey. I would call Brick in the morning, finding out what he'd discovered. Then I'd make whatever plans would be needed.

I took a sip of the drink, realizing the burn sliding down the back of my throat that usually made me feel alive was doing exactly the opposite. The taste was flat, almost repulsive. Chuckling, I thought about tossing it into the fire, glass and all, but additional bouts of anger weren't going to do me any good.

Sighing, I placed the glass on the mantel, shoving my hands into my trousers. I'd carried her to bed after she'd fallen asleep, her soft murmurs enticing the hell out of me. But I'm simply tucked her in, pulling the covers over her. Was there a possibility she was still playing me, planning on leaving in the night? Maybe. However, my instinct told me that something had changed, her fear of me remaining but our connection growing stronger.

Plus, she wanted this mystery solved as much as I did.

Another ache remained, another concern that was also grating on me, keeping me on edge. If I was the target, there was plausible reason to expect that whoever wanted me dead wouldn't find every weakness. Now I had two.

A single loud crack outside drew my attention immediately. I snapped the Sig off the hearth, releasing the safety and heading in the direction of the sound. I'd closed all the blinds, had checked the entire area before dark had fallen. While there were trees all around the small bungalow, there was no chance of limbs hitting the roofline or anything else.

With only the glow of the fire going, I flipped the lock, carefully opening the door. Thank God the damn thing didn't creak. With the gun in both hands, I walked outside, moving immediately into the shadows and listening.

A few seconds of silence passed. Other than the light whistle of the wind whipping through the trees, there was no other sound. But I remained, allowing my eyes to become accustomed to the darkness. After another three or four minutes had passed, I eased off the small porch, making a sweep of the front then moving around to the side. When I heard the noise again, I snapped my weapon in that direction, ready to fire.

Hissing when some animal raced away, scuttling over what had to be several fallen limbs from the trees on the side of the house, I almost laughed. I waited for another few minutes before returning to the house, engaging both locks.

This shit was going to stop.

Still frustrated, I moved toward the hallway, stopping long enough to glance into the second bedroom, even turning on the light. As I walked in, another sense of sadness pulled at my mind as well as my heart. Some people enjoyed having families, never knowing what kind of evil lurked in every shadow and around every corner. They went about their daily lives, pretending that their little world was protected. There wasn't a single person on this earth that I couldn't hunt down, destroying their fragile lives with one decision or the pull of a trigger.

That meant it was true on the flipside. If someone was out to destroy my life, they would continue to try until they succeeded.

I moved toward the small bed in the room, brushing my fingers across the headboard, the sweet carvings of furry animals delighting any child.

Until they turned into ravaging creatures with sharp canines.

I almost laughed at the imagery, my body tensing the longer I stood in the room. After a few seconds, I backed out, flipping off the light and shutting the door. I didn't need another reminder of what I didn't have in my life.

Having a family wasn't in the cards for a man like me.

As I shifted my attention to the other room, I was glad I'd left the light on by the bed. At least I could tell she was resting peacefully from the doorway. Still, I was drawn further inside, walking to the other side of the bed where she lay sleeping. As I peered down, I reached toward her face, curling my fingers at the last minute and pulling my arm away.

Who are you? Why are you stuck in the middle of this?

I glanced toward the picture, taking it into my hands and staring at the happiness all three of them exuded. Goddamn it. Maybe I didn't want anyone to experience the kind of joy they obviously were. Another round of anger swept through me like a lightning rod. Disgusted, I almost dropped the frame in my effort to return the photograph to its rightful place.

Huffing, I headed for the door, prepared to keep watch all night.

Then I heard the rustle of covers and stopped just inside the doorway.

"You were outside," Walker said, her tone soft and inviting.

"Yes. I heard a noise."

"Is that what you have to do every day of your life, check behind you?"

I chuckled under my breath. "At times."

"Doesn't that get old?" she asked as she yawned.

"At times."

This time, she laughed. Then the covers rustled again. "Why don't you get some sleep? You can stay right here. I promise I won't bite. I mean..." Her laugh had a nervous twinge, the sound seductive, my cock aching all over again. Given I was the carnivore, I would be the one doing the biting. At least the thought gave me a smile.

My entire body tensed from her simple question. There was nothing I wanted more than to crawl into bed with her, but that wasn't in our best interest. "Go back to sleep. I'll be just outside."

"Don't go, Maksim. I'm no fool. When we leave this space, I'll become just a nuisance that you've had to deal with all over again. I know that. However, tonight is... different. Isn't it?"

Her question was too difficult to answer. I fisted my hand, the other wrapped tightly around my weapon. How many nights had I spent without my gun by my side, another in the drawer, and still at least two more in close proximity? I always had to be prepared, even though I thought I'd had tight security on my house. What a crock. Maybe there would never be any location safe enough to allow my guard to fall.

When I didn't answer her right away, I could tell she was mumbling under her breath.

"What you're doing is just existing, Maksim. Not living. All the power and money that you have yet I feel so sorry for you."

I rubbed my eyes, the ache behind them likely to remain for days if not weeks. Of course she was right, but I'd attempted to have a life once upon a time. I hadn't just failed. I'd allowed that guard to fall, pretending that nothing bad could happen.

And I'd been wrong.

So damn wrong.

I took another step toward the door, determined to keep my resolve, but goddamn it, I wanted her all over again. The warmth of her body. The touch of her hand. All the need I'd insisted she would feel was exactly what I was feeling myself. I was such a fucking fool.

Tension was a part of my life as well but the only time I hadn't felt the kind of muscle ripping strain on my entire system had been only a few hours before. Jesus Christ. I wasn't just falling hard for the girl. I was falling in love with her.

As I turned slowly, I could feel the increase in my heartrate, my pulse ticking quickly. Seeing her long raven hair splayed out over the pillow was too much for me to take. I advanced like the damn predator I was, jerking off my shoes and trousers, throwing back the covers.

She'd pulled out one of the tee shirts I'd packed for her, the soft material outlining her voluptuous body far too well. She scooted toward the other side, raising onto her elbow and staring at me with such intensity that I was sucked of all the anger and venom. I carefully placed the weapon inside the nightstand drawer. No one was getting inside this room.

When I crawled under the covers, she was the one who pulled them over my heated body, acting as if she was going to tuck me in. Then she lowered her head, keeping her gaze pinned in my direction, a slight smile on her lovely face. The woman had no idea how enthralling she was, the hint of vulnerability adding to the draw of her kind demeanor and flawless porcelain skin.

I turned on my side to face her, the warm amber glow hiding a portion of her features. I wasn't the kind of man who could handle small talk, but I was tired of grilling her about things she obviously didn't know. "I'm curious. Did you always want to be a nurse?"

"Oh, hell, no."

Her answer surprised me, enough so I burst into laughter. "I wasn't expecting that."

"When I was a kid, the sight of blood made me faint. I wanted to be a ballerina, but Mom couldn't afford lessons so by the time I was ten, I knew that wasn't going to work out. What did you want to be, certainly not a doctor?"

"I don't know really. My father always geared me toward following in his footsteps. That's all I ever knew."

"And your mother left Russia?"

I realized that only one other person had asked me the question before. "She couldn't stand the Bratva life. When she was offered a scholarship to an American school, her father allowed her to go with the condition she return. Of course, she refused. By that point, she was already engaged."

"But she loves her country enough to teach you about your heritage."

"True, but I think she felt like it was her duty, although some stories were amazing ones. Like you, she wanted to become a ballerina. She had a chance until her father pulled her out of the lifestyle, telling her it was too dangerous. That's when she knew she couldn't stand living the way she had for the rest of her life."

Walker crowded closer, enough so I found it next to impossible to keep my hands off her luscious body.

"Yet after she told you about her experiences, you chose the life. Why?"

"I don't have the kind of answer you need me to tell you. You can't mold me into the hero you obviously need in your life. I'm not a good man and I never have been. My darkness has always driven me toward what my mother hoped wasn't in my blood, but it was."

"I don't need a hero, Maksim, and I'm a pretty good judge of character. You are a good man, although for some reason you're hiding behind a façade, but I think that's all about pain you've experienced in your life. You let your demons guide you instead of you pushing them away.

Until you do so, you won't truly understand what's most important to you."

My resolve started to crumble around her again. Using my knuckle, I eased hair away from her face, brushing my fingers down her cheek to her neck. She didn't tense or pull away, but she sighed as if the weight of the world was on her shoulders. She truly thought she could fix me, pulling me away from the only world where I'd felt that I'd fit in. How tragic it would be for her when she realized that her first assumptions were correct.

She fingered my chin, sliding the tip of her finger back and forth across my jaw, the two-day stubble that was unusual for me to keep. "You'd look very good with a beard."

I pulled her hand into mine, pressing a kiss against her palm. "That's never going to happen."

"You know what they say. Never say never."

"I'll try and remember that." As I gazed into her eyes, I wanted nothing more than to keep her protected. That might become impossible. "You're Italian."

"How ever did you guess?" she asked, giggling for the first time. "Yes, so it would seem, but certainly not on my mother's side. She's a natural blonde with huge blue eyes. Look what happened to me."

"I think you grabbed the better end of the deal."

"You do, huh?"

"Yes, I do."

She pulled her hand away, continuing to trace my face. "Whatever happens, Maksim, I don't care about money or who my father is. I'd be lying if I said the condo wasn't an incredible gift, but I'm not certain I could ever stay there again after what happened with Jack. I don't need a fortune, just enough to pay my bills and maybe get a nicer car one day. I'm a simple girl who happens to love her job."

"What else do you love?"

"I don't know. Does it matter?"

I tweaked her nipple as a reminder I was very much in charge.

"Fine. I like rain showers in the spring and the first snow of the season. I adore Christmas lights and window shopping, hating that so much has gone to the internet. What do you want to know?"

"Anything you want to tell me," I said in a husky voice, my cock aching and my balls tight as drums. Just her scent alone was enough to push me over the edge, taking her without hesitation. I could tell by the way her lower lip twitched that she knew all the carnal thoughts racing in the back of my mind.

"I love the color purple. My favorite food is pizza. I love almost any kind of wine and my favorite thing in the world is experiencing a new winery."

"How old are you?"

The look she gave me could turn a man into stone. "You know better than to ask a lady her age."

All I had to do was give her an intense look although she rolled her eyes.

"I'm twenty-seven. How old are you?"

"Older."

She made certain that her expression was harsher than mine, which allowed me to laugh.

"Almost thirty-one."

"A babe in the woods. Now, it's your turn."

"What do you want to know?"

She inched even closer until I could feel her hot breath, the tickle drawing my beast closer to the surface. When she lifted her head, brushing her lips across my chin, electricity skittered into every muscle and tendon. "Whatever you want to tell me."

"Mmm… I like steak, the rarer the better. I don't like rain and snow I could do without. Give me a hot day on the beach and I'm happy. However, going to a winery does sound enjoyable."

"Hmm… Then maybe."

I couldn't stand it any longer. The draw to her, our intense connection was stronger than anything I'd felt, including with the one woman I'd thought I'd spend the rest of my life with. As I rubbed my hand down Walker's back, she shuddered audibly, the sound driving me crazy.

"Being around you is dangerous," she murmured.

"Perhaps but being around you is an addiction."

She sighed, crawling her fingers down my chest, dipping them under the covers. When she wrapped her hand around my cock, I couldn't resist issuing several deep growls.

"Be careful, little bird. I could eat you alive."

"Go ahead and try. I'm tougher than you think."

There was no sense in trying to resist her any longer. I shifted Walker onto her back, moving over her and pushing my hand against the bed, hovering over her. As I brushed my fingers down her face, she shivered visibly, stroking my shaft until I was hard as a rock.

"I don't need you to be tough, Walker. I need you to let yourself go."

"I'm not certain I can do that around you."

I laughed softly, enjoying every sensation tingling my fingers. "You already have." As I crushed my lips over hers, she arched her back, opening her legs in a blatant offer. I felt every movement as she positioned the tip of my cock just past her swollen folds. I wanted nothing more than to erupt deep inside of her, filling her with my seed. Everything about this moment was cathartic, as if in taking her this way meant there was no turning back.

The deep cravings I had for her, the intensity of the electricity we shared was something that would likely never be denied again. I wanted all of her. Every touch. Every private moment.

Every inch.

My possessive nature took over and the moment I thrust the entire length of my cock inside her tight channel, I threw my head back and roared. The sound was strangled, yet a crazy admittance that I didn't want to live without her.

She moaned into the kiss as her muscles expanded, accepting the thickness even as my shaft continued to expand. When she wrapped her long legs around me, I pressed my fist against the bed, sliding my tongue past her still swollen lips. There was nothing like the taste of her, sweet like honey. My mind exploded with all the nasty things I wanted to do to her.

With her.

I could share everything with her, even though I knew that wasn't in either of our best interests. Yet she was the one, the creature who'd finally smashed all the chains. I remained floored at how much I cared about her and as I plunged deep and hard, every part of her reacted to the brutal fucking, the skin on her face shimmering, her breathing skipping several beats.

She swept her tongue back and forth across mine as she slid her hand over my shoulder, digging her long nails into my neck. The way she held me tightly was a clear indication of our strong connection. I slowed my actions, driving inside in slow and deliberate actions. When I finally broke the kiss, I pressed my lips against her cheek, taking shallow breaths. Everything about her was intoxicating, keeping my body tense, my heart thudding to the point I had difficulty breathing.

I pulled further away, enjoying nothing more than being able to gaze into her eyes. Her pupils were dilated, her long lashes skimming across her rosy cheeks. How could I avoid falling in love with her?

The question remained in the forefront of my mind as I continued fucking her—making love to her.

With her.

I pulled first one of her arms over her head then the other, intertwining our fingers as I continued thrusting. We locked eyes, which we'd done before, but this time was entirely different. It was as if we were both peeling away layers of anger and fear, years of countless searching for the right one. I almost laughed at my realization, but nothing about this was amusing.

She was mine.

Mine to take and taste.

Mine to love.

And no one was going to take her away from me, so help me God.

Mere seconds later, she tensed, her breathing rapid. She squeezed her knees against my heated body, arching her back as much as our hold would allow, her mouth pursing. I could tell she was close to an orgasm.

"Come for me, baby. Let yourself go."

She purred softly, tossing her head back and forth as her pussy muscles clamped around my cock. As her body started to tremble, I pumped deep and hard, wanting nothing more than the feel of the lovely woman letting go.

"Oh. Maksim," she murmured, her eyes now half closed. As she continued shaking, she did everything she could to jerk out of my hold, her body convulsing. There was nothing more beautiful than when she released, a climax sweeping through her.

I finally closed my eyes, driving into her with wild abandon. Everything about this moment was perfect. She was a gentle soul, a gorgeous flower allowing a monster to drink her nectar. I wanted nothing more than to consume her, savoring every moment as the shower of electricity continued to pelt through both of us.

"Yes. Yes. Yes!" She jerked hard against me, her fingers digging into mine.

I could tell a single orgasm powered into a second. I wanted nothing more than for her to enjoy every moment, but I was ready to lose control, my cock aching to erupt.

Walker managed to free one of her hands, sliding it down my back and pulling me closer. That's all I could take. As my balls filled with cum, I threw back my head, refusing to accept that I might lose her.

No. That wasn't going to happen.

As of now, not a single soul on this fucking planet would take her away from me.

If they tried, they would die by my hands.

"I could fall in love with you," she breathed.

As I erupted, I let go of her hand, enjoying the way she clung to me. Even though I'd never felt closer to anyone in my life, when I heard her soft murmur, I realized that I would be her ultimate demise.

And that wasn't acceptable.

Maksim!

The single word jerked me from a deep slumber. As my eyes snapped open, I took several strangled breaths, blinking as I tried to focus. What the hell? A rush of memories floated into my mind, and I jerked my head to the side, now gasping for air.

Who the fuck had called out my name?

After controlling my breathing, I realized that Walker was still sleeping peacefully. I was shocked I'd actually fallen asleep, the slight hint of morning light coming in through the blinds disturbing. My intent had been to leave her sleeping, returning to the living room. I raked my hand through my hair, angry that I'd lost control.

I turned my attention toward Walker once again, easing my arm from under her. The words she'd said still burned in the back of my mind. How could she love someone like me? That didn't make any sense, especially given everything that had occurred between us. My nerves remained on edge. Waking up because my name had been called was unusual, but my gut told me something was wrong.

Very wrong.

I slipped out of the covers, checking the drawer to the nightstand to make certain my weapon was exactly where I'd left it. Whatever the bad feeling remaining in the back of my mind, I knew it was a sign.

I gave her another look before rising to my feet, grabbing the gun before grabbing my trousers. It didn't matter that it was early in the morning. I needed to find out what the hell had gone on since I'd left.

As I headed for the living room, an odd sense of foreboding settled in. I yanked my phone out of my pocket, taking the time to jerk on my pants before calling Brick.

While he answered in the second ring, I could tell I'd awakened him.

"Maksim. Are you okay?"

"I'm fine. Tell the identity of the assholes who died at that park."

"You ain't gonna like this but same as with the assholes at the hotel. I can find nothing on them."

"Call in the member of law enforcement who can run their fingerprints. I'm finished with this game."

"Okay, I can do that."

"Any other disturbances?" I moved toward the windows in the front, peering out from around the blinds. From what I could tell, there was no activity. Everything appeared to be quiet. That didn't settle my nerves in the least.

"No. Nothing else happened. I checked the streets, trying to find information but nobody is talking."

Of course they weren't.

"That means no one is talking about the attack at the hotel either?"

"Hell, no. I confronted three of our informants who had nothing for me. Trust me, Maksim, I did everything I could to make certain they weren't lying to me. Whoever is threatening us doesn't want to identify themselves just yet."

I thought about what he was telling me as well as listening for any inflection in his tone of voice that would indicate he was betraying me. While I found nothing to show he was a traitor, my gut continued to warn me. However, there were few people I could trust, and I doubted Ivan would understand why I was keeping Walker alive.

The quicksand was getting deeper by the minute.

"Brick. I need you to search a name, birth records for me."

"Sure, boss. Who?"

"Find out everything you can about a birth that occurred in New York. The name is Rafaela Walker Sutherland." As I gave him two years when the birth could have occurred, I could hear him whistling through his teeth.

"You think this girl is somebody?"

"Yeah, I do. See if you can find a birth father."

Brick exhaled. "That might take some time."

"I don't give a shit." I shifted toward the door, making certain she hadn't heard me.

"Then I'll give it my full attention. You know Ivan will be looking for you. What do you want me to tell him?"

"Nothing. I'll handle it. Call me when you know something and Brick, don't fail me. I'm finished with this ridiculous ruse. Do you hear me?"

"Loud and clear, boss."

I'd thrown out a gauntlet. If the man was dirty, I'd know it soon enough. Nothing made any more sense than it had the night before. I refused to continue being shoved into this position. No one was going to threaten my world.

Or the woman I loved.

When I heard my phone ringing, I hesitated until I noticed the caller. Several ugly thoughts remained in the back of my mind as I answered the call. "Sandy. It's early. What's wrong?"

"Maksim. I didn't want to call you."

"But you did, which means something is wrong."

"There have been some strange cars in the neighborhood. I didn't think anything of it until this morning," Sandy answered, as if she was under duress.

"What do you mean strange cars?"

"They arrived yesterday morning. Two men sitting in a dark SUV. They just left a few minutes ago. Who does that? Does it mean anything?"

Every nerve stood on end.

"You need to get the hell out of there. Now!"

"We can't. Jasmine is sick again. She's running a fever."

My fucking God. Every aspect of my life was being ceremoniously challenged, someone prepared to take everything that mattered to me.

"You need to listen to me carefully because I'm not going to say this twice. For once you will do as I say. You need to get to a safe place. All three of you."

"What the hell is going on?"

"You're in danger. I'm coming to get Jasmine. Then you and Miles are going to get the hell out of town until I tell you it's safe."

Sandy snorted. "I can't do that. You can't just take her."

"Hear me, Sandy. While I understand she's ill, there are men who want to hurt her, which I refuse to allow to happen."

"Maksim. This isn't just a common cold. There's something else wrong."

"Then I'll get her help. Just do this. Grab her things and go to a store or the mall and stay out of sight. I don't give a shit where you go. Just do it now then tell me where you are." When she hesitated, I couldn't keep my voice low. "Now! This is a matter of life and death."

"Okay. Okay! But you will bring her back. She belongs with us."

"Fine. Just do it." Like hell she belonged with them. I'd allowed the situation to get out of hand for far too long. As I hung up the phone, I couldn't stop the bellow from erupting.

"What is wrong?" Walker asked from behind me. "Who is Jasmine?"

I took several deep breaths, trying to abate the rage while my mind continued spinning.

"She's important to you. Isn't she?" Walker badgered, coming closer. "That's what this house is about. Right?"

There was no way to avoid this. None. As I turned to face her, I could see the concern in her eyes. "Fine, Walker. You want to know my big secret, then I'll tell you because I don't have another choice. Jasmine is my daughter."

CHAPTER 15

$\mathcal{M}$aksim

Nothing was going to stop me from getting to my daughter. The assholes had gone too far, pushing my last button.

"Your daughter?" Walker asked, her tone incredulous.

I moved around her, heading for the bedroom. "I don't have time to explain."

"Well, you need to make the time. What the hell is going on? That's the girl in the picture. Isn't it?"

Walker's demands infuriated me, but at this point, she had a right to know. I turned sharply, trying my best to calm the building rage. "Yes, that's Jasmine in the picture. She lives with her grandparents. They've been threatened and we're going to get her."

"Wait a minute. I heard she's sick. What's wrong with her?"

"Get dressed, Walker. I don't have time to waste." I yanked the keys off the table, shoving them into my pocket. If my calculations were correct, we didn't have a single minute to lose. Now I knew without a doubt that Brick was involved, the bastard obviously managing to track my fucking phone. What the hell had been wrong with me? I'd led the motherfucker right to us.

While she finally understood, backing away toward the bedroom, I continued to have trouble breathing. I should have known the fuckers would try to harm my child, the little innocent creature who never left my mind, her existence haunting me.

I grabbed what few supplies would enable us to stay on the road, praying to God that Jasmine wasn't succumbing to the kind of illness that would necessitate a hospital. There was no way I could leave her anywhere and keep her safe.

After tossing the items into a bag, I moved toward the window, tugging on the blinds. I scanned the area, making certain our location hadn't been compromised, my gut still churning. Being in this position was dangerous as hell. While the bungalow was nestled behind a group of trees, there was a clear shot down the long driveway to one of the main roads.

When a dark vehicle passed the driveway at a slow rate of speed not once but twice, my instinct told me that it was vital we get the hell out of town.

"Walker. We're leaving now." I took long strides toward the room, catching something out of the corner of my eye. "No!" I lunged toward her, dragging her down to the floor just as something was tossed in through the window. Instantly, the room was ablaze, the Molotov cocktail tossed in erupting upon contact.

As Walker screamed, I kept my body covering hers, scrambling to get us out of the room. Within seconds, the accelerant used allowed the fire to jump from the floor to the bed, igniting the flammable source then licking up the walls.

I heard a second crash coming from another part of the house and knew that the entire place would go up within seconds. We had one shot at getting the hell out of here and the odds weren't in our favor.

"Stay low and whatever you do, don't let go of my hand," I instructed, wrapping my fingers around hers and jerking her toward the door.

"The fire is too hot," she exclaimed.

"We don't have a choice. We're going to the bathroom. It's closest to the garage." I didn't wait for her to respond, shielding her body as I jumped through the flames, crouching low as I stormed into the smaller room, shutting the door. She jerked out of my hold, her breathing ragged. I turned to face her, gripping both her arms. "Just try and relax. We need to get out this window but there are at least two assassins, maybe more. We have one crack at getting away."

"The keys. Do you have the keys?" she asked, her entire body shaking.

"Don't worry, little bird. Wait right here." I squeezed her arms then moved to the side of the window, barely able to make out much of the yard. Another crash caused her to yelp, and I was able to gather the stench of smoke as it rolled in underneath the door. We were running out of time.

When I tried to open the window, I realized the goddamn thing was stuck, the aging building likely compressing all the windows.

"We need to get out of here," she whispered.

"Hide your face," I instructed, not waiting until I turned my head, cracking my elbow against the glass. Thank fucking God it shattered. I busted out the rest, hissing when she started to cough from the acrid stench. "Come on. You can do this." As with all the buildings, the window was close to the ceiling, but I was easily able to climb out, immediately reaching for her. When she hesitated, I gave her an intense look. "Come on, baby. You can do this. We have to go. Trust me."

She closed her eyes for a couple of seconds then crawled onto the sink, reaching through to my arms.

Pop! Pop!

Fuck.

"Come on. You can do it." As soon as I had her in my arms, I yanked out my Sig, aiming in the direction of the gunfire, squeezing off several shots as we raced toward the garage. I didn't bother unlocking the garage door itself, instead kicking in the smaller door to gain entrance.

Pop! Pop! Pop!

She squealed only once when I shoved her inside, the girl smart enough to immediately head for the car. I raced to the other side, jumping in and wasting no time before throwing the gear into reverse. "Just stay down." As soon as I slammed on the accelerator, one of the perpetrators raced in through the open door. They managed to get off two additional shots, one catching the back window before I slammed into the garage door, the aging wood splintering upon impact.

"Go. Go. Go!" she yelled, ignoring my command and peeking out the window.

"Stay the fuck down, Walker." I shoved her down, hissing from the sight of the cozy house burning to the ground. Someone was going to pay dearly for what the fuck they'd done to my life.

I jerked the car one hundred and eighty degrees, hissing when I noticed another one of the assholes directly in front, ready to fire off another round. I jammed the gear into drive then slammed my foot against the accelerator, ready to fire off a round if necessary. When the fucker didn't move, I hit him head on, the force of impact tossing him to the side.

As the Mercedes jerked to the right, I corrected, noticing another one of the assholes in a vehicle quickly approaching. I yanked the weapon into my hand, pressing on the button for the window then swerving to the side. After firing several shots in quick succession, several smashing through the windshield, I didn't wait to witness the aftermath, heading directly for the main road.

The third fiery explosion indicated I'd been a good shot.

And I didn't let off on the gas for several minutes until I was certain we wouldn't be ambushed again. At least I knew the location like the back of my hand, making certain I knew every road long before I'd allowed Jasmine to be taken to the location.

There was also a shortcut to get to New Buffalo where Sandy and Miles lived. I only prayed they'd managed to get away from the house before sons of bitches returned. Miles wasn't stupid. He'd be the one driving. He knew everything about my life, including the danger they could face if anyone found out about Jasmine. Both of us had done everything in our power to keep that from happening, even if in doing so, I'd been forced to give up custody for the betterment of the child.

Fuck that.

Jasmine was much safer with me.

When I made another turn, I finally slowed down to the required speed. The last thing we needed was to be pulled over by an officer of the law. While Ivan owned the majority of cops in many jurisdictions, this area didn't happen to be one of them. I took a deep breath, finally placing the weapon on the console. When I looked in her direction, it was easy to tell she was shaking uncontrollably.

"Hey. Everything is okay," I said as gently as possible.

"For how long? Until they find us again?" She shot her head in my direction, her eyes shimmering from tears she refused to shed.

"I won't sugarcoat the situation any more than I did everything else I've told you. They will continue the hunt until we're dead, but I'm not going to allow that to happen."

"You're one man, Maksim. One man. I don't care how many weapons you have, unless you have your army of soldiers with you, they will succeed at some point."

"It seems you don't know me very well, Walker. Come on. We have an hour drive. You might as well be comfortable."

She exhaled, the sound exaggerated then crept onto the seat. As she held her arms, she stared out the passenger window. The fact she remained quiet was almost as disturbing as what had occurred only moments before.

I rubbed my jaw as I took another look into the rearview mirror. "You asked why I changed majors in college. Did some of it have to do with my father's insistence that I join him in the field of medicine? Yes, it did, but that wasn't the only reason."

After barely darting a look in my direction, she shifted even closer to the door.

"I met someone in one of my classes. She was truly a bright shining star. Anyway, we got closer, finally entering into a full relationship that continued for over a year. We were happy. However, she came down with cancer and everything changed." I took a deep breath, finding it difficult to think about the past.

"I'm so sorry, Maksim. What was her name?"

"Maggie. She fought very hard but eventually had to drop out of school. I went to see her as often as possible, but I couldn't keep up the schedule with school. I finally took a leave of absence. Her condition worsened and she almost died. Even though she managed to recover, I didn't have the stomach to return to a profession after watching everything she'd suffered through. I switched to business, even though I couldn't have cared less about school in general."

I was surprised when she reached over, placing her hand over mine. For some reason, the comfort was almost too intimate for me to tolerate. Anger remained, vicious and biting, my hatred for every doctor still in the front of my mind.

"What happened?" she asked after a quiet tension eased between us.

"Months went by. Finally, Maggie went into remission and bounced back to her old self, but her parents didn't want her returning to school, let alone remaining in a relationship with me. She reluctantly agreed, which put me into a tailspin. I was close to graduation and stayed until I was finished, but I was angry at the world, lashing out at anything and anyone I could. Ivan had already reached out to me, asking me to consider a change in careers." I had to laugh. A career. I hadn't truly understood what it meant to be involved with the Bratva. What a fool I'd been.

"That's very sad. Jasmine is the child you had with Maggie, isn't she?"

"Yes. We weren't supposed to see each other, but I ran into her at a coffee shop and one thing led to another. We stoked our relationship, enjoying three beautiful months together. Then she found out she was pregnant. Of course, there were complications since her immune system had been damaged. She refused to terminate the pregnancy against her parents' wishes. Her entire pregnancy remained difficult, and she was hospitalized at seven months. The doctors induced delivery a week later." I heard my voice change, the slight cracking as another wave of sadness settled in.

"Oh, God," she whispered, squeezing my hand.

I brushed my finger across hers, trying to stay focused. There was nothing worse than remembering. "Maggie had a stroke during delivery, and she never recovered. She was placed on a ventilator."

"And the baby?"

"Jasmine was born with certain medical issues because of her premature birth. Even today, if she gets a cold, it can turn into pneumonia very easily. Her heart was damaged, and she is on several medications. The doctors hope she'll grow out of it but that remains to be seen."

"Maggie died?"

"Her parents made the decision to have her removed from the ventilator ten days later. She died never meeting her baby girl. The bad blood remains between us. I was already in the life of the Bratva by then and they knew it. They went to court, convincing a judge that I wasn't the kind of role model for Jasmine and the man agreed. I have very limited visitation rights. The only good thing that came out of it is that until today, Jasmine's life was never in jeopardy. I did everything in my power to make certain no one knew about her. Only Ivan does and my Capo, which makes this situation intolerable."

The quiet settling between us was as horrible as the goddamn memory.

"I don't know what to say to you except I'm so sorry for everything you've been through. That's why you don't trust anyone."

I rubbed my finger across my lips, pressing down on the accelerator.

"That's exactly why, Walker. This entire situation has brought up the same bad blood all the way around in my mind. Secrets kept, lies being told. I refuse to have my little girl hurt in any of this. And I won't allow anyone to hurt you either. You do matter to me, whether you like it or not." I shifted my gaze in her direction, noticing a change in her eyes, that same rebellious look I'd seen the first minute I'd met her, only this time it wasn't directed at the man who'd captured and kept her.

"Then we get Jasmine. I'll take care of her, Maksim. I'm not sure how, but I will. Please tell me where we're going."

I thought about her question and there was only one logical answer. "We go to New York, and we find out who the hell is responsible for this."

She took a deep breath then nodded. "Okay. I'll find a way to get through to my mother."

"You're going to need to, Walker, because our choices are limited."

As I continued the drive, I realized that she would need to do that in a timely manner. As I pulled out my phone, all the red flags from before remained. While Brick knew about Jasmine, he had no idea where she lived. However, Ivan could easily find out. Would the Bratva leader betray me or was he also being played? I dialed Sandy's number. Thank God the woman answered on the first ring.

PIPER STONE

"We're here and I don't think we've been followed but I don't like this at all, Maksim," she said, the same tart tone in her voice.

"You don't have a choice, Sandy. Only I can protect her at this point and the only way to do so is to take her to an undisclosed location and you need to do as I told you and get out of town."

"I want to be able to talk to her on a regular basis."

"That's not going to be possible until I handle a situation. You're going to need to trust me, Sandy, because after I pick her up in twenty minutes, there will no further communication for some time. Do you understand what I'm saying?"

I could hear Jasmine crying in the background, and it burned me deep within. No one threatened a child and lived.

"I hate you for this and for the life you lead," she hissed.

"Sandy. While I appreciate everything that you've done for Jasmine, this is something only I can handle. I know what's best for *my* child. Now, where are you?" After a moment of hesitation, she told me the location. Even then, I bristled inside. If they were fucking with me, I wasn't certain how I was going to react.

"Fine. But when this is over, I'm going to make certain you never see our baby girl again. Do you hear me, Maksim?"

"I hear you, Sandy." As I ended the call, I turned my head toward Walker. Certain choices needed to be made and even if they damned me to hell, I would do everything in my power to save the two people who meant the most to me in my life.

* * *

Walker

Love.

While my mother had never tried to find anyone special in her life after whatever had happened with my father, she used to always tell me that the act of loving someone was more powerful than anything in the universe. I'd never fully understood what she was saying given what I thought was her hatred of all men, but as I pressed my hand against Jasmine's cheek, I finally comprehended what she'd tried to tell me. It wasn't just the romantic love with someone but the intense emotions surrounding the love of a child or a pet, a friend or another family member.

I could easily see Maksim's love for his daughter in everything he did and the look in his eyes. For a brutal and unforgiving man, he was kind and gentle around her.

The same way he'd been with me the night before. My thoughts drifted to the passion we'd shared, the quiet banter that had nothing to do with what was happening around us. I still found it impossible to accept that I cared for the man, but there was no denying that fact any longer. He was a decent person underneath the layers of violence and anger, unable to cope with a tragedy that had made his heart harden, which had allowed him to be sucked into the world of the mafia.

Now he was doing everything he could to protect us. He'd tossed his phone, purchasing a burner, finding an out of the way hotel to spend the night. We would head into New York in the morning, locating my mother, which was something I dreaded, and I wasn't certain why.

Maybe it was because I'd stopped wondering about my father a long time ago, realizing that I was never going to hear any stories or be given any pictures. I'd made up a persona for him, pretending he was a prince from another country, but I was beginning to believe that wasn't the case.

I eased away from the bed, tucking the covers a little more tightly around her sleeping frame, brushing hair from her eyes before heading for the window where Maksim had been standing for over an hour. His entire body was tense since he remained on watch, prepared for anyone who dared break into the hotel room. At least he'd hidden his weapon in a drawer, refusing to allow Jasmine to face any additional fear.

When I placed my hand on his shoulder, his muscles jerked from the heavy adrenaline flowing through him. He sighed before glancing in my direction.

"Her temperature is down. I think with a good night's sleep and another dose of medicine the fever will break by morning."

I wasn't certain if my words had any affect until a slight smile finally crossed his face. He glanced over his shoulder, nodding several times as if accepting the news but barely hearing me.

"Thank you for taking care of her," he said quietly.

"I think Sandy overreacted this time. Her heartbeat is strong and regular. Even with this condition you mentioned, she's a little fighter. You should probably have her tested again. You're right that some children grow out of these conditions. I have a good feeling."

I slid my palms against his chest, finding comfort in the heat building between us. While the sparks remained, the touch we shared was so much more than before. I could feel his emotions changing, even though his rage was just under the surface. "You have ideas in mind for what's going on. Don't you?"

He shot the sleeping girl another look before answering. "I think your father was involved with an organization out of New York."

I wasn't in the least bit surprised by his assumption. "Mafia?"

"Yes. As I told you before, we have many enemies. Every connection that I've made, from where Samuel came from as well as his buddies to where you lived before moving to Chicago, is the same."

"New York."

"Correct. You're not surprised."

"Nothing surprises me any longer, Maksim. In a sense, my mother lied to me all these years by not telling me the truth."

"She was likely trying to protect you."

"Instead, she didn't give me the ammunition I needed to know when I was being placed in harm's way. I know she loved my father. I could see it in her eyes what few times I brought him up. I also know she was destroyed by him, crippled emotionally. However, I don't think he left us, at least not in the way she threw out the one time she told me anything about him." I allowed my thoughts to drift to that ugly conversation which now seemed like a lifetime ago. At least it wasn't as fuzzy in my mind as it had once been.

He rubbed his fingers across my face, lowering his head and pressing his lips against my forehead. "Love doesn't always follow the kind of path you hope it will. Sometimes it's brutal and ugly. Other times it's deceitful and wrong. But love is truly powerful."

Laughing softly, I couldn't believe what he'd just said. "That sounds like something my mother told me once."

"Then listen to her. I shut down after Maggie's death. That enabled me to live in a world that cared about no one."

"That's not you, Maksim. You can change. You can do something else."

I could tell by the look on his face that even if that's what he wanted, it would never happen. The Bratva would never release him. He was a prisoner just like he'd made me.

"We will expose the truth," he stated.

"Then what?"

"Then the Novikov family ends the battle our way."

Shuddering, I thought about what he was saying, and something dawned on me, a name suddenly coming to the surface of my mind. A scene with my mother I'd blocked out.

Until now.

"Hey, Mom," I said as I entered the room, instantly realizing she was crying. "What's wrong?"

"Nothing," she whispered, rubbing her eyes then shifting her head in my direction. Her bright smile was completely fake, tear continuing to slip past her lashes.

I glanced at the television, reading the headlines. 'Tony Marciano gunned down in Chicago.' Why did this bother her?

"Who is he, Mom?"

She stood, immediately switching away from the news. "That's nothing. Really. Why don't we grab something to eat?"

Exhaling, I pressed my hand across my lips, stunned that I hadn't been able to remember the conversation for years. "Does the name Marciano mean anything to you?" When he didn't say anything at first, I tilted my head and could tell by his expression that the name not only meant something but that he'd been correct in his assumptions.

"The Marciano crime syndicate has been considered the most powerful mafia organization on the East Coast. Why do you know that name?"

"Because my father was named Tony Marciano," I said, now remembering everything about that moment. She'd been shaking, pale. "There was a news broadcast after he was gunned down. She was very upset. I didn't understand why. Now I do. And that's why *she* left him. I can't believe I just remembered that."

Maksim closed his eyes, his chest heaving. "I need to make a phone call, Walker. Stay in this room with my daughter."

"Okay, but I deserve to know what's happening. What are you going to do?"

He threw another look toward Jasmine before locking eyes with mine. "I need to confirm the information but if what your mother told you is true, your father was Antonio Marciano."

"Of the Marciano crime syndicate," I said, suddenly feeling nauseous.

"Yes, Antonio was the first-born son of a powerful and savage man named Luigi Marciano."

"That makes me Luigi's granddaughter."

"Yes. Unfortunately, your father was murdered several years ago." He closed the distance, keeping his voice low.

"Murdered." A cold chill trickled down my spine. "By whom?" He didn't say anything at first, exasperating me even more. "By whom? Tell me!"

"By the hand of Ivan Novikov."

CHAPTER 16

$\mathcal{M}$*aksim*

Revenge.

I'd told Ivan that revenge was often best served cold, and I'd truly begun to believe that. As I stood outside the small motel, I realized that while Ivan's decision to kill the son of an enemy had been necessary in his mind, it wasn't every aspect of what had been happening. Everything had gotten very personal, family ties meaning much more than I'd ever understood.

But I knew one thing for certain.

Walker wasn't the target. However, she had been lured to Chicago for a reason, groomed for another purpose.

The Marciano family wanted to take her from her life. Why hadn't they done so before?

The answer? Because they hadn't known she existed until recently. Maybe. If so, then how had that been kept a secret? Or was it because a deal had been struck, her true identity used as a bargaining chip? Those were the only two answers that made any sense.

And I was beginning to put the pieces together, only I didn't like what I was thinking.

I was surprised that Ivan answered the call given my use of a burner phone. "Ivan."

"I was hoping you'd call, Maksim. Brick told me what happened at your house and at the park. Are you alright?"

I was surprised there was no animosity in his voice for going against him with regard to Walker. "We're fine. However, there's something you should know."

"Do you mean that Samuel Rossi was born as Nikolai Samuel Marciano, brother of Antonio Marciano, the man I killed several years ago, only months before Samuel came to work for me. Correct?"

"You discovered the truth."

"I turned over some rocks to find the answers I needed. You were correct in that this is an act of revenge. It would seem that the Marciano family decided that the best way to destroy me was from the inside out. The shit at the Diamond Club. The crap with the real estate development. All their doings. Even the attack on you, all meant to put the fear of God into me. I assume that when he was removed from the situation, the family decided to finish the battle more directly. I suspect there will be more hits."

"I would agree with you. Have you increased security?"

Ivan snickered. "Of course I have. It's time for you to return home. I need you by my side."

"I'm not ready to do that yet, Ivan. There are more answers that need to be obtained."

"That means you already have an idea of what's going on. Don't you, Maksim?" His tone was terse.

"You once asked me to trust you when I wasn't certain whether or not I should accept your kind offer of joining your organization. Now, I'm going to ask you to do the same."

He hesitated, his deep breaths indicating his continuing frustration with me. I wasn't sorry at this point. Whatever was going on had everything to do with the Novikov organization.

"You're bound for New York. Aren't you?"

"Yes."

"And you refuse to rid yourself of this woman," he stated.

"She's important to us, Ivan, but even more than that. She's special to me."

He sighed, then huffed under his breath. "You're a powerful leader, Maksim, much more so than I'd imagined all those years ago. And to be truthful, you've taught me as much as I've taught you over the years. Perhaps it's past time for someone else to take the reins, moving our organization into another century since I seem to be lamenting over the past."

"I've never known you to lament over anything."

"That's where you're wrong, my boy. I allowed the Bratva to control my life instead of following my heart. While I've loved my wife, the arrangement made for us to marry wasn't in our best interests. I've tried to make her happy over the years, but true love was never something that I wanted. So I allowed her to suffer while I built my empire. If you truly care about this woman, then do what's right for you, but I will caution you. If you love her then you will need to find a way to keep her safe. The world you've committed yourself to won't allow for any weakness. You already know that by what's happened with your daughter."

I bristled when he brought her up, but I knew he was right. The best thing that I'd done for Jasmine was to let her go. Perhaps that's what I needed to do with Walker. I couldn't be with her, especially if her identity was true. The two families would never allow our relationship to continue.

"I'll keep that in mind."

"If you're asking me to trust you, then know that I do. Just remember everything I've told you. The Marciano family will not allow you seek your own revenge."

What he meant to say was there was a good possibility that I would be killed in my efforts to seek the truth.

So be it.

"Understood."

* * *

"Daddy. Daddy. Come play with me!" Jasmine's little voice pained me more than it should have, her excitement at not only feeling better but being taken to one of her favorite places weighing heavily on my mind.

"I'll be right there," I said, although I could barely drag my enthusiasm to the surface.

Walker touched my arm and when I glanced in her direction, I could see her expression of encouragement.

"She loves you," she said, although so quietly I could barely hear her.

"She doesn't know her father is a monster."

"Well, that man doesn't exist, at least today. Enjoy being with your daughter."

"You should know that Samuel was your father's brother, not his friend." I was troubled by her lack of reaction. The only way I knew she'd heard me was by the single sigh she issued.

"I was nothing but a pawn," she finally whispered.

"I think it was more than that. I honestly believe your father wanted you to have the best things in life."

"But Samuel stole money from your organization. Right?"

I shook my head. "I think it was out of revenge."

"That still doesn't answer why Samuel would lure me to Chicago into the lair of the asshole who killed his own brother. Revenge or not, that doesn't make sense."

"No, it doesn't."

"But you think the letter addressed to my mother fits all the pieces together." She finally looked into my eyes.

"Yeah, I do." Even if I was right, I wasn't certain either one of us were going to like the answers.

"Daddy!" Jasmine screeched, the sound making both of us laugh.

I took another sip of the wretched coffee the fast-food restaurant served then followed my daughter into the protected play area. I couldn't stop the training that had been mandatory on day one of my employment with the Bratva, scanning the parking lot outside the small location. I could feel Walker's presence behind me, yet she remained standing in the doorway of the play area, allowing me to enjoy the moment alone with the little girl who'd never been far from my mind.

"Daddy. Slide with me!" Jasmine insisted and all I could do was smile. She acted as if she'd never had a fever in the first place. She stood on the top of the colorful slide, her face beaming as if she'd found a secret hiding place.

"Daddy won't fit, baby girl. Why don't you come to me? I'll catch you instead." I moved to the end of the plastic platform, my muscles remaining tense after no sleep and constant worry. After Jasmine gave me one of her famous pouting looks, she slumped down on the slide, raising her arms and giggling as she headed in my direction. As I scooped her into my arms, hugging her tightly, I swung her around in a full circle. "That's my girl, but it's time to go."

"Oh, Daddy. Just one more?" she pleaded.

"Hmmm…"

"Why don't I go down with her?" Walker asked, her expression warm.

"I would like to see that," I answered, barely able to keep my extreme desire from giving me away.

"Come with me, Jasmine. Let's show that old man of yours what girls can do." Walker rolled her eyes as she reached for Jasmine's hand. I was surprised when Jasmine accepted it without any hesitation. My baby girl had been so sheltered in her life that meeting strangers was difficult for her, yet she'd taken to Walker from the minute we'd picked her up from the parking lot.

I leaned against the bank of windows, watching as Walker carefully guided Jasmine up the set of stairs, making certain my little baby held onto the railing. Then

Jasmine settled into her lap at the top, giggling the entire time.

"Whee!" Walker said, winking before pushing them away from the landing. As they slid down, I was overcome by the way the two of them interacted and by the sizzling sensations jetting through me. I wanted a family.

No, I needed to feel grounded for the first time in so damn long.

Walker couldn't contain a grin as she rubbed Jasmine on the top of the head, guiding them both in my direction. "She's such a little actress."

"Yes, she is," I said, laughing. "But we need to go."

"Daddy? You're mean."

Jasmine had a way of making all the shadows disappear from my life, reminding me that every day was far too short.

However, that didn't change anything. We were headed for New York. And we would find the answers we required.

"I know, baby girl, but Daddy has business to deal with." After I said the words, Walker and I locked eyes, hers full of concern. Even though the woman standing in front of me should do everything in her power to get away from me, she walked closer and all I could think about was how much I wanted this woman in my life.

Permanently.

"Let's roll!" I said, the phrase something I'd said on so many occasions when she was little, the inflection of my voice alone keeping Jasmine excited. She clapped her hands, waiting as patiently as a three-year-old could do as we tossed what was left of our breakfast into the trash.

As Walker secured her into the car seat, I studied the surrounding area, still fearful we'd been followed. I didn't like the odds of what we were facing.

"We're less than two hours away from my mother's house," Walker said a few seconds later.

"That's good. Are you going to be okay with this?"

"Do I have a choice?"

I shook my head, still looking from one side of the road to the other. "No. There's no other choice right now."

"Then I'll do what's necessary. What if we do find out the truth? What about Jasmine's safety?"

"I assure you that I'm not going to put either one of you in harm's way. I'll make certain you're both safe. Then I'll take care of what needs to happen."

"By yourself?"

While I could hear the concern in her voice, she had no idea what I was willing to do at this point in order to keep her safe.

And to end this nightmare.

"I do what's necessary."

"That would make you a fool," she hissed.

There were several things I wanted to say to her, but Jasmine's chatter to one of her stuffed animals dragged my attention away. The entire situation was absurd, but given what Ivan had told me, I knew we were getting close to discovering the truth.

"You will follow my directions, Walker. Whatever happens, you're the only one I can trust to protect Jasmine. Will you do that for me?"

While she shivered visibly, she nodded. "Of course I will. But don't you dare get yourself killed."

While I had no intentions of allowing that to happen, sometimes things didn't go as planned.

"Let's do this," I said with no hesitation.

* * *

Walker

Learning bits and pieces about a portion of my family I never knew was disturbing as hell. There was no denying I was still anxious, my stomach churning. While I wanted to weed through the years of silence, I was also terrified of what I'd learn. I knew Maksim feared the Marciano family was going to try to overthrow Ivan, finalizing their act of revenge by killing everyone of importance, including the man I cared about far too much.

He'd shared with me everything about what he knew regarding Samuel, Jack, and a man I'd never met by the name of Gregor Chamberlain. I found it interesting that Samuel had been like my father, attempting to find another life outside of the mafia family they'd grown up in. I had to admit, I wanted to know everything about how my mother had met him and how long they were actually together. I needed the pieces of the jagged puzzle to fit, even though I was terrified about learning anything else.

Still, that's all I could think about.

My mother still lived in the same small town I'd grown up in. Even though it was only a little over an hour away from New York City, it was worlds away from the Big Apple. Everything seemed to go in slow motion. People didn't lock their doors at night or worry about horrible crimes. I'd grown up thinking it was suffocating. What I wouldn't give to find a town just like it near Chicago.

As I directed Maksim down the small street toward my mother's house, my nerves were about to get the better of me. While I'd asked him about warning her that she could be in danger, he'd insisted that allowing her the chance to run and hide wasn't an option. He'd also assured me that her life wasn't in any danger and that if it had been, she'd already be dead. When I saw her car was in the driveway, I almost issued a sigh of relief.

Almost.

The early morning hours had been just as surreal as the night before, his actions with Jasmine continuing to confuse the hell out of me. When he pulled into the driveway, I could tell he was still antsy, concerned someone had followed us.

"I'm going in first," he said as he pushed his weapon into his pocket.

Just the sight of him performing the action was a reminder we were all in danger. I gave a quick look into the back seat, happy that Jasmine was oblivious to what was going on.

"No, you're not. My mother doesn't know you," I chastised, already opening the passenger door.

"There could be someone inside. I won't allow you to go in by yourself."

"Stop it, Maksim. This is something you wanted to do so you need to allow me to handle it first." I shot him a hard look before easing onto the concrete driveway. Jasmine's small voice gave me another pang in my heart.

"What are we doing here, Daddy?" she asked, her little voice yet another reminder the man was out of his mind for risking her life.

"We're visiting a friend of Walker's," he answered, his deep baritone more like a soft song whispered to his child.

"Yay! I like meeting people."

I remained antsy as I closed the car door, finding it difficult to take steps toward the small house I'd grown up in. I even found myself hesitating before knocking on the door. The last time I'd been here, which had been months before, I'd simply walked inside. Now I felt like a stranger. My hands were perspiring as I waited for her to answer. When I heard footsteps, I backed away, tossing Maksim a quick look.

As the door opened, there wasn't joyful surprise in seeing me standing on the doorstep.

There was apprehension and fear. She immediately took a step outside, noticing that I wasn't alone.

"Why are you here?" she asked, the pulse on the side of her neck irregular.

I was shocked at her tone and her attitude, uncertain how to answer at first. "Is that a way to greet your daughter?" My mother had always been prim and proper, never leaving the house without makeup or a perfectly pressed outfit. I couldn't remember a single time as a child she'd gone out of the house, even to the backyard, without looking stunning.

On this day, she looked haggard, and I could swear she'd aged by several years in a few short months.

"Who is that man?" she demanded, surprising me even more.

"A friend of mine. Can we come in?"

She hesitated and my gut told me at that very minute that she had a feeling why I'd returned. "Okay, but you can't stay long."

I held my tongue as I turned my head in Maksim's direction, another round of creepy crawlies scuttling through me.

She backed away into the shadows almost immediately, folding her arms as if protecting herself. I waited until Maksim approached with Jasmine in his hold.

"Is everything okay?" he asked softly.

"I don't think so."

"Do you want me to wait outside?"

"No. I don't know what's going on, but I doubt we'll have another chance to get to the truth." I wasn't certain my mother would tell us anything. I guided them inside, closing the door behind us. All the blinds were closed, which also wasn't like her at all. "Maksim and Jasmine, this is my mother, Andrea."

My mother barely acknowledged our presence until Jasmine pulled away from Maksim's hand, taking deliberate steps in her direction and holding out her little hand. "If you're a friend of Walker's, then you're a friend of mine."

I couldn't fight back a laugh from the little girl's words, my mother also caught off guard, but it seemed some of her hard shell cracked and she leaned down, a smile crossing her face.

"Well, I think it's an honor to meet such a beautiful little girl." While my mother said the right words, I could tell she remained nervous as hell, darting quick glances in Maksim's direction. Someone had terrified her. I knew her far too well.

Jasmine giggled as she shook my mother's hand, then pulled away, moving toward the bookshelf in the living room. I'd forgotten several of my childhood books had been left there, maybe something my mother could hold onto.

"Can I look?" Jasmine asked.

"Of course you can, honey," I answered, waiting until a book had been selected, the girl absorbed in the pictures before I inched closer to my mother. "We don't have much time, Mom. For some reason, I think you know why we're here."

"No. I don't, but you should go," she answered, still as nervous as I'd ever seen her.

"Why?"

"Because you don't belong here any longer."

When she tried to turn away, I gripped her arm, keeping my voice low. "Do you have the letter I gave you?"

"What letter?" When she paled, I took a deep breath.

"You know exactly what letter I'm talking about. The one I tried to give you that came from Samuel's attorney. You refused to look at it and I meant to take it with me, but I guess I dropped it." I noticed a strange yet fleeting look in her eyes. "Wait a minute. You did take it. Didn't you?"

She closed her eyes briefly, her hand shaking as she brushed her fingers through her hair. "You dropped it."

Bullshit.

She'd wanted to read it after all.

"And you not only kept it, but you read the contents." When she didn't answer, I had to fight everything I had inside of me to keep from screeching. "Didn't you?"

"You said so yourself, you were curious. So was I," she finally answered.

"What did you find inside?"

"Nothing of importance."

I closed my eyes, the dull throbbing in my temple increasing. "Mother. This is very important. Some things have happened, and I need that letter. Please get it for me."

"Why?"

I'd never been rough with my mother in my life, but right now, I was as exasperated as I'd ever been. I pulled her into the doorway of the kitchen, far enough away from Jasmine's ears that the little girl wouldn't hear us. "I know about my father."

"What do you mean you know?"

As Maksim came closer, she seemed more uncomfortable that when he'd entered her home. "His name is Antonio Marciano. Right?"

A look of real horror crossed her face. I'd never seen her appear so devastated in her life. She tried her best to pull away from me, her mouth twisting from the repulsion of what I'd said.

"I told you that you shouldn't have interfered! I told you!" Her entire body was shaking, but I knew my mother's anger. Her outburst wasn't about fury but about fear.

Maksim exhaled from the doorway, a clear sign that he was getting antsy.

"Just say it. I need you to tell me that's who my father was."

She teared up, all the years of keeping the ugly secret finally taking its toll. As she lowered her head into her hands, I tried to remain patient. I could tell how much she was hurting, but I also knew we were running out of time. I didn't need Maksim to tell me that.

"Please, tell me. You know I deserve to know."

After sucking in her sobs, she lifted her head, brushing my long strands behind my shoulder like she always used to do. "You look so much like him, Rafaella."

I was stunned she called me by that name, something I hadn't heard since I was a little girl. "So it's true."

"Yes."

"Then talk to me. Tell me about him. How did this happen?" I no longer cared that my tone was demanding.

"You don't know this, but I grew up in Boston. That's where I was living when I met your father. I didn't know who he was, or I wouldn't have gotten involved, but he was so charming and handsome. The man swept me off my feet with dozens of roses and gifts. How he loved to give me things. And restaurants. I'd never been to such incredible places in my life before him. I fell head over heels in love." Her eyes had shone brightly when talking about him, but almost as soon as she'd lit up, her slight moment of happiness faded, her eyes full of nothing but haunted sadness.

"That sounds wonderful." She'd never once told me about Boston, and she certainly didn't have an accent. Given my grandparents were dead and she'd had no siblings, it had never occurred to me she'd lived anywhere else.

She lifted her head, sucking in her breath then tossing Maksim another look. I could swear she knew that he was the same kind of man, but she didn't know him any better than she had my father. "It was all a lie. He was a murderer. He'd come into town to kill a man the very night he met me. Of course, I didn't know that at the time. He told me he had business and that he lived in New York City. That was the single truth. Everything else was a lie and I bought it because I thought I'd found the perfect man. I'd read about the murder in the papers, but it didn't dawn on me because your father told me he

305

was a salesman. Isn't that ridiculous?" She laughed bitterly.

"How did you find out?"

"Someone had a copy of the *New York Times* at work and his picture was on the front page along with his father. There he was, the prince of the Marciano mafia family. I was sick, refusing to see him but your father wasn't going to allow that to happen. I pretended like I didn't care until he left to go back to New York. I left Boston the day after, never looking back. I changed my name because it was much easier then and went as far as the money that I'd saved would take me. I had friends here at the time who took me in. For a long time, I didn't leave their house. You see, I'd found out I was pregnant and didn't want to be alone. I was scared."

"I'm surprised he never knew."

"I don't know if he looked, but I didn't care."

She laughed, brushing her fingers across her lips, obviously thinking about something. I shot Maksim a look and his imploring eyes begged me to get on with it. My God. That's one reason Samuel gave me that condo.

"Mama, you need to listen to me. The letter is important. You were right about keeping me from going to Chicago. The gift was… Let's just say it wasn't without strings."

"Goddamn it! I knew better. I knew it!" she wailed, fisting her small hands. "What happened? What did Samuel do to you?"

"So you know who Samuel is?"

"Of course I know," she spat, recoiling almost the instant she did.

"Why didn't you tell me that? Why? You allowed me to go to that city without all the information and..." I looked away, refusing to yell at her. She'd been through enough. I was a big girl.

"You're right. I should have been honest with you years ago, but the truth is that I wasn't ready to face the past. I didn't honestly think you'd go. You're a levelheaded girl. When someone gives you an expensive condo as a gift, I would have thought you would have laughed, not accepted. But you had the job of your dreams and it all seemed to make sense to you. I hoped that maybe Samuel was actually doing what your father would have wanted."

"So you know Antonio is dead."

My mother looked away again, another reflection of the past giving her a smile. "He got what he deserved in my opinion."

"Mama. There are some bad people after me, maybe from my father's family. I don't know what they want but the letter is the only chance we have at finding out."

"Ms. Sutherland. The letter really is important to us," Maksim said in a caring and quiet tone.

She looked confused, uncertain of what to do.

"Please, Mama. Whatever is in that letter might answer so many questions. You already read it. You know that."

"It's from your father telling me that he knew all along about you and that he stayed away out of respect for me. What difference would it make now?"

"Please."

Another ten seconds passed.

"Fine." She bolted around me, yanking open one of the drawers in her side cupboard, jerking out the envelope that had been lying directly on top. Even from where I stood, I could tell the flap had been ripped open, a portion of the letter showing. She stood where she was, the letter fisted in her hand. As she looked back and forth between Maksim then back to me, I realized she was debating what she wanted to tell me.

"It's okay, Mama. Just let me read the letter."

"Who is he?" she demanded, throwing her arm out in Maksim's direction.

"I already told you, he's a friend of mine."

"Don't lie to me. Don't you ever lie to your mother."

The vehemence in her voice was something I rarely heard. She was on the edge, her trembling only getting worse. "Maksim is with the Novikov Bratva out of Chicago. My father's family is considered an enemy and because of who I am, I'm being used as a pawn for some reason. That's why this letter is important."

After reluctantly handing me the letter, she walked closer to him, shifting her gaze into the living room. "Is that your daughter?"

"Yes, ma'am, she is."

"Then do yourself a favor and give her to someone who can raise her far removed from your lifestyle. I did what I could to protect my little girl. And I failed."

I could tell the words hit him hard by the look in his eyes. As I unfolded the letter, scanning it twice, I realized that it was nothing more than a love letter, hoping that one day she would find it in her heart to tell me about my father. There was nothing that I read that helped us in any way.

As Maksim moved closer, taking it from my hand, I felt an odd sense of being let down as well as grateful for knowing the truth. The knot in my stomach remained, but slowly I was already starting to accept who my father had been. However, I was frustrated that there wasn't something else in the two pages.

I heard the slight growl he emitted and knew he was disgusted.

"Now, just go. Okay?" my mother stated with far too much emphasis.

"Why?" I demanded. She was suddenly finding it difficult to look into my eyes.

"You have another life to live."

When she tried to walk away, I blocked her. "Did something else happen?"

"No!"

She answered far too quickly.

"Mother. If something happened or someone hurt you, then you need to tell us."

"Why, so Maksim will come to my defense?" Her laugh was almost as if she was becoming unhinged.

I gripped her arms, shaking my head out of exasperation. "Did someone hurt you?"

"I can't. I just can't," she said, sobbing all over again.

"Jesus. Who threatened you? Who?"

"If I tell you then they'll kill you and you have a new life ahead of you, a marriage. I just…"

Marriage?

Maksim lifted her chin with his knuckle, giving her a respectful nod. "I will never allow anything to happen to you or to Walker, but you need to be honest with us. Who issued the threat, Andrea?"

"Some man with a gun. Okay? He came to visit me after you'd left."

I held my breath as I looked at Maksim. "What did this person say to you? Did he hurt you?"

"No, he didn't hurt me. But I knew he would if I said anything. He told me that if I tried to contact you again or convince you to return that they would kill you. Why? Who do they want you to marry? He said a deal had been made. What deal?"

Maksim pulled her into a hug, turning his head so he could look me squarely in the eyes. "I promise you that you'll be protected for the rest of your life." He reached out for me, taking my hand and at that moment, I realized I never wanted him to let me go.

With him, I felt safe.

And loved.

CHAPTER 17

" $\mathcal{L}$ ies and secrets are like cancer in the soul. They eat away what is good and leave only destruction behind."

—Cassandra Clare

Maksim

If I should have taken a single piece of advice my mother had given me, it was that secrets and lies were a black hole sucking away your soul. I knew that to be true more than most. Now I hated everything about lying to myself, the destruction that doing so had already caused and not only in my life.

I'd been forced to place my trust in someone, and I'd relied on my instinct to do so.

Now I had to pray that I'd made the right decisions. If not, I'd just sealed Walker's fate as well as that of Andrea and my sweet Jasmine. At least they were safe for now, the location far removed from what I knew would be a bloodbath.

But the situation had to be handled without any further waste of time or hesitation.

The call had been terrible to make, the answer even worse. But I'd learned something valuable about loyalty, trust, and respect. While blood was thicker than water, it was all about the way a person handled themselves and the business that truly mattered. Once any of the three were destroyed, they could never be restored.

A line had been crossed.

A deal made with the devil.

Now it was time to face the consequences.

I got out of the car, waiting as several vehicles spilled into the parking lot of one of the warehouses we owned. I held my loaded weapon in front of me, waiting with as much patience as I could tolerate. Night would soon fall and while I didn't mind the darkness, I was antsy to get this taken care of. I had a different life to lead.

As the two dozen men approached, I looked from one to the other, finally settling my heated gaze directly on Brick. I could tell he knew what I was thinking and that I'd questioned his loyalty.

He bowed his head, the respect noticed by everyone else in the group who did the same.

"Mr. Calderon," Brick said, awaiting whatever order I would give him.

I walked closer to the man I knew I could trust but made certain that every other soldier heard every word of what I was about to say.

"I checked on that birth certificate," he added, hoping that following my orders would help. "It's just like you thought, although someone tried to change it."

I took a deep breath before saying anything.

"I value loyalty more than anything. Loyalty leads to trust, trust to being considered a member of the family. Betrayal leads to death, and I assure you that it won't be quick or without a heightened level of pain. What we're about to do will be difficult if not deadly for some of you. Therefore, you have a single chance at walking away and I'll allow you to live. However, if you stay, I expect nothing less than absolute allegiance. Is that understood?"

I kept my eyes locked on Brick, taking a deep breath. When I let it go, he shuddered, knowing that he'd crossed the line in providing information to the wrong man. In doing so, he's almost cost the woman I loved her life. However, he'd also trusted in someone within the organization, not realizing that everything he'd told the man had been used. My whereabouts. My intentions. Everything.

"Absolute devotion, Maksim," Brick stated. "And that goes for all of us."

The chorus of similar words was all I needed. Time was still not in my favor.

"Excellent. Then you know what must happen."

"Yes, sir."

"Then we go hunting until it's done and Brick. You're coming with me."

"You got it, boss. There are four soldiers protecting your mother and father. No one will be able to get to them."

I'd done everything I could to protect those I loved. My choices had placed them in harm's way, my mother refusing to continue being a part of a family that she loved, yet a lifestyle she feared. And I'd placed her once again in the middle of a turf war, only on the soil of the country she'd adopted and fallen in love with.

Just like my father.

While the man would never be able to understand the reasons behind the decisions I'd made, that would never stop me from doing everything I could to protect them.

There was no need to provide additional commands. They'd been laid out to Brick after our initial discussion, and he'd delivered the information. While some of my soldiers had once been loyal to Ivan's regime, they'd all pledged an oath to serve my command.

Now they knew what would happen if they crossed it.

Brick dispatched several of the men to different locations, my soldiers prepared to eliminate those who'd joined Vadim's treachery.

As I drove, I thought about Walker and the last words she'd said to me. They would burn me until I returned or was forced to take my last breath.

"Come back to me, Maksim. You have a home."

A home.

I wasn't certain any longer what that meant.

But I was determined to find out.

My job was a simple one.

Eliminate the traitor.

Vadim.

I remained quiet as I drove to Ivan's house, still seething from everything that had occurred. That Vadim had entered into a deal with the Marciano family, using marriage to the daughter of the once notorious mafia prince as the binding tie was treacherous and disgusting. Vadim had looked the other way when Samuel had taken the money because he'd orchestrated it.

Unfortunately, Samuel had placed his trust in Vadim given the deal made between the two families. I did find it interesting that Samuel had been used as a scapegoat in the entire scam, his murder at Vadim's hands the only piece of the puzzle that remained missing.

"Did you hear about Luigi Marciano's murder?" Brick asked. "That idiot Riccardo Marciano is running things now. I heard he's a real savage."

Savage. That's the way I'd described Vadim.

I turned my head, my stomach churning, the last pieces suddenly snapping into place. "When?"

"Two days ago. He was gunned down in his own home." Suddenly, Brick exhaled. "Wait a minute. You don't think that something happened to Ivan. Do you?"

"Jesus Christ. That's exactly what I know happened." I'd called Ivan, wanting nothing more than to have a chance to see him face to face. He must have called Vadim in his rage. Dear God. What had I done to the man?

As soon as I turned into the driveway, I knew my gut had been right. There were none of Ivan's usual guards standing at his entrance.

"What the fuck?" Brick hissed as he leaned forward.

"Get some of the others here," I barked. They'd been sent to hunt down those most loyal to Vadim. I couldn't risk a single one of them remaining in our employ. But I'd miscalculated Vadim's hatred of his family or his need to grab every aspect of Ivan's power.

I jerked the car to a stop, jumping out as soon as I'd cut the engine and running toward the front door. The massive wooden piece had been left ajar. Fuck. Fuck! I eased to the side, giving Brick a hard look as he flanked the other side. After I pushed against it, I hesitated before rushing inside.

There was no spray of bullets, no soldiers jumping out of the shadows, but I sensed a horrific tragedy.

And I'd been right. Just taking two additional steps, I could see a trail of blood.

"Dear God. That's one of the housekeepers," Brick snarled.

I glanced down at the woman, hissing under my breath. We were too late. I swung my weapon from side to side, moving into the family room, a roaring fire still going in the stone fireplace. There were no words to describe the sight of my aunt. She'd been sitting by the fire, a glass of wine in her hand. And she'd been reading a book. I walked closer, disgusted to the point all I could think about was torturing Vadim, taking days and days to do so, ignoring his cries for leniency.

Fuck him.

At least she'd been shot in the back of the head, never seeing her own son's merciless betrayal.

The stench of blood hung in the air, the coppery sweet odor an indication that everyone in the house had been gunned down. For what? The deal made with the Marciano family? Would Vadim take the house or had this been offered to the only surviving member of the Marciano syndicate? The single person left? A brutal man

Vadim's age. From what I knew about Riccardo Marciano, he was cut from the same cloth as Vadim, greedy as hell. That was the only answer that made any sense.

"Take that side," I directed him as I headed for the man's office, bursting inside. My blood turned to ice as I stared at the horror scene. Blood was everywhere, covering every surface. Ivan's most trusted soldiers had been lured in, all four of their bodies riddled with several bullets.

And Ivan.

He'd been like a surrogate father to me, even though he never attempted to be anything but my mentor as well as my uncle. He was in the same place I almost always found him, behind his beloved ornate desk that he'd had shipped from Honduras. I could still remember his gleeful smile the day it had arrived, the satisfaction he'd had when resting behind the massive piece of furniture for the first time.

It had suited him.

A man of honor.

A man of respect.

And a man I loved.

Now, instead of commanding an empire, he was slumped over, his face resting in his own pool of blood.

As I moved closer, I heard Brick from behind. I'd never realized how strong his love of the family was until at that moment when I heard a single sob erupt from his throat.

Ivan had treated him well, ensuring him that I would also do the same in my leadership position.

"Jesus. Fucking. Christ. Vadim did this?" he asked, although he already knew the answer.

"Yes," I hissed, moving very slowly around the desk, easing him back by the shoulder. His eyes remained open, the last thing he'd seen a reflection in his lifeless eyes.

Treachery.

Closing my eyes, I said a silent prayer that God would be kind to the man who'd nurtured me. While I wasn't a praying man, on this day, I felt something change deep inside of me, an entirely different kind of rage taking over.

I eased my hand down his eyelids, giving him the final nod of respect. "Rest in peace, Uncle. Your death will be avenged." Seconds later, I snapped my head toward Brick. "Hunt. The. Fucker. Down."

As we ran toward the front door, a sick feeling swept through me. The man would attempt to take everything that mattered to me.

Soldiers burst in through the door, both men out of breath.

"He's not at his house," one of them yelled, his face twisted from the realization of what had happened and what was yet to come.

I threw back my head and roared. I'd found a safe haven, or so I'd thought, but the house was one Ivan had offered. Was it possible Vadim had discovered where I'd hidden Walker and Jasmine?

"What now, boss?" Brick asked, his voice as strangled as before.

"I want every single soldier employed by Vadim killed. Find out where Vadim went. Torture his men if you need to. We're going to finish this."

"You heard the man. Rusty. Giovanni. Hunt down Vadim. And hold him. This is Maksim's call how he wants to handle the asshole," Brick ordered.

"We'll find him," Rusty snarled. "But it will be difficult not to slice his throat."

"Don't!" I yelled. "The man is mine."

There was no time to waste, no lamenting over lost family or broken ties. This was about saving Walker, ensuring she could live the rest of her life as she wanted, not as Vadim demanded. If I had to guess, the deal of joining forces had been predicated on Vadim's marriage to Walker. As such, the son of a bitch would stop at nothing to get what he wanted.

There would be no law enforcement agency, no cop on the beat who would stop me from getting to Walker. As I slammed my foot on the accelerator, weaving in and out of traffic, my entire system remained on edge. There was a chance it was already too late.

It seemed like hours passed when it had been only twenty minutes, but in that time, whatever change had begun inside my system, my heart and my soul, was now complete. I was now and would be in the future nothing but a killing machine when necessary, incapable of showing mercy for anyone who dared to try to destroy the family.

Family.

The word remained in the forefront of my mind. A portion had already been stripped away from me.

Tension remained in the car, Brick antsy to exact his own revenge. I remained on edge, only focused on getting to Walker and my daughter. They had to be okay. Blinded from rage, I continued driving recklessly, daring anyone to try to stop me. As I swung around the last corner, the house located at the end, visions of Walker's face filtered into my mind. I could almost hear her laugh, could swear her scent remained with me, covering every inch of my skin.

And my heart longed to touch her once again, if only to say goodbye in order to free her to live her life. I would accept those consequences for my actions and none other.

There was an odd sense of quiet on the secluded street, the house on the lake one that Ivan had purchased to get away from his responsibilities. He'd shared the news of the purchase with me over a glass of whiskey almost two years before, purposely telling me that no one, including my amazing aunt knew of the location. It was his private retreat, the only place where he could be himself.

I would never forget that day, the trust he'd placed in me to keep his secret. But my gut told me that Vadim had turned over every rock, finding everything he could about just how powerful his father had become. The plan had been in motion for a long time, every player who'd been involved ceremoniously eliminated.

My fucking God. If the two factions came together, every other family would be targeted, their hunger for power knowing no bounds.

"You need to have my back, Brick," I said in a low and husky voice, turning toward him slightly.

"You need to trust me, Maksim. You're now the *Pakhan*. I will protect your life with mine if necessary."

Pakhan. I'd never considered the job, although there was no one else to take it. I refused to allow the Novikov organization to wither because of one man's greed.

"Then so be it."

As I suspected, the front door of the cottage had been kicked in, but there were no cars. There were two points of access, the road allowing anyone inside to see an approaching vehicle. The only other way was by boat, although the waters of Lake Michigan were torrid at this time of year. However, it offered exactly what Vadim had been seeking, an element of surprise.

A sudden calm washed over me as I exited the vehicle, scanning the perimeter. There were no outside guards. It would appear that Vadim had been expecting my arrival, his final act of betrayal something he wanted to make certain I was a part of.

I snapped another clip of ammunition into my Sig before heading for the front door. As soon as I walked inside, the sound I heard was the most disturbing of all.

Jasmine's giggle.

Brick hissed beside me, and I pressed my arm against his chest. We had to be very careful how we handled this, or my baby girl would be a victim of crossfire and Vadim knew I wouldn't risk her life under any circumstances. I'd swept the entire cottage when I'd brought Walker, her mother, and Jasmine only a few hours before. I'd even left a weapon for Walker, knowing she wouldn't hesitate to use it if necessary.

I took a deep breath before following the sound of Jasmine's sweet voice into the living room.

"It's about time you got here," Vadim said as he chuckled.

"Maksim!" Walker exclaimed.

"Shush, darling," Vadim told her, jerking her closer to him.

My rage rose to the surface again, but I shoved it aside, thankful that up to this point there hadn't been any bloodshed or injuries inflicted. While there were two of Vadim's soldiers in the room, the only visible weapon was the one Vadim held out of sight from Jasmine yet pointed at Walker in a casual manner.

"Daddy!" Jasmine yelled and held up a stuffed animal. "Look what Unkie Vadim brought for me." She jumped up, racing toward me and Vadim stood where he was, a smile on his face.

"Hiya, baby girl. That's a very nice bear. Did Walker show you your room?" I kept my eyes locked on my little bird, praying to God that she was really alright.

"Yes. It's purty. Purple!"

"Could you do me a favor and go play for a little while? Daddy and Uncle Vadim need to have an adult discussion." I leaned down, tugging on one of her locks of hair, trying to keep an emotionless smile on my face. I would rip the man apart for putting a child in this situation.

Jasmine gave me a pouting look, stomping one foot then broke into a smile of her own. "Okay, Daddy. But you owe me."

I laughed on purpose, hating how hollow it sounded, taking a deep breath as she scampered out of the room. "Let Andrea go with the child. She has nothing to do with this." The last thing I wanted was for Walker's mother to witness what had to happen.

"I don't think so, cousin. She's likely to escape. I think one big family gathering is very special. Don't you?"

"Goddamn it, Vadim. Let. Her. Go."

He reared back, glancing at Andrea. "Fine, but if the woman tries to run, I will kill her. It's that simple. However, since she's going to be my mother-in-law, I'll grant you this single wish."

The taste of blood formed in my mouth as the anger continued to increase.

I moved toward Andrea, taking her by the arm and helping her to her feet. "Can you take care of Jasmine for me?"

Andrea swallowed, tossing a nasty look in Vadim's direction. "I'll protect her with my life, Maksim."

As she walked out of the room, I moved closer to the asshole, trying to remain calm. "You killed your own mother and father. You are one sick fuck."

He laughed, enjoying the moment. "They were in my way. It was that simple. I tried to convince my dearly departed father to step down. I told him I'd allow him to live, but he refused me. He even tried to have his soldiers gun me down. Imagine that. I simply couldn't trust him any longer."

"You're a fucking bastard."

"Yes, my father taught me well that if you want more power, you simply take it."

I'd spent a significant number of years learning about our enemies, able to detect their stench before walking into a room. At this moment, Vadim was drunk on power he hadn't earned.

"Why the games?" I asked, giving him a hard look.

"I found them fun. Plus, my partner in crime was vacillating about what he wanted to do."

"Interesting. What exactly do you and Riccardo have planned?" While I was curious, I simply wanted the man to keep talking. I inched closer, my action something he either didn't notice or give a shit about. He thought he was invincible.

He laughed, raking the forearm holding his weapon across his brow. The slight tremor in his hand meant one of two things. His adrenaline was far too high, or he was uncertain of what I could and would do. It was an advantage, albeit slight.

"First, I'm marrying this luscious creature. That will forge my relationship with the Marciano family. After that? I'll allow your imagination to envision the possibilities. Let's just say I'll become one of the most powerful men in the world."

"And what happens when Riccardo realizes you killed his brother?"

I could tell my question angered him. As if I gave a shit.

"We eliminate our enemies, Maksim. That's what my father taught us."

"Samuel made a promise to Antonio. He was determined to protect Walker."

"You mean Rafaella?" he asked, fisting Walker's hair and dragging her closer.

"Don't touch me, you fuck!" she snarled, slamming her fist into his gut.

He continued laughing, pulling her even closer, nipping her earlobe as if she already belonged to him. "She is a lovely creature and you're right. The reason I killed Samuel is that he and his buddies tried to protect her against her rightful husband. I assure you that Riccardo had no issue with the elimination of his brother, the very one who'd left the family fold years before, even changing his name to try and erase his heritage. That kind of treachery wasn't acceptable."

Riccardo Marciano was as hungry for power as Vadim, killing his father and allowing the murder of his only remaining brother in his quest for taking the Marciano throne. What a tangled, vicious web both men had weaved.

It was time to stop the madness.

"You can't have Walker. She belongs to me," I stated, giving the woman who I'd fallen in love with a longing stare. In her eyes, I could see a mixture of ragged emotions as well as a determination to get out of the man's clutches.

"That's where you're wrong, cousin."

Vadim made the mistake of snapping his weaponed hand in my direction, believing that he could get off a clear and easy shot, eliminating his final enemy without a fight.

The man was wrong.

He'd forgotten that I'd become a crack shot, spending hundreds of hours perfecting the skill. With a simple lift of my arm, I managed to get off two shots before he was able to react.

As Brick roared, the sound of gunfire exploding just behind me, I lunged forward, dragging Walker out of Vadim's clutches and pummeling us both to the floor. While I kept my body over hers, I twisted, prepared to fire again.

But it wasn't necessary. Brick had my back, terminating the two soldiers Vadim had counted on.

"No. No!" Walker scrambled underneath me, her entire body undulating. It was the first time I noticed she had the gun I'd given her nestled in her hand.

"Shhh... It's okay. You're okay," I whispered, pressing my hand against the side of her face.

"Jasmine! We need to get to Jasmine." She continued to struggle, her eyes becoming wild with fury.

She managed to push hard against me, jerking to a sitting position, doing everything she could to get out of my hold. And the second her eyes lit up like a firecracker, the air in the room was sucked into a vacuum.

"No!" she bellowed. "You're not going to destroy anyone else I care about. You threatened my mother, the man I love and his beautiful child. That will never happen again."

"I wanted you to suffer while I killed them one by one. My wedding gift to you," Vadim hissed then made the mistake of bursting into laughter.

As everything moved into slow motion, she raised her arm, firing off several shots in rapid succession.

As Vadim's body slowly slid to the floor, his smile began to fade.

Then all was quiet.

CHAPTER 18

 *alker*

Family.

Maybe I'd taken the concept for granted my entire life. My beautiful mother had given up the love of her life in order to protect the child growing inside of her. She'd had the instinct that raising me in that violent world wouldn't be best for her little girl. In turn, she'd never been able to get over the man who'd swept her off her feet.

The past week had been nothing but an eventful, exhausting blur. Police. Interrogations. Being moved from one location to another. Nowhere felt safe except for Maksim's arms. Yet there was a distance growing between us, his requirement to try to heal the horrific rifts and holes within the Novikov organization not only taking a

331

significant amount of time but also a huge toll on the man who'd turned to stone.

Blurred images of me firing off countless shots, every bullet slamming into Vadim remained in the forefront of my mind. I'd never shot anyone before, but the moment he'd reared up, his weapon pointed at Maksim's head, I'd reacted on instinct and the fury that had furrowed within me since finding Jack's body on my living room floor.

There'd been explanations, Maksim allowing me to understand that in the world of powerful mafia men, even family wasn't immune to betrayal. Samuel had learned of my father's—his brother's—death years before, the Marciano family certain Ivan had issued a command, requiring the assassination of the man I'd never met. From what Maksim had been able to decipher, Samuel had already left the family operation, trying to pursue a life of his own with the love of his life. Then she'd died unexpectedly. That had removed the last barrier stopping the man's desperate attempt at seeking revenge against Ivan.

From there, Samuel had enlisted the help of his old marine buddies, concocting what they'd thought was a perfect way of exacting retaliation. However, he'd under-estimated Vadim's greed as well as his determination to destroy everything that was important to a man he knew would ascend to the throne.

And Maksim had almost died trying to protect me.

I took a deep breath, glancing up at the bright sun. The day was frigid, yet with the sky a bright blue, not a cloud in sight, I was tingling from the warmth.

I felt his presence behind me and sighed. As Maksim wrapped his arms around me, pulling me against the heat of his chest, I felt a combination of absolute happiness as well as a tremor of fear regarding the future.

At this point, I didn't think we'd have one. How could we? I longed to return to my normal life and to a job I adored.

Yet the pull to be with the man I loved was strong, keeping me on edge, butterflies remaining in my stomach.

"What do you think?" he asked before nuzzling against my neck.

"An incredible winery. I'm surprised you remembered."

He chuckled, the sound creating a beautiful set of vibrations dancing down the length of my body. "I remember everything you've ever told me."

"You have, huh? What's my favorite color?" I asked, purring afterward.

"Purple, my little bird. You're not that tough to figure out." As he spun me around several times, all I could do was laugh.

"Don't make me spill my wine. This is my favorite one so far." I pushed my hand against his chest, immediately kneading his thick shirt, drinking in his rugged scent. The recent light snow added to the festive ambiance, every structure of the small yet bustling winery glistening from the icicles forming overnight.

"Then I'll buy a case. No, make that three cases. Is that enough?" He lowered his head, his chest heaving.

I wanted nothing more than to claw my fingers through the three layers he'd worn, finally pressing my palm against his chest. Maybe that would come later. "Make that four and we have a deal."

His laugh was genuine, his eyes twinkling in the sunlight. This had been our first time together and alone, my mother insisting that she babysit Jasmine. The two of them had developed quite a bond and I'd been surprised when she'd told me that Maksim was a keeper. I certainly hadn't expected that.

"You drive a hard bargain, but I'll grant your wish, even if you haven't been a good girl."

"Bullshit," I mewed, sucking in my breath before he captured my mouth. I could kiss the man all day long, enjoying the way I felt in his arms. As I slid my arm around his neck, tangling my fingers in his hair, he pulled me off the ground, swinging me around as he'd done before. He dominated my tongue, growling around the moment of passion. His cock was hard, the scent of his testosterone only fueling the desire that always built into a frenzy around him. I was breathless and lightheaded, wanting nothing more than to find a quiet place while the man ravaged my body for his pleasure alone.

When he finally broke the kiss, we both took a deep breath. I pushed against him, my face flushed. For some reason, just being around him made me nervous today. He'd remembered one of the few things I enjoyed doing, trying to make the day very special for us both.

But I had a feeling there was something important he wanted to tell me, and I already knew what that was.

He took my hand, heading toward the vineyard itself. "When do you start work again?" he asked after we'd walked for a full minute.

"Day after tomorrow."

"I'm glad. I know you want to get back to your life."

"I do. Plus, the hospital needs me."

"I'm still concerned Riccardo will try and contact you. He is your uncle."

"He means nothing to me, Maksim. He's my birth father's brother. So what?"

Maksim's sigh was rattled, and I could tell he was thinking about his own uncle. Ivan's death had been hard on him, but Vadim's betrayal had changed him. I was no longer certain who he was, not that I'd really known him at any point. I had to keep reminding myself of that for fear of losing what was left of the woman inside, the person I'd been before all the horrors.

"Remember that family is important. He's still blood."

"Blood isn't always thicker than water."

Chuckling, he squeezed my hand, finishing off the small amount of wine. "I think you're right."

"What are you going to do with Jasmine?"

"Well, I won't have an opportunity to decide. Sandy and Miles decided to take me back to court. They want my parental rights terminated."

"What?" I jerked free and turned to face him. "You are fighting it, right? They can't do that!"

"They have every right to do that. I'm not a good influence in Jasmine's life. I put her in danger, which they were quick to tell their attorney."

"Maksim. You're her father. She belongs with you."

"She has a heart condition on top of everything."

I shook my head. "She is growing out of it. The tests came back late yesterday."

He breathed a sigh of relief then snarled. "You're smart enough to know how these things work. I currently don't have a home that's suitable for her and I doubt the judge wants to hear that I'm waiting for renovations to be complete because of gunfire. They want a stable environment and a real family, which I know isn't going to happen." The way he looked into my eyes let me know he was letting go, freeing his little bird. "Besides, I have new responsibilities and the danger level is just going to increase."

Tears formed in my eyes. "You're going to remain *Pakhan*. Aren't you?" It was the moment I knew was coming but had feared for several days. There'd been so many meetings with soldiers, men coming and going from the temporary location he'd rented for all of us, including my mother. He'd done everything in his power to make us feel safe while he'd picked up the pieces, making certain the business Ivan had built over the last four decades continued to run smoothly. And I'd seen the light leave his eyes. The one of hope.

And I feared the one of love.

He took my hand into his, rubbing his thumb back and forth across my knuckles. "It's something I have to do. There's no one else left. The men respect me."

"That means you're giving up everything you care about."

Maksim lifted his head, looking into my eyes. When he shifted his hand to my cheek, the pain on his face brought tears to my eyes. "I love you with all my heart, Walker, but I can't expect you to stay with me. How could you after everything I've put you through? You're a beautiful, vibrant woman who deserves a much better life than what I can give you."

"So this is goodbye."

He took a deep breath, holding it for several seconds, then glanced at the sky. "I'm giving you the choice and I know it's not an easy one to make. You need to realize that I'm not a good man and that you can't change me or what I must do in the future."

"You *are* a good man, but you won't allow yourself to believe that. You won't fight for your daughter, and you refuse to fight for me." The combination of anger and despair was too much.

"I fight for the battles that I can win and the ones that are worth fighting for." As he lifted his head, his eyes locking onto mine, I realized that he'd shut down altogether. He'd brought me to a lovely public location to tell me that what we'd shared hadn't meant anything to him. What a fool I'd been.

Well, no more.

I was finished with being anyone's pawn.

And I was through with Maksim Calderon.

* * *

Maksim

"Are you ready for today, boss?" Brick asked as he came into my office.

I took a deep breath, trying to find the right words to answer him. Was anyone actually ready to lose the last thing that mattered in their lives? "It has to happen."

"You sure you don't want to postpone the court case? Maybe get yourself a new attorney?"

Three weeks had passed since the horrible call from my attorney. Three weeks since I'd sent Walker back to her real life, but I'd watched after her, making certain no one from the Marciano family tried to derail her plans at having a normal life. Still, I wouldn't put anything past Riccardo, which is why I'd issued a tough but necessary command.

Within hours, Riccardo would be gunned down on the streets of New York, becoming just another victim of a random attack. While I might regret my decision, I knew it was the only way she could keep that normal life she so desperately wanted.

Even if I'd suffered every day since lying to her at the winery.

She'd made plans to sell the condo. I couldn't blame her. She'd found a little house in an okay section of Chicago, convincing her mother to move in with her. I was glad they had each other. As far as my baby girl, I'd returned her to the care of Sandy and Miles, almost breaking down when Jasmine had burst into tears. Her screams for her daddy remained with me every night, preventing me from sleeping. That wouldn't change for a long time to come.

I raked my hand through my hair, no longer able to feel anything. I was cold inside, dead. Nothing mattered but business.

"Is anyone ready to end the only good part of your life?"

I could tell he had no idea what to say. "I'm sorry, boss. Do you want me to drive you? I'm happy to be there if you need someone."

Chuckling, I grabbed my keys and sunglasses, heading away from my desk. "I appreciate your offer, Brick, but this I need to handle on my own."

"You should take some time for yourself after this is all over."

I stopped just inside the doorway, thinking about what he said. "Maybe I'll do that, Brick. Maybe I will." But I knew I wouldn't. There was a significant amount of work to be done.

At least the drive was without incident, although I couldn't remember making the turns or being on the highway. All I could think about was what it would feel like to have a family. I'd tried to recoup some of that feeling by spending time with my mother and father. At least I hadn't gotten into an argument with my dad. In fact, he seemed happy to see me for the first time in as long as I could remember.

Still, that couldn't make up for the significant void I felt or the knowledge it was best for me to remain alone.

Goddamn it. I loved Walker.

As I walked into the courts building, sadness replaced anger. I'd failed the little person who needed me the most.

One day, I would get her back. I would take Walker's advice. I would find a judge who could help me.

The moment I walked into the assigned courtroom, my attorney breathed a sigh of relief, walking toward me with a quick pace.

"You worried me, Maksim. I was afraid you weren't going to show."

"Stop worrying, Michael. I realize that I have to take responsibility for my actions." I shifted my gaze toward Sandy and Miles. While it was obvious that they knew I was in the building, the inability to look at me was infuriating. They were ripping my heart out and they didn't have the decency to acknowledge their actions. I noticed the bailiff's approach, first talking with the attorney working with Sandy and Miles then heading in our direction.

"Mr. Moorechower, a word, please," the bailiff said quietly.

"Stay right here," Michael said with emphasis in his voice.

I didn't bother taking my seat, preferring to stand at this point. When Michael started to return, I could tell by the look on his face that he was baffled.

"What's wrong?" I growled.

"It would seem there's been a development. We're wanted in the judge's chambers."

"What? All of us?"

"No, just us."

What in the hell was going on? As I walked toward Jasmine's grandparents, I stopped in front of them, crouching down. I could hear Michael's disgusted deep breath. "I just want you to know that I'm not angry with either one of you. I know how much you love Jasmine and I only want what's best for her."

While Miles turned away, I was surprised when Sandy reached down, grasping my hand. "I know you do, Maksim. I can see why Maggie loved you so much. We just know that Jasmine needs to grow up a normal little girl."

"I know." I squeezed her hand before rising to my feet. I had to make peace with this. I refused to put Jasmine in the middle.

When we were in the judge's office, I realized just how uncomfortable I felt. I continued to think about Walker's words, her insistence that I was a good man. Well, this was my single attempt at doing the right thing.

When I heard the door open behind me, I didn't bother glancing to see who else had arrived. I wasn't certain I wanted to know.

Then I felt her, the woman I loved. Walker. As I slowly turned my head, I was floored at seeing her. She was dressed in scrubs, slightly out of breath and her skin was flushed, giving her a beautiful rosy color. As she walked forward, her eyes never left mine.

"Please remain standing," the bailiff stated as the door to the judge's private chambers opened, the judge walking straight to his desk.

"Please, everyone take a seat," the judge said. After we were all seated, he glanced at Walker, immediately nodding in recognition as well as acknowledgement. What the hell had she done? He finally turned his head, his expression not nearly as pleasant as the man stared at me.

"Mr. Calderon. Ms. Sutherland. I realize that this has been a difficult time for both of you, so I won't delay in providing my decision."

Michael pressed his hand against my chest when I moved to the edge of my chair, about ready to launch into the man.

"The facts of this case are different from others and quite frankly disturbing on several levels. I'm well aware of who you are, Mr. Calderon, and what you do for a living. That being said, Jasmine is your biological daughter who has expressed interest in returning to her home to live with her father. While I wouldn't ordinarily put but so much faith in the testimony of a three-year-old, I found her remarkably intelligent and mature for her age."

What the hell was he getting at? I remained tense, barely able to contain my anger.

"However, I wasn't inclined to grant her wishes given the circumstances," the judge continued.

"Judge Jericho," Michael started until the judge threw up his hand, giving my attorney a nasty look.

"Let me finish, Counselor. That is until I received a rather presumptuous visit from Ms. Sutherland. I will say that while I certainly didn't appreciate your tactics in demanding that you be allowed to have a conversation with me, I did appreciate your tenacity, which is why I granted a few minutes together in the first place."

"What does Ms. Sutherland have to do with this?" Michael asked. Now I was the one who pushed my arm against his chest.

The judge lifted his eyebrows before continuing. "You're very lucky to have a woman like Ms. Sutherland in your life, Mr. Calderon. It is quite apparent how strongly she feels about you as well as the child. She mentioned how you were with Jasmine and exactly how she feels about you. Even for an old man like me, I was touched. I was also happy to hear about your upcoming engagement. I do believe that having two people in Jasmine's life is a necessity. Still, I can't ignore the concerns as expressed by Mr. and Mrs. Cooper." He seemed uncomfortable, still weighing his decision.

I slowly turned my head, amazed at what Walker had done. As she darted a look in my direction, I almost laughed as a slight rush of color crested along her jaw and cheeks.

"I've decided to award permanent custody to Mr. Calderon on the condition that Mr. and Mrs. Cooper be given full visitation rights. There will also be a subsequent meeting in one year from this date to make certain that Jasmine is thriving. Is my decision understood?" He looked me directly in the eyes, his expression unreadable.

"Absolutely, Your Honor. And thank you."

"Bailiff. Please send in Mr. and Mrs. Cooper."

As we were guided through the door, Michael pushed me past Sandy and Miles, refusing to allow me to stop and talk with them. I'd never felt such a rush of emotions in my life and as I walked into the corridor, a moment of utter happiness rushed into my system.

Walker finally walked out the courtroom door, remaining where she was.

Michael noticed my stare and shook his head. "We have some paperwork to deal with, Maksim. Don't get off track. I'll wait outside but you and I need to talk."

"Sure thing, Michael." I watched him walk away then moved closer to her. Finding the right words was next to impossible. "Is that your way of asking me to marry you?"

She laughed softly, the flush still remaining. "I improvised when I finally got an audience with the judge. I'm sorry. I just... I knew Jasmine should be with you, but other than telling him I was your fiancée, everything I told him was the truth."

"Such as?"

"That you're a kind and loving father, watching out for Jasmine in every aspect, encouraging her to become her own person while keeping her out of harm's way."

I inched closer, the scent of her perfume instantly intoxicating. "And what else?"

"That you made me happy."

"Oh, really?" I slid my arms around her, pulling her close.

"Mmm-hmmm... And that I couldn't wait to be your wife."

"What else?"

"You're needy," she whispered.

"Yes, I am. You make me that way."

I entwined my fingers in her hair, tugging on the pin holding her long strands in a bun. She swung her head back and forth, rising onto her tiptoes as she slipped her arms around me. "That you were one of the kindest, most generous people I'd ever met."

As I lowered my head, my body began to shake from the rush of adrenaline. "Lady, I can't live without you."

"Then don't."

As I crushed my mouth over hers, I knew that being with her was more important than anything in my life.

Money.

Power.

While I would do my duty, ensuring the Novikov organization flourished, my love and my loyalty would be given to the two women who mattered the most in my life.

And for the first time, I was whole.

Happy.

And in love.

* * *

Walker

Life was a beautiful yet delicate flower that needed to be nurtured from time to time. Love was much the same way. The days and nights I'd spent without Maksim had almost broken me in two. I'd worked long hours, hoping I could break free of the spell that kept me enthralled, but I hadn't. And in my heart, I'd known that he needed Jasmine with him like I needed him.

As I walked into his office, I couldn't help but smile. He'd fixed up his lovely home, selling it almost immediately, replacing it for one much smaller but with a gorgeous back yard complete with a playset for Jasmine and a swing attached to two large trees just for me. He'd kept his promise to the judge, allowing Sally and Miles to see Jasmine whenever they wanted. They finally seemed okay with the arrangement.

The gorgeous man stared at me with such intensity that I suddenly couldn't breathe. I walked closer, tingling all over from the way his gaze traveled down every inch of me, his nostrils flaring.

"Daddy! Walker!" Jasmine squealed as she ran into the room, lunging in my direction.

"Goodness," I said, laughing as I caught her in my arms. "Look at you. What a pretty little dress."

"Daddy bought it for me."

"Uh-huh. I think Daddy spoils you." As Brick walked in, he appeared flushed from trying to keep up with her.

"I'm sorry, boss. She got away from me," Brick muttered.

Maksim laughed. "Don't worry about it, Brick. However, will you do me a favor?"

"Sure, boss. Whatever you need."

"Why don't you take the lovely Ms. Calderon to the store and have her pick out two flavors of ice cream."

"Really?" she asked, her eyes lighting up.

"Yes, we'll have a little celebration later in the garden. Would you like that, baby girl?" Now Maksim was the one lit up like a firecracker, which he did every time one of us walked into the room.

"Yes. Yes. Yes. Yes!"

"Then be a good girl and don't give Brick any trouble."

Brick rubbed over his eyebrow, taking a deep breath. The poor guy hadn't anticipated being a pseudo babysitter until certain details were finalized in his... no, our lives. He held out his hand, waiting until Jasmine ran toward Maksim, hugging his legs. When she scampered out of the room, I pressed my hand over my mouth to try to keep from laughing.

I failed.

"What's so funny?" he asked, growling afterward.

"You. Brick. The entire situation."

"Oh, yeah?" He swept me into his arms, peering down at me with a stern look on his face. "And you're one disobedient woman."

"What does that mean?"

"You constantly ignore the rules. You don't listen to me."

"You're a tough man to ignore."

He laughed, shaking his head. "Let's go out to the garden." As he took my hand, opening the set of French doors leading out onto the stone patio, I took a deep breath of the afternoon air. It was a gorgeous March day, a few of the trees already budding. He led me to the swing, finally letting me go.

"What's wrong?"

"You know we're going to need to make the judge happy."

"Meaning what?"

"Getting married."

I pressed my hand against his chest, pursing my lips. "Are you asking me to marry you?"

"Would you accept if I did?"

"Why don't you try me?"

"Ms. Rafaella Walker Sutherland, will you do me the honors of becoming my wife?"

"Yes," I answered without hesitation, the butterflies in my stomach finally set free.

"To love and cherish, honor and obey?" he threw in, a twinkle in his eyes.

I narrowed my eyes, huffing. "Wait a minute. Who said anything about obey?"

"I did. And you will. Yes?"

When I tried to push away from him, he yanked me tightly against him.

"You're such a bad man."

He grinned like a kid when I said that. "Answer me."

"Fine. Yes. I will. Now, be good and let me go."

"Nope. I can't do that. Not until you get the spanking you deserve."

"What?"

His grin remained as he tossed me over the wooden swing, immediately yanking my dress over my hips and exposing my naked bottom, the G-string covering nothing.

"If you're a good girl, you're get a reward after this," he said, the husky tone of his voice setting me on fire.

"Ice cream?"

He laughed, the deep baritone sending a wave of shivers dancing down the backs of my legs. "Of sorts." As he brought his hand down, moving from one side to the other, I kicked out, which was exactly what he was expecting. "Be still or I'll have to pull off my belt."

"You wouldn't."

"Do you want to make a bet?"

"No. No, sir. Not a bit." As the force of his hand moved the swing back and forth, I closed my eyes, the pain quickly turning into raging desire, my pussy quivering as my nipples became fully aroused.

The man refused to stop, one coming after another until I was wet and hot all over, my bottom aching from his forceful smacks. He spanked me long and hard, covering every inch of real estate on my bruised and aching buttocks.

"So mean. So horrible," I muttered.

"Keep that in mind," he murmured, his breath sounds becoming even more ragged. When the barrage of brutal strikes stopped, I took a deep breath, blinking several times.

When he helped me to my feet, I bit my lower lip to keep from moaning at the sight of his gorgeous, throbbing cock, pre-cum already dripping from his sensitive slit.

"Oh, you are a bad man," I whispered, reaching for his shaft, stroking the base.

"As I've told you many times, that's something you need to keep in mind. I will take you whenever and wherever I desire." His wry smile and intense look took my breath away. When he sat down on the swing, gripping my hips and pulling me closer, he issued a series of low and deliciously husky growls.

As always, he made me shiver to my core, but as the electricity built to a frenzied state, I couldn't wait to have him inside of me. I straddled his legs, bucking against him.

He was also a man with no patience. His fingers digging into my skin, he positioned the tip of his cock just past my swollen folds.

"Something else for you to remember, my little bird. You belong to me." As he pulled me down, thrusting the entire length of his shaft deep inside, I threw my head back, allowing several whimpers to float toward the sky.

The beautiful blue cloudless sky.

"I love you," I whispered, feeling more alive than I'd ever been in my life.

As he yanked me up from the deep arch, holding the back of my head, I realized something very important.

Love wasn't simple nor was it easy, but for every difficulty, every battle that needed to be fought, the only thing that mattered was family.

And I'd found mine.

The End

AFTERWORD

Stormy Night Publications would like to thank you for your interest in our books.

If you liked this book (or even if you didn't), we would really appreciate you leaving a review on the site where you purchased it. Reviews provide useful feedback for us and our authors, and this feedback (both positive comments and constructive criticism) allows us to work even harder to make sure we provide the content our customers want to read.

If you would like to check out more books from Stormy Night Publications, if you want to learn more about our company, or if you would like to join our mailing list, please visit our website at:

http://www.stormynightpublications.com

BOOKS OF THE ALPHA DYNASTY SERIES

Unchained Beast

As the firstborn of the Dupree family, I have spent my life building the wealth and power of our mafia empire while keeping our dark secret hidden and my savage hunger at bay. But the beast within me cannot be chained forever, and I must claim a mate before I lose control completely...

That is why Coraline LeBlanc is mine.

When I mount and ravage her, it won't be because I want her. It will be because I need her.

But that doesn't mean I won't enjoy stripping her bare and spanking her until she surrenders, then making her beg and scream with every desperate climax as I take what belongs to me.

The beast will claim her, but I will keep her.

But that can wait. Tonight I'm going to wring one ruthless climax after another from her quivering body with her bottom burning from my belt and her throat sore from screaming.

She will know she is mine before she even knows she is my bride.

Savage Prince

Gillian's father may be a powerful Irish mob boss, but he owes a blood debt to my family, and when I came to collect I didn't ask permission before taking his daughter as payment.

It was not up to him… or to her.

I will make her my bride, but I am not the kind of man who will wait until our wedding night to bare her and claim what belongs to me. She will walk down the aisle wet, well-used, and sore.

Her dress will hide the marks from my belt that taught her the consequences of disobeying her husband, but nothing will hide her blushes as her arousal drips down her thighs with each step.

By the time she says her vows she will already be mine.

BOOKS OF THE MERCILESS KINGS SERIES

King's Captive

Emily Porter saw me kill a man who betrayed my family and she helped put me behind bars. But someone with my connections doesn't stay in prison long, and she is about to learn the hard way that there is a price to pay for crossing the boss of the King dynasty. A very, very painful price…

She's going to cry for me as I blister that beautiful bottom, then she's going to scream for me as I ravage her over and over again, taking her in the most shameful ways she can imagine. But leaving her well-punished and well-used is just the beginning of what I have in store for Emily.

I'm going to make her my bride, and then I'm going to make her mine completely.

King's Hostage

When my life was threatened, Michael King didn't just take matters into his own hands.

He took me.

When he carried me off it was partly to protect me, but mostly it was because he wanted me.

I didn't choose to go with him, but it wasn't up to me. That's why I'm naked, wet, and sore in an opulent Swiss chalet with my bottom still burning from the belt of the infuriatingly sexy mafia boss who brought me here, punished me when I fought him, and then savagely made me his.

We'll return when things are safe in New Orleans, but I won't be going back to my old home.

I belong to him now, and he plans to keep me.

King's Possession

Her father had to be taught what happens when you cross a King, but that isn't why Genevieve Rossi is sore, well-used, and waiting for me to claim her in the only way I haven't already.

She's sore because she thought she could embarrass me in public without being punished.

She's well-used because after I spanked her I wanted more, and I take what I want.

She's waiting for me in my bed because she's my bride, and tonight is our wedding night.

I'm not going to be gentle with her, but when she wakes up tomorrow morning wet and blushing her cheeks won't be crimson because of the shameful things I did to her naked, quivering body.

It will be because she begged for all of them.

King's Toy

Vincenzo King thought I knew something about a man who betrayed him, but that isn't why I'm on my way to New Orleans well-used and sore with my backside still burning from his belt.

When he bared and punished me maybe it was just business, but what came after was not.

It was savage, it was shameful, and it was very, very personal.

I'm his toy now, and not the kind you keep in its box on the shelf.

He's going to play rough with me.

He's going to get me all wet and dirty.

Then he's going to do it all again tomorrow.

King's Demands

Julieta Morales hoped to escape an unwanted marriage, but the moment she got into my car her fate was sealed. She will have a husband, but it won't be the cartel boss her father chose for her.

It will be me.

But I'm not the kind of man who takes his bride gently amid rose petals on her wedding night. She'll learn to satisfy her King's demands with her bottom burning and her hair held in my fist.

She'll promise obedience when she speaks her vows, but she'll be mastered long before then.

King's Temptation

I didn't think I needed Dimitri Kristoff's protection, but it wasn't up to me. With a kingpin from a rival family coming after me, he took charge, took off his belt, and then took what he wanted.

He knows I'm not used to doing as I'm told. He just doesn't care.

The stripes seared across my bare bottom left me sore and sorry, but it was what came after that truly left me shaken. The princess of the King family shouldn't be on her knees for anyone, let alone this Bratva brute who has decided to claim for himself what he was meant to safeguard.

Nobody gave me to him, but I'm his anyway.

Now he's going to make sure I know it.

will teach her to obey, but what happens to her sore, red bottom after that will teach the real lesson.

She will be used mercilessly, over and over, and every brutal climax will remind her of the humiliating truth: she never even had a chance against me. Her body always knew its master.

Claimed as Revenge

Valencia Rivera became mine the moment her father broke the agreement he made with me. She thought she had a say in the matter, but my belt across her beautiful bottom taught her otherwise and a night spent screaming her surrender into the sheets left her in no doubt she belongs to me.

Using her hard and often will not be all it takes to tame her properly, but it will be a good start…

Made to Beg

Sierra Fox showed up at my door to ask for my protection, and I gave it to her… for a price. She belongs to me now, and I'm going to use her beautiful body as thoroughly as I please. The only thing for her to decide is how sore her cute little bottom will be when I'm through claiming her.

She came to me begging for help, but as her moans and screams grow louder with every brutal climax, we both know it won't be long before she begs me for something far more shameful.

MORE MAFIA AND BILLIONAIRE ROMANCES BY PIPER STONE

Caught

If you're forced to come to an arrangement with someone as dangerous as Jagger Calduchi, it means he's about to take what he wants, and you'll give it to him... even if it's your body.

I got caught snooping where I didn't belong, and Jagger made me an offer I couldn't refuse. A week with him where his rules are the only rules, or his bought and paid for cops take me to jail.

He's going to punish me, train me, and master me completely. When he's used me so shamefully I blush just to think about it, maybe he'll let me go home... or maybe he'll decide to keep me.

Ruthless

Treating a mobster shot by a rival's goons isn't really my forte, but when a man is powerful enough to have a whole wing of a hospital cleared out for his protection, you do as you're told.

To make matters worse, this isn't first time I've met Giovanni Calduchi. It turns out my newest patient is the stern, sexy brute who all but dragged me back to his hotel room a couple of nights ago so he could use my body as he pleased, then showed up at my house the next day, stripped me bare, and spanked me until I was begging him to take me even more roughly and shamefully.

Now, with his enemies likely to be coming after me in order to get to him, all I can do is hope he's as good at keeping me safe as he is at keeping me blushing, sore, and thoroughly satisfied.

Dangerous

I knew Erik Chenault was dangerous the moment I saw him. Everything about him should have warned me away, from the scar on his face to the fact that mobsters call him Blade. But I was drawn like a moth to a flame, and I ended up burnt... and blushing, sore, and thoroughly used.

Now he's taken it upon himself to protect me from men like the ones we both tried to leave in our past. He's going to make me his whether I like it or not... but I think I'm going to like it.

Prey

Within moments of setting eyes on Sophia Waters, I was certain of two things. She was going to learn what happens to bad girls who cheat at cards, and I was going to be the one to teach her.

But there was one thing I didn't know as I reddened that cute little bottom and then took her long and hard and oh so shamefully: I wasn't the only one who didn't come here for a game of cards.

I came to kill a man. It turns out she came to protect him.

Nobody keeps me from my target, but I'm in no rush. Not when I'm enjoying this game of cat and mouse so much. I'll even let her catch me one day, and as she screams my name with each brutal climax she'll finally realize the truth. She was never the hunter. She was always the prey.

Given

Stephanie Michaelson was given to me, and she is mine. The sooner she learns that, the less often her cute little bottom will end up well-punished and sore as she is reminded of her place.

But even as she promises obedience with tears running down her cheeks, I know it isn't the sting of my belt that will truly tame her. It is what comes next that will leave her in no doubt she belongs to me. That part will be long, hard, and shameful... and I will make her beg for all of it.

Dangerous Stranger

I came to Spain hoping to start a new life away from dangerous men, but then I met Rafael Santiago. Now I'm not just caught up in the affairs of a mafia boss, I'm being forced into his car.

When I saw something I shouldn't have, Rafael took me captive, stripped me bare, and punished me until he felt certain I'd told him everything I knew about his organization... which was nothing at all. Then he offered me his protection in return for the right to use me as he pleases.

Now that I belong to him, his plans for me are more shameful than I could have ever imagined.

Indebted

After her father stole from me, I could have left Alessandra Toro in jail for a crime she didn't commit. But I have plans for her. A deal with the judge—the kind only a man like me can arrange—made her my captive, and she will pay her father's debt with her beautiful body.

She will try to run, of course, but it won't be the law that comes after her. It will be me.

The sting of my belt across her quivering bare bottom will teach Alessandra the price of defiance, but it is the far more shameful penance that follows which will truly tame her.

Taken

When Winter O'Brien was given to me, she thought she had a say in the matter. She was wrong.

She is my bride. Mine to claim, mine to punish, and mine to use as shamefully as I please. The sting of my belt on her bare bottom will teach her to obey, but obedience is just the beginning.

I will demand so much more.

Bratva's Captive

I told Chloe Kingstrom that getting close to me would be dangerous, and she should keep her distance. The moment she disobeyed and followed me into that bar, she became mine.

Now my enemies are after her, but it's not what they would do to her she should worry about.

It's what I'm going to do to her.

My belt across her bare backside will teach her obedience, but what comes after will be different.

She's going to blush, beg, and scream with every climax as she's ravaged more thoroughly than she can imagine. Then I'm going to flip her over and claim her in an even more shameful way.

If she's a good girl, I might even let her enjoy it.

Hunted

Hope Gracen was just another target to be tracked down… until I caught her.

When I discovered I'd been lied to, I carried her off.

She'll tell me the truth with her bottom still burning from my belt, but that isn't why she's here.

I took her to protect her. I'm keeping her because she's mine.

Theirs as Payment

Until mere moments ago, I was a doctor heading home after my shift at the hospital. But that was before I was forced into the back seat of an SUV, then bared and spanked for trying to escape.

Now I'm just leverage for the Cabello brothers to use against my father, but it isn't the thought of being held hostage by these brutes that has my heart racing and my whole body quivering.

It is the way they're looking at me...

Like they're about to tear my clothes off and take turns mounting me like wild beasts.

Like they're going to share me, using me in ways more shameful than I can even imagine.

Like they own me.

Ruthless Acquisition

I knew the shameful stakes when I bet against these bastards. I just didn't expect to lose.

Now they've come to collect their winnings.

But they aren't just planning to take a belt to my bare bottom for trying to run and then claim everything they're owed from my naked, helpless body as I blush, beg, and scream for them.

They've acquired me, and they plan to keep me.

Bound by Contract

I knew I was in trouble the moment Gregory Steele called me into his office, but I wasn't expecting to end up stripped bare and bent over his desk for a painful lesson from his belt.

Taking a little bit of money here and there might have gone unnoticed in another organization, but stealing from one of the most powerful mafia bosses on the West Coast has consequences.

It doesn't matter why I did it. The only thing that matters now is what he's going to do to me.

I have no doubt he will use me shamefully, but he didn't make me sign that contract just to show me off with my cheeks blushing and my bottom sore under the scandalous outfit he chose for me.

Now that I'm his, he plans to keep me.

BOOKS OF THE DARK OVERTURE SERIES

Indecent Invitation

I shouldn't be here.

My clothes shouldn't be scattered around the room, my bottom shouldn't be sore, and I certainly shouldn't be screaming into the sheets as a ruthless tycoon takes everything he wants from me.

I shouldn't even know Houston Powers at all, but I was in a bad spot and I was made an offer.

A shameful, indecent offer I couldn't refuse.

I was desperate, I needed the money, and I didn't have a choice. Not a real one, anyway.

I'm here because I signed a contract, but I'm his because he made me his.

Illicit Proposition

I should have known better.

His proposition was shameful. So shameful I threw my drink in his face when I heard it.

Then I saw the look in his eyes, and I knew I'd made a mistake.

I fought as he bared me and begged as he spanked me, but it didn't matter. All I could do was moan, scream, and climax helplessly for him as he took everything he wanted from me.

By the time I signed the contract, I was already his.

Unseemly Entanglement

I was warned about Frederick Duvall. I was told he was dangerous. But I never suspected that meeting the billionaire advertising mogul to discuss a business proposition would end with me bent over a table with my dress up and my panties down for a shameful lesson in obedience.

That should have been it. I should have told him what he could do with his offer and his money.

But I didn't.

I could say it was because two million dollars is a lot of cash, but as I stand before him naked, bound, and awaiting the sting of his cane for daring to displease him, I know that's not the truth.

I'm not here because he pays me. I'm here because he owns me.

BOOKS OF THE CLUB DARKNESS SERIES

Bent to His Will

Even the most powerful men in the world know better than to cross me, but Autumn Sutherland thought she could spy on me in my own club and get away with it. Now she must be punished.

She tried to expose me, so she will be exposed. Bare, bound, and helplessly on display, she'll beg for mercy as my strap lashes her quivering bottom and my crop leaves its burning welts on her most intimate spots. Then she'll scream my name as she takes every inch of me, long and hard.

When I am done with her, she won't just be sore and shamefully broken. She will be mine.

Broken by His Hand

Sophia Russo tried to keep away from me, but just thinking about what I would do to her left her panties drenched. She tried to hide it, but I didn't let her. I tore those soaked panties off, spanked her bare little bottom until she had no doubt who owns her, and then took her long and hard.

She begged and screamed as she came for me over and over, but she didn't learn her lesson...

She didn't just come back for more. She thought she could disobey me and get away with it.

This time I'm not just going to punish her. I'm going to break her.

Bound by His Command

Willow danced for the rich and powerful at the world's most exclusive club… until tonight.

Tonight I told her she belongs to me now, and no other man will touch her again.

Tonight I ripped her soaked panties from her beautiful body and taught her to obey with my belt.

Tonight I took her as mine, and I won't be giving her up.

BOOKS OF THE MONTANA BAD BOYS SERIES

Hawk

He's a big, angry Marine, and I'm going to be sore when he's done with me.

Hawk Travers is not a man to be trifled with. I learned that lesson in the hardest way possible, first with a painful, humiliating public spanking and then much more shamefully in private.

She came looking for trouble. She got a taste of my belt instead.

Bryce Myers pushed me too far and she ended up with her bottom welted. But as satisfying as it is to hear this feisty little reporter scream my name as I put her in her place, I get the feeling she isn't going to stop snooping around no matter how well-used and sore I leave her cute backside.

She's gotten herself in way over her head, but she's mine now, and I protect what's mine.

Scorpion

He didn't ask if I like it rough. It wasn't up to me.

I thought I could get away with pissing off a big, tough Marine. I ended up with my face planted in the sheets, my burning bottom raised high, and my hair held tightly in his fist as he took me long and hard and taught me the kind of shameful lesson only a man like Scorpion could teach.

She was begging for a taste of my belt. She got much more than that.

Getting so tipsy she thought she could be sassy with me in my own bar earned Caroline a spanking, but it was trying to make off with my truck that sealed the deal. She'll feel my belt across her bare backside, then she'll scream my name as she takes every single inch of me.

This naughty girl needs to be put in her place, and I'm going to enjoy every moment of it.

Mustang

I tried to tell him how to run his ranch. Then he took off his belt.

When I heard a rumor about his ranch, I confronted Mustang about it. I thought I could go toe to toe with the big, tough former Marine, but I ended up blushing, sore, and very thoroughly used.

I told her it was going to hurt. I meant it.

Danni Brexton is a hot little number with a sharp tongue and a chip on her shoulder. She's the kind of trouble that needs to be ridden hard and put away wet, but only after a taste of my belt.

It will take more than just a firm hand and a burning bottom to tame this sassy spitfire, but I plan to keep her safe, sound, and screaming my name in bed whether she likes it or not. By the time I'm through with her, there won't be a shadow of a doubt in her mind that she belongs to me.

Nash

When he caught me on his property, he didn't call the police. He just took off his belt.

Nash caught me breaking into his shed while on the run from the mob, and when he demanded answers and obedience I gave him neither. Then he took off his belt and taught me in the most shameful way possible what happens to naughty girls who play games with a big, rough Marine.

She's mine to protect. That doesn't mean I'm going to be gentle with her.

Michelle doesn't just need a place to hide out. She needs a man who will bare her bottom and spank her until she is sore and sobbing whenever she puts herself at risk with reckless defiance, then shove her face into the sheets and make her scream his name with every savage climax.

She'll get all of that from me, and much, much more.

Austin

I offered this brute a ride. I ended up the one being ridden.

The first time I saw Austin, he was hitchhiking. I stopped to give him a lift, but I didn't end up taking this big, rough former Marine wherever he was heading. He was far too busy taking me.

She thought she was in charge. Then I took off my belt.

When Francesca Montgomery pulled up beside me, I didn't know who she was, but I knew what she needed and I gave it to her. Long, hard, and thoroughly, until she was screaming my name as she climaxed over and over with her quivering bare bottom still sporting the marks from my belt.

But someone wants to hurt her, and when someone tries to hurt what's mine, I take it personally.

Alpha's Mate

I didn't ask Nicolina to be my mate. It was not up to her. An alpha takes what belongs to him.

She will plead for mercy as she is bared and punished for daring to run from me, but her screams as she is claimed and rutted will be those of helpless climax as her body surrenders to its master.

She is mine, and I'm going to make sure she knows it.

He is her daddy.

He is the one who punishes her when she's been a bad girl, and he is the one who takes her in his arms afterwards and brings her to one climax after another until she is utterly spent and satisfied.

But something shady is going on behind the scenes at Dominick's company, and when Jenna draws the wrong conclusion from a poorly written article about him and creates an embarrassing public scene, will she end up not only costing them both their jobs but losing her daddy as well?

Conquering Their Mate

For years the Cenzans have cast a menacing eye on Earth, but it still came as a shock to be captured, stripped bare, and claimed as a mate by their leader and his most trusted warriors.

It infuriates me to be punished for the slightest defiance and forced to submit to these alien brutes, but as I'm led naked through the corridors of their ship, my well-punished bare bottom and my helpless arousal both fully on display, I cannot help wondering how long it will be until I'm kneeling at the feet of my mates and begging them take me as shamefully as they please.

Captured and Kept

Since her career was knocked off track in retaliation for her efforts to expose a sinister plot by high-ranking government officials, reporter Danielle Carver has been stuck writing puff pieces in a small town in Oregon. Desperate for a serious story, she sets out to investigate the rumors she's been hearing about mysterious men living in the mountains nearby. But when she secretly follows them back to their remote cabin, the ruggedly handsome beasts don't take kindly to her snooping around, and

Dani soon finds herself stripped bare for a painful, humiliating spanking.

Their rough dominance arouses her deeply, and before long she is blushing crimson as they take turns using her beautiful body as thoroughly and shamefully as they please. But when Dani uncovers the true reason for their presence in the area, will more than just her career be at risk?

Taming His Brat

It's been years since Cooper Dawson left her small Texas hometown, but after her stubborn defiance gets her fired from two jobs in a row, she knows something definitely needs to change. What she doesn't expect, however, is for her sharp tongue and arrogant attitude to land her over the knee of a stern, ruggedly sexy cowboy for a painful, embarrassing, and very public spanking.

Rex Sullivan cannot deny being smitten by Cooper, and the fact that she is in desperate need of his belt across her bare backside only makes the war-hardened ex-Marine more determined to tame the beautiful, fiery redhead. It isn't long before she's screaming his name as he shows her just how hard and roughly a cowboy can ride a headstrong filly. But Rex and Cooper both have secrets, and when the demons of their past rear their ugly heads, will their romance be torn apart?

Capturing Their Mate

I thought the Cenzan invaders could never find me here, but I was wrong. Three of the alien brutes came to take me, and before I ever set foot aboard their ship I had already been stripped bare, spanked thoroughly, and claimed more shamefully then I would have ever thought possible.

They have decided that a public example must be made of me, and I will be punished and used in the most humiliating ways imaginable as a warning to anyone who might dare to defy them. But I am no ordinary breeder, and the secrets hidden in my past could change their world... or end it.

Rogue

Tracking down cyborgs is my job, but this time I'm the one being hunted. This rogue machine has spent most of his life locked up, and now that he's on the loose he has plans for me...

He isn't just going to strip me, punish me, and use me. He will take me longer and harder than any human ever could, claiming me so thoroughly that I will be left in no doubt who owns me.

No matter how shamefully I beg and plead, my body will be ravaged again and again with pleasure so intense it terrifies me to even imagine, because that is what he was built to do.

Roughneck

When I took a job on an oil rig to escape my scheming stepfather's efforts to set me up with one of his business cronies, I knew I'd be working with rugged men. What I didn't expect is to find myself bent over a desk, my cheeks soaked with tears and my bare thighs wet for a very different reason, as my well-punished bottom is thoroughly used by a stern, infuriatingly sexy roughneck.

Even though I should have known better than to get sassy with a firm-handed cowboy, let alone a tough-as-nails former Marine, there's no denying that learning the hard way was every bit as hot as it was shameful. But a sore, welted backside is just the start of his plans for me, and no matter how much I blush to admit it, I know I'm going to take everything he gives me and beg for more.

Hunting Their Mate

As far as I'm concerned, the Cenzans will always be the enemy, and there can be no peace while they remain on our planet. I planned to make them pay for invading our world, but I was hunted down and captured by two of their warriors with the help of a battle-hardened former Marine. Now I'm the one who is going to pay, as the three of them punish me, shame me, and share me.

Though the thought of a fellow human taking the side of these alien brutes enrages me, that is far from the worst of it. With every searing stroke of the strap that lands across my bare bottom, with every savage thrust as I am claimed over and over, and with every screaming climax, it is made more clear that it is my own quivering, thoroughly used body which has truly betrayed me.

Primitive

I was sent to this world to help build a new Earth, but I was shocked by what I found here. The men of this planet are not just primitive savages. They are predators, and I am now their prey...

The government lied to all of us. Not all of the creatures who hunted and captured me are aliens. Some of them were human once, specimens transformed in labs into little more than feral beasts.

I fought, but I was thrown over a shoulder and carried off. I ran, but I was caught and punished. Now they are going to claim me, share me, and use me so roughly that when the last screaming climax has been wrung from my naked, helpless body, I wonder if I'll still know my own name.

Harvest

The Centurions conquered Earth long before I was born, but they did not come for our land or our resources. They came for mates, women deemed suitable for breeding. Women like me.

Three of the alien brutes decided to claim me, and when I defied them, they made a public example of me, punishing me so thoroughly and shamefully I might never stop blushing.

But now, as my virgin body is used in every way possible, I'm not sure I want them to stop...

Torched

I work alongside firefighters, so I know how to handle musclebound roughnecks, but Blaise Tompkins is in a league of his own. The night we met, I threw a glass of wine in his face, then ended up shoved against the wall with my panties on the floor and my arousal dripping down my thighs, screaming out climax after shameful climax with my well-punished bottom still burning.

I've got a series of arsons to get to the bottom of, and finding out that the infuriatingly sexy brute who spanked me like a naughty little girl will be helping me with the investigation seemed like the last thing I needed, until somebody hurled a rock through my window in an effort to scare me away from the case. Now having a big, strong man around doesn't seem like such a bad idea...

Fertile

The men who hunt me were always brutes, but now lust makes them barely more than beasts.

When they catch me, I know what comes next.

I will fight, but my need to be bred is just as strong as theirs is to breed. When they strip me, punish me, and use me the way I'm meant to be used, my screams will be the screams of climax.

Hostage

I knew going after one of the most powerful mafia bosses in the world would be dangerous, but I didn't anticipate being dragged from my apartment already sore, sorry, and shamefully used.

My captors don't just plan to teach me a lesson and then let me go. They plan to share me, punish me, and claim me so ruthlessly I'll be screaming my submission into the sheets long before they're through with me. They took me as a hostage, but they'll keep me as theirs.

Defiled

I was born to rule, but for her sake I am banished, forced to wander the Earth among mortals. Her virgin body will pay the price for my protection, and it will be a shameful price indeed.

Stripped, punished, and ravaged over and over, she will scream with every savage climax.

She will be defiled, but before I am done with her she will beg to be mine.

Kept

On the run from corrupt men determined to silence me, I sought refuge in his cabin. I ate his food, drank his whiskey, and slept in his bed. But then the big bad bear came home and I learned the hard way that sometimes Goldilocks ends up with her cute little bottom well-used and sore.

He stripped me, spanked me, and ravaged me in the most shameful way possible, but then this rugged brute did something no one else ever has before. He made it clear he plans to keep me...

Auctioned

Twenty years ago the Malzeons saved us when we were at the brink of self-annihilation, but there was a price for their intervention. They demanded humans as servants… and as pets.

Only criminals were supposed to be offered to the aliens for their use, but when I defied Earth's government, asking questions that no one else would dare to ask, I was sold to them at auction.

I was bought by two of their most powerful commanders, rivals who nonetheless plan to share me. I am their property now, and they intend to tame me, train me, and enjoy me thoroughly.

But I have information they need, a secret guarded so zealously that discovering it cost me my freedom, and if they do not act quickly enough both of our worlds will soon be in grave danger.

Hard Ride

When I snuck into Montana Cobalt's house, I was looking for help learning to ride like him, but what I got was his belt across my bare backside. Then with tears still running down my cheeks and arousal dripping onto my thighs, the big brute taught me a much more shameful lesson.

Montana has agreed to train me, but not just for the rodeo. He's going to break me in and put me through my paces, and then he's going to show me what it means to be ridden rough and dirty.

Carnal

For centuries my kind have hidden our feral nature, our brute strength, and our carnal instincts. But this human female is my mate, and nothing will keep me from claiming and ravaging her.

She is mine to tame and protect, and if my belt doesn't teach her to obey then she'll learn in a much more shameful fashion. Either way, her surrender will be as complete as it is inevitable.

Bounty

After I went undercover to take down a mob boss and ended up betrayed, framed, and on the run, Harper Rollins tried to bring me in. But instead of collecting a bounty, she earned herself a hard spanking and then an even rougher lesson that left her cute bottom sore in a very different way.

She's not one to give up without a fight, but that's fine by me. It just means I'll have plenty more chances to welt her beautiful backside and then make her scream her surrender into the sheets.

Beast

Primitive, irresistible need compelled him to claim me, but it was more than mere instinct that drove this alien beast to punish me for my defiance and then ravage me thoroughly and savagely. Every screaming climax was a brand marking me as his, ensuring I never forget who I belong to.

He's strong enough to take what he wants from me, but that's not why I surrendered so easily as he stripped me bare, pushed me up against the wall, and made me his so roughly and shamefully.

It wasn't fear that forced me to submit. It was need.

Gladiator

Xander didn't just win me in the arena. The alien brute claimed me there too, with my punished bottom still burning and my screams of climax almost drowned out by the roar of the crowd.

Almost…

Victory earned him freedom and the right to take me as his mate, but making me truly his will mean more than just spanking me into shameful surrender and then rutting me like a wild beast. Before he carries me off as his prize, the dark truth that brought me here must be exposed at last.

Big Rig

Alexis Harding is used to telling men exactly what she thinks, but she's never had a roughneck like me as a boss before. On my rig, I make the rules and sassy little girls get stripped bare, bent over my desk, and taught their place, first with my belt and then in a much more shameful way.

She'll be sore and sorry long before I'm done with her, but the arousal glistening on her thighs reveals the truth she would rather keep hidden. She needs it rough, and that's how she'll get it.

Warriors

I knew this was a primitive planet when I landed, but nothing could have prepared me for the rough beasts who inhabit it. The sting of their prince's firm hand on my bare bottom taught me my place in his world, but it was what came after that truly demonstrated his mastery over me.

This alien brute has granted me his protection and his help with my mission, but the price was my total submission to both his shameful demands and those of his second in command as well.

But it isn't the savage way they make use of my quivering body that terrifies me the most. What leaves me trembling is the thought that I may never leave this place… because I won't want to.

Owned

With a ruthless, corrupt billionaire after me, Crockett, Dylan, and Wade are just the men I need. Rough men who know how to keep a woman safe… and how to make her scream their names.

But the Hell's Fury MC doesn't do charity work, and their help will come at a price.

A shameful price…

They aren't just going to bare me, punish me, and then do whatever they want with me.

They're going to make me beg for it.

Seized

Delaney Archer got herself mixed up with someone who crossed us, and now she's going to find out just how roughly and shamefully three bad men like us can make use of her beautiful body.

She can plead for mercy, but it won't stop us from stripping her bare and spanking her until she's sore, sobbing, and soaking wet. Our feisty little captive is going to take everything we give her, and she'll be screaming our names with every savage climax long before we're done with her.

Cruel Masters

I thought I understood the risks of going undercover to report on billionaires flaunting their power, but these men didn't send lawyers after me. They're going to deal with me themselves.

Now I'm naked aboard their private plane, my backside already burning from one of their belts, and these three infuriatingly sexy bastards have only just gotten started teaching me my place.

I'm not just going to be punished, shamed, and shared. I'm going to be mastered.

Hard Men

My father's will left his company to me, but the three roughnecks who ran it for him have other ideas. They're owed a debt and they mean to collect on it, but it's not money these brutes want.

It's me.

In return for protection from my father's enemies, I will be theirs to share. But these are hard men, and they don't just intend to punish my defiance and use me as shamefully as they please.

They plan to master me completely.

Rough Ride

As I hear the leather slide through the loops of his pants, I know what comes next. Jake Travers is going to blister my backside. Then he's going to ride me the way only a rodeo champion can.

Plenty of men who thought they could put me in my place have learned the hard way that I was more than they could handle, and when Jake showed up I was sure he would be no different.

I was wrong.

When I pushed him, he bared and spanked me in front of a bar full of people.

I should have let it go at that, but I couldn't.

That's why he's taking off his belt…

Primal Instinct

Ruger Jameson can buy anything he wants, but that's not the reason I'm his to use as he pleases.

He's a former Army Ranger accustomed to having his orders followed, but that's not why I obey him.

He saved my life after our plane crashed, but I'm not on my knees just to thank him properly.

I'm his because my body knows its master.

I do as I'm told because he blisters my bare backside every time I dare to do otherwise.

I'm at his feet because I belong to him and I plan to show it in the most shameful way possible.

PIPER STONE LINKS

You can keep up with Piper Stone via her newsletter, her website, her Twitter account, her Facebook page, and her Goodreads profile, using the following links:

http://eepurl.com/c2QvLz

https://darkdangerousdelicious.wordpress.com/

https://twitter.com/piperstone01

https://www.facebook.com/Piper-Stone-573573166169730/

https://www.goodreads.com/author/show/15754494.Piper_Stone

Made in the USA
Columbia, SC
12 February 2022

56080774R00220